Critical acclaim for Joh...

VOTAN

'The narrative is terse ~~...~~ the events barbarously splendid ... an imagination as rich as it is original'
The Times

'The best thing about the Dark Ages is that, where fiction is concerned, you can do what you like with them. There are legends and a few odd facts, for the rest, one man's imagination is as good as the next man's. And John James' is splendid'
Daily Telegraph

'The aim of this *tour de force* is to scrape away the centuries-old varnish of legend to reveal the vibrantly crude colours of reality beneath ... A remarkable achievement'
Sunday Telegraph

NOT FOR ALL THE GOLD IN IRELAND

'Crackles with atmosphere and splendidly imaginative writing'
Guardian Journal

'Fast-moving and ingeniously plotted ... a brilliant picture of these barbaric regions'
British Book News

'A thoroughly enjoyable novel, full of exuberance and colourful fantasy'
Manchester Evening News

Also by John James

VOTAN
NOT FOR ALL THE GOLD IN IRELAND
and published by Bantam Books

John James

MEN WENT TO CATTRAETH

BANTAM BOOKS

TORONTO · NEW YORK · LONDON · SYDNEY · AUCKLAND

MEN WENT TO CATTRAETH

A BANTAM BOOK 0 553 17360 X

Originally published in Great Britain by Cassell & Company Ltd.

PRINTING HISTORY
Cassell & Company edition published 1969
Bantam edition published 1988

This book is set in 10/11 Souvenir

Bantam Books are published by Transworld Publishers Ltd., 61-63 Uxbridge Road, Ealing, London W5 5SA, in Australia by Transworld Publishers (Australia) Pty. Ltd., 15-25 Helles Avenue, Moorebank, NSW 2170, and in New Zealand by Transworld Publishers (N.Z.) Ltd., Cnr. Moselle and Waipareira Avenues, Henderson, Auckland.

Reproduced, printed and bound in Great Britain by
Hazell Watson & Viney Limited
Member of BPCC plc
Aylesbury, Bucks, England

In Memoriam

Roger Berkshire

AUTHOR'S NOTE

This is a work of the imagination, not of history, nor yet a translation. We know nothing about the Battle of Cattraeth, neither when it was fought, nor against whom, nor where, apart from what we read in the surviving ninety-seven elegies which go under Aneirin's name. We do not even know how long after the battle they were written down in their present form. But this is the setting in which the battle must have taken place.

The chapter headings and their translations are taken from the edition of John Williams ab Ithel, published in 1852.

CHAPTER ONE

Carasswn disgynnu yg Cattraeth gessevin
Gwert med yg kynted a gwirawt win

I could wish to have been the first to shed my blood
in Cattraeth
As the price of the mead and the drink of wine in the Hall.

I wish that I had been the first to shed my blood before Cattraeth. But it is now that I pay the price for the wine and mead of the feasts in Mynydog's Hall. Late, indeed, I came to the feasts.

I came in the afternoon to sight of the Rock of Dumbarton. I had with me Aidan, son of Cormac King of the Northern Coasts, whose Judge I had been through the winter. Not a King like you find in the South. We walked across all his Kingdom to hear his people's quarrels and judge them and settle the prices in five days. He had perhaps, in a desperate time, four hundred men who could bear arms, and those arms would only be their axes, or scythe-heads tied to long poles. There were only five swords in the whole Kingdom, and one cape of mail that Cormac wore. But he was a King, just as Evrog the Wealthy was King in Dumbarton, and Uther in Camelot, Theodoric in Rome and Zeno in Byzantium and Clovis in Gaul.

I climbed the rock of Dumbarton with Aidan before me and Morien the charcoal-burner whose father no one knew behind me. Steep that rock is, and the path is beaten earth, not stone cut into steps as they say is the path to Camelot. All the harder for an enemy, Evrog used to say. All the harder for his own men, labouring up with bags of salt and casks of water, with carcasses of meat and dried salmon and bales of hay for the horses. All the harder too for the horses when they were brought down to exercise in the plain. And hard for me.

Yet that hard climb up the rock was for me the beginning of my journey to Cattraeth. From this place, Evrog ruled his vast Kingdom, Strathclyde and Galloway to the borders of Cumbria. He was hard pressed by the Scots who came flooding in from Ireland, and it was certain that if they did not come to stay this year, then they would some day soon. So had Cormac's father come thirty years ago. In the East, Evrog was always at loggerheads with Mynydog King of Eiddin, although they never came quite to open war: their enmity was more a matter

8

of pinpricks and cattle-raids and hiring poets to sing satires and scurrilous verses against each other. And now, the Savages who had taken the attention of the King of Eiddin for long enough were come far west enough to attack Galloway from the South. This was, I thought, a more serious thing than any settlements of the Scots from Ireland, because they were all Christian and worshipped the Virgin: and the people there are the same as we are, only differing in their way of speech, honouring poets and smiths and all makers far above any soldier or King. But the Savages do not live in this Roman way, and there is no understanding them.

Yet Evrog was cheerful enough all the time I knew him, saying that there was no other way for a King to live in such a situation. If once he stopped to shed a tear he would weep for ever.

Evrog's Gatekeeper knew me well. He was Cynon, son to Clydno who was King Mynydog's Judge. Cynon had been to the South beyond the wall, and had learned to read several words of obvious utility like *deus* and *rex* and *poena* and *tributum* from Cattog the Wise in the School of Illtud. He had seen great cities with his own eyes, Chester and Gloucester and Caerleon. But he had not wished to be a Bishop, as he could easily have been, since he had no wish to live walled up and at the beck and call of any little monk who wanted to be ordained, so he came home, and was now Captain of the Household to Evrog. Now, they tell me, Cynon is a great man, and for all that his arm is crooked at the elbow and cannot strike a blow, he stands as Judge at Arthur's throne. Seeing me, as he was coming out of the Hall to blow the horn for the King's dinner, he shouted out the words I did not want to hear, 'Make way for Aneirin! Behold the Chief Bard of the Isle of Britain. Stand aside all, that the greatest Poet of Rome may pass!'

Once I would have thought that my due, less than my due indeed, and everyone in the Island knew it, and there was no boasting in acknowledging the truth. But now – I

9

was no longer a Bard, though the bitter words were spoken and could not be called back.

I walked through the gate into the Dun of King Evrog, all set around with spiked logs the height of a man, with stables for a hundred horses and three hundred men, safe against the Irish. Evrog's Hall was not of stone as are palaces in the South, with pillars of marble and roofs sheeted with gold and the walls covered with magic pictures. Not even Evrog here in the North could pay for those workmen from far away to bring their magic to his Dun: no man born in the Island has the art now of cutting stone by spells. He had lately new built the Hall in the Roman manner, with straight sides and a rounded end in which he set his High Table. The logs of the walls were thick and the chinks well stuffed with mud and seaweed, and the thatch was of oatstraw, which is better than reeds.

Evrog was wealthy. He showed his wealth, hanging tapestry from the walls and weapons from the pillars. He showed forty swords, and with mail and axes and spears he could send forth a Household, mounted, of a hundred men, and this was, at the time, more than any King had ever done in the Island from the beginning of time. So the whole of this immense Hall, forty or fifty paces long, glittered with iron. It glittered, because beside the fire in the centre Evrog would burn rush lights, dipped in tallow, twenty or thirty at a time, to light the feast. You will understand therefore that a feast in Evrog's Hall was a scene of magnificence such as few even in the South see more than once in a year.

I went in and sat low at the table. All Evrog's great landowner's were there, looking at me, and knowing me, and saying nothing, seeing that I was sitting where I wanted to sit. They thought perhaps that I was come to recite a Satire on Evrog paid for by Mynydog, or even by some Irish King, that would do half the business of a war. I have destroyed whole armies in my time with my verses: before I rode to Cattraeth.

Then Cynon, standing now at the High Table, for

10

would you have him sit outside all the time and miss his supper, blew his horn again, and the great ones of Evrog's Court filed in.

Evrog's Judge came first, and then his Butler and his Treasurer, his Steward and his Manciple, his Bailiff and the Master of his Horse, the more important coming later. There was a harper in the Hall, but no Bard, since Evrog's Bard had died the year before, so that Evrog entered, and his Queen with him, and his principal guest last of all.

When the Queen went to pour the first cup for Cynon, and then for her King, as is right, I bowed my head low so that the man who now sat at Evrog's right should not see me. But he did see me, and spoke to the King. Then Cynon, drinking, blew the Horn for the third time, and the King called out, 'The knife is in the meat, and the drink is in the cup. Let no man enter but who is skilled in craftsmanship and pre-eminent in his art. And if there is any one such in the Hall, let him come and sit at my right hand.'

Now, these are conventional words which every King in all the Empire says when he sits to eat. But this evening, Evrog shouted it out, and Cynon answered loudly, because in those days he had knowledge and no wisdom, like myself, 'Forward Aneirin! Forward the Pre-eminent Chief Poet of the Isle of Britain.'

The men around me seized my elbows and pushed me forward. There was no use my protesting or refusing. They would only have lifted me up and carried me bodily to the High Table. They would have taken my denials only as posings, as if I were any common bard who earned his bread by measure, singing from Hall to Hall and Court to Court. I, Aneirin, never said that I was anything but a great poet: the truth was too clear for anyone to deny. Now I was no longer a poet. But to have explained that to the men around me was too difficult. It was easier to obey than to make a scene.

At the High Table, I sat where they put me, where *he* had first sat, though I had to wait a little while they

11

brought in from the King's sleeping house, the Chair he himself had awarded me, the Chair in which no one else was ever allowed to sit. And they made *him* sit on the King's other hand, who ought to have sat in the highest place of honour. For he was Precent.

A strong man was Precent. Not tall, he was a head shorter than I was but strongly built. Heavy, and strong above all. Some men of that build are only fat, but Precent, why he could carry off a young ox, and the yoke and chains on it. He used to have sport, seeing how thick a rod of iron he could twist like a rope. The short black hairs bristled on his arms, and his black curls were blacker, sleeked down with goose-grease. His black eyes sparkled in the light of the wax candles they had placed on the table in front of the King, two of them in a precious bronze candlestick. There is no one who knows where bronze is mined or from what kind of rock it is smelted.

Now the Queen was withdrawn, Peredur served us with mead; young Peredur that is, Evrog's seventh son, who is now such a great man in Arthur's Hall. He was named after his uncle, Peredur Ironarms, Master of Evrog's Horse.

Oh, a strong man was Precent, in all civilized arts. A strong man for breaking a horse, for throwing a steer for gelding. A strong man was he for riding all day with the herd or for running the fells to gather in the sheep. He was a man strong for stalking deer all day in the drizzling rain, or for pitching sheaves into a wagon in the harvest sun. Today he had ridden from Eiddin all the width of Alban, and still there he sat at table, bright as a button. He was young, and so were we all then, young and strong.

Precent talked to Evrog all through the meal, or across us both to the Queen who sat by me. I kept my head down and said nothing. The others did not find this strange, even though they had not seen me all winter. They did not ask me where I had been. Only Precent said to the King, 'Aneirin's got the awen on him tonight. There's a fine poem we'll get from him when he has finished eating.'

12

But I knew I could never have the awen on me again.

When the meal was finished, Evrog beat on the table. While the mead went round again, and the Queen withdrew, as was the custom in Strathclyde, the King said loud so that all could hear the distinction between conversation and an announcement made, 'Now that the great and principal guest, unexpected though he was, has been fed, tell me, Precent, King of the Picts: why is it you have come tonight into the Kingdom of Strathclyde seeing that for so long you were gatekeeper to my rival Mynydog?'

Precent went red in the face, and cleared his throat loudly, and drowned the frog in mead. He was always longwinded in his speeches, and clumsy in his choice of words, so I hoped that he would offend nobody: and while he talked I would withdraw my mind and think of Bradwen in Eiddin. Precent began well enough.

'A man I am, a man. Gatekeeper to Mynydog I was, and it is some of you I have kept out of his sheepfolds before now, as well you all know. With what little strength I have, I did what I could.'

'Who stole the gadflies off Morddwydtywyllon's cow?' someone shouted. I think it was Peredur Ironarms, because he was always put out to think there could be anybody stronger than he was. It rather put Precent off his speech, and he shouted angrily, losing his composure and thickening his Pictish vowels.

'It is not a matter of cows I am come about, but the matter of the life and death of the Isle of Britain.' His bellow cut through the laughter, and the men below us quietened, sensing in his tone some emotion they had not expected in him.

'It is more than cows you will get if you listen to me. Glory and honour and praise I am come to tell you about, and offer to you all for little effort. Mynydog King of Eiddin is a generous man, though no one calls him "wealthy" to his face, and a proud man too. Those who do him service in one campaign may swagger and be proud all the rest of their lives and tell their children, "I was there." It is men he wants, warriors excelling in weapons, youths exulting in war.'

'Aye, he wants us to steal our own cows for him,' sneered someone from lower down the hall. Precent pretended he didn't hear it, but nevertheless he countered at once.

'In battle against the bloody Loegrians let us loose our blades, not shedding brothers' blood. Savages from over the Ocean, in the salt seas washed, not in sweet baptism bathed, they neither serve the Holy Virgin nor venerate her saints. They persecute her Bishops and betray her priests, thieves of bells are they and burners of thatch. There is nothing that the Holy Virgin desires more than that we should kill them and drive them from this Island.'

A noble of Mynydog's ought to know that, I thought. There was a hermit in the wood behind Mynydog's Hall, and the King had spent good silver to send this man to Iona and have him made a priest, and had bought a book for him to read, so that he could tell Mynydog the days for Easter and Assumption and the other great feasts, and so that he could have his dead prayed for. Not to be outdone, Evrog had sent one of his nephews, Gelorwid, to Iona, but him, for some reason, I could see sitting in the Hall that night, not dressed as a hermit. Precent went on.

'I know that now the Savages trouble you little. It is the Scots out of Ireland who, you think, are your only foes. But believe you this. If the Savages from over the sea are not fought and beaten and crushed and driven utterly out of this island, then when the Kings of Ireland come again with their armies, it is the Savages they will fight before this rock, and not Romans. Because we will be dead before our time. And that will be not in ten generations or in two, but it will be the year after next if they wait so long. Carlisle has fallen. Will Dumbarton be the next?

'Strike not at the nearest foe, but at the most dangerous. Mynydog will fight them, whether you wish or not. If there is any man here who thinks himself skilful and strong enough to come and fight the Savages with us, let him stand up and ride out with me, to share in the glory and honour and profit of this war. But do not come if there is any thought in your minds that it will be an easy campaign against a weak foe. Cunning in the field they are, and ruthless in war. How cruel, let Aneirin tell you. Silence for Aneirin, Pre-eminent Chief Bard of the Isle of Britain!'

I did not stand. I looked bleakly at the table before me, seeing the grain of the scrubbed pine. I had known it, I ought not to have come into a King's Hall, or into the company of anyone who knew who I was, till I had first come again to Bradwen. I sat and stared at the backs of my hands on the table. At last I said, and they all hushed to listen to me, as if I had been singing them an englyn, or intoning a triad, 'I am not a Bard. I am no longer a poet. I will make no more songs. I have sung for the last time.'

The silence continued, only for the sound of indrawing breath. Evrog asked, 'What do you mean?'

'I mean what I say,' I told him. This was the first time I had told the truth about this in public. It was the first time I had told a King I would make no more poems, no more music to glorify his Kingdom, no more satires against his enemies. I still looked at my hands on the table. I would not look into the faces in front of me. To think that I, Aneirin, who had sung to every King in the North, was abashed in front of this audience.

'You all know the law as well as I do. Naked weapons must not be brought into the presence of a Bard. More. If a sword is drawn before a Bard, and blood is shed in his sight, then he is unclean, and he may not sing again that night. Think, then, what happened to me. More than swords were bared before me. Spears and saxes fought above me. The blood of my friends and my kinsmen flowed over me. The blood of Savages stained me. And that not once but twice. How then can I be a poet again? How can I ever sing again in all my life?'

'Nonsense,' Evrog told me. He could treat it lightly. The generous King had never felt terror, shame, pain like this. 'Nonsense,' he said, 'I'll have my priest up here to cleanse you in the morning. And if he can't do it, we'll take you to the Monastery, where they have a Bishop, and he will be able to do something. You have been baptized, haven't you? If we have to do that all over again, then I'll stand Godfather and the Queen will be your Godmother. Then you can come here and be my Bard – I can't get used to being without one.'

I shook my head. Even if it were possible, was he really thinking that he could get the greatest poet of the Roman world to be his household Bard, to write satires on his enemies and lullabies for his grandchildren in return for bed and board? It was not possible.

'Priests and Poets have nothing to do with each other. The Church hates poetry. Priests are men of writing. Bards sing, they do not write. A priest would only read something over me out of a book. What good would that do?'

Precent spoke quickly. Trying to cover my embarrassment, unerringly he chose the wrong thing to say.

'Look, all of you! If there is nothing else will make you angry, see what the Savages have done to the greatest Poet of the age. A Poet is the greatest ornament any Kingdom can have, and Aneirin is so great that he belongs not to any one King, but to all the Romans of the Island. Think of all he did in those first few years of his flowering, while still a lad. Who of you has never sung his songs at the reaping, or never recited his verses to the plough team? Who has not walked a dozen miles to hear him sing to the harp or to challenge him to compose on a theme at first hearing? And now, he sits here and says he will not sing again.

'Look at him, Aneirin, Son of Manaw Gododdin, grandson to Cunedda, cousin to Mynydog Gododdin King of Eiddin. The blood of the greatest houses of North Britain, of South Britain within the wall, of Ireland, flows in his veins. Sent from the South to be fostered he was, as I was from among the Picts in the house of Eudav the Tall, who lived beneath the Wall. Safe we were there, our parents thought, from the Irish, to learn all the arts of civility. We grew up there, he and I and Bradwen the daughter of Eudav.

'Ah, what a youth was Aneirin. Did you know there was one, once, who could outrun Precent? There he sits now as often he sat at the end of the long field, waiting for me to catch up. Did you know there was once one who could outwrestle even Precent? There he hangs down his head, as once he pressed my shoulders to the grass.'

Now, Precent was launched. Three cups of mead, we used to say, and Precent will charm the horns from a stag. Six cups of mead, and Precent will charm the moon from the sky. And not all by boredom, either, though partly – it is not a finished orator you would be calling him.

'All this he set aside to be a bard. These hands you have heard on the harp-strings, how often have they guided the team across the headlands. That voice you have heard sing, it has called the cattle home many a time, or spread the news of cattle-thieves on the moors – aye, and raiders from Strathclyde at that. His first songs I heard when we were still children, when we spent the happy summers in the leafy huts, watching the sheep on the green fells.

'It was to Eudav's house that Aneirin would return, long after he became a man, long after he became welcome in every Hall and every Dun North of the Wall, long after the Kings in the South would have given much to have him live there, in Cardigan or Camelot; long after I had returned to my father's seat among the Picts, long after Bradwen herself had gone to Mynydog's Court. And that was when the Savages first came so far North. They came through the Wall. They burnt Eudav's house above Eudav's bloody trunk, and his head they carried away before his cattle. And with the cattle they took away Aneirin, to be their slave and their butt.

'That was a year ago. We heard of it, all of us, all across the Kingdom of Eiddin, across the lands of the Gododdin, into the realm of the Picts. Before the harvest was in the ear, I, Precent, made war. I brought my own men,

17

Romans and Picts together, and we gathered men in Eiddin. I led the Household of Mynydog the ever-victorious, pre-eminent in war. A hundred men in mail I led out, an invincible array. Who could stand before us? Who could resist us? The Savages fled, the Pagans would not wait for us. We swept across the land of Mordei, and brought the bones of Eudav for Bradwen to bury in Eiddin. And southwards from Eudav's Hall, where they thought they were safe, the Savages were clearing the blessed forests to plant their vile wheat. There we found Aneirin, the greatest poet of the world. In fetters and in misery they kept him in a hole in the ground. We brought him gently back to Eiddin where we hoped to keep him and heal him. Before we knew, he had gone from us, into the North, silent. From then till now we have heard nothing of him. Now I find him in Strathclyde, and he says that he will not sing again because of what the Savages did to him. Do you want to hear him sing again? Then listen to me!

'Mynydog has decided. For once and for all, the menace of the Savages must be driven from the borders of Eiddin and of Strathclyde. The House of the Gododdin will do that. The King of Eiddin has begun to call about him a Household of the young men of his Kingdom, and not of his Kingdom only. It is a Household such as the world has never seen before. Any young man from any place may come to join it, if only he is a Roman and worships the Virgin. If a man is thought fit to join us, then Mynydog will give him a sword and mail, a helmet, two shirts and a cloak. And Mynydog will entertain his Household in his Hall for a year and a day from the time he began to call them together. And when the time is over, and it will not be so long now, and not many feasts for you to take part in, then Mynydog's Household will honour their vow and go down to clear the land of Mordei from the Savages for ever, and further all across Bernicia to meet the army of Elmet. There is still room at our feasts for those who are fit to join us. Who will come?'

There was silence, a long silence. Precent would not have made such an appeal in that Hall, unless he had agreed it before with the King. Yet there was silence. Even after Evrog said, 'If I were young, I would go. But now I am too old, and if I must die, then it will be on the steps of my own Dun,' still there was silence. Precent looked at me, asking me, silently to speak. I looked at my hands. Wars had nothing to do with me. I was going to Bradwen in Eiddin, not to war. Someone asked from the bottom of the Hall, 'And have anybody come to join you from other Kingdoms, real like?'

'Oh, come and see them,' Precent invited. 'Men there are from Mona, who speak strange and sibilant, as if they had adenoids. Syvno has brought them, and you all know of him, whose father was Astrologer to Vortigern the Good. And men from the Mountains that look on Mona, who cannot understand how it rains so little in Eiddin.' This caught at me, these would be my own people. 'And men from Dyfed and Gwent, forest walkers who have stripped every hedge in Eiddin to make their ash bows. Don't like wind, they don't. And men from the Summer Country, where Uther Pendragon rules.'

This last took them all, caused head wagging and whispering.

'More, there are men from over the seas. There are soldiers from Little Britain, in Gaul, who went over with the Legions to conquer Rome, and did it, and never came back till now. Not many of them with us, but some.'

There was more murmuring. But still no one said he would come. Peredur Ironarms put it bluntly, what the hindrance was.

'Do you expect that we will come to ride under you as Captain of Mynydog's Household? How many of my cousins have you not killed, Pict King?'

'I am not the Captain of this Household. I will ride, but I will serve.' There was a sound of astonishment. 'There will be another Captain. His name I will not tell you. If you

19

are too proud to ride except for a name, then it is too proud you are to ride at all.'

And then Evrog spoke again.

'Too old I said I was to go. But if any man of my household wants to go, he may, and he can return to me when the campaign is over, and keep all his booty, and he may boast as he likes of what he did, and no man may contradict him, who did not go with him. And I will send Mynydog thirty suits of mail, and helmets for thirty men, and thirty swords' – and here there was another taking of breath through the Hall, because this was a royal gift again, and would leave half the pillars bare – 'and twenty billets of good iron to beat spearheads out of, and forty horses all broken with their harness and saddles and three sets of shoes apiece. And this so that my Cousin may grant arms to his Household.'

Never had anyone thought that Evrog and Mynydog could be on such terms of friendship. There must be peace for one to send such gifts to the other, at this moment when the Irish raged along the coasts. Cynon stood.

'If Mynydog raises such a Household, what do I do here?'

This, I guessed, had already been arranged. Evrog told him, 'You need not ask arms of Mynydog. I have given you a sword and mail to guard my gate. Take them, and bring them back again to me.'

Peredur Ironarms was on his feet.

'So long as Precent is not leader of the war band,' he said in that lazy insolent way that his nephew, I hear, has after him, 'it will be no objection my friends will be having if I ride alongside this Pict to look after him.'

There was a roar of laughter at this, and Precent went a purple colour, but still he sat chewing the ends of his moustaches and answered mildly,

'We will ride together then, and count the heads of the Savages we drive onto each others' swords.'

Now it was this mildness of Precent's, this willingness to

accept provocation, that convinced the men of Strathclyde that there was something special about the expedition. Gelorwid, Evrog's other nephew, stood up, and talked like a hermit preaching a sermon, but that was the fault of the way he had been brought up. 'There is the evil that Morgan preached, that a man can choose his life, and take good or evil as he wishes. But every man does only what God has laid up for him. It may seem to him that he chooses. God in the beginning laid out the world and fixed for every man the way he should go, and how he should die. Maybe, I will be a priest and a hermit after all, maybe not. God has already chosen for me.' His face and his voice brightened. 'I have learnt a few prayers, and I will come and say those to you. Looking at the men who insist on going, I am sure that a little virtue and doctrine will be necessary. And I have not forgotten the swordplay I learnt at my father's knee, when I was able to beat Peredur when I liked, and I am sure that I can now—'

With that there was a hubbub, but several of the rougher grooms bellowed from the back of the Hall, so as to cut down the opposition, 'Quiet all of you, give the lad a chance, let him talk!'

They hoisted Aidan onto the table, and he cried out in his Irish-accented British tongue, his voice not long past breaking, 'I am a King's son, and I deserve a sword and a coat of mail, even if I have three elder brothers who are without arms. I will come with you and fight because I want a sword!'

There was a shout of applause, and now there were a whole crowd of men shouting to be heard. Among them, I could recognize Morien, shouting, 'I shall burn them out, burn them out!'

Then the songs began, and the Harper tried to choose the tunes but he was shouted down as they sang the old songs, songs of war made long before I ever sang of peace, 'Heads on the Gate', and 'The Toad's Ride', The Hunting of the Black Pig', and 'Blood on the Marshes'. Tomorrow would be the preparation, the saddling of the horses and the packing of soft bags, the farewells to mothers and the parting gifts from sweethearts, the choosing of clothes for riding and of clothes for feasting, and the giving away of things one would need after because they would be easy to loot and better for it. But tonight was the time for singing and drinking, and the old songs rolled in the rafters. Under the sound of the music and laughter, Precent and Evrog leant towards me.

'Will you come too?' Precent asked. 'Foster-brother, dearer than a brother, will you ride into Mordei and the land of the Savages? Will you guard my back?'

'In war,' I asked bitterly, 'what would I do? What place has the ox in the stampede?'

'If you are a poet, come and sing for us and make our deeds immortal. If you are not a poet, come and kill Savages.'

'I do not know,' I said. It was true. I could not think what I would do, except that I would not ride to war against the Savages. 'I will come to Eiddin, if I can.'

'I will give you a horse,' offered Evrog. 'You may have it whether you go to war or not, whether you go to Eiddin or not. It is yours for all the pleasure you have given me over the years.'

'Then I will come to Eiddin,' I agreed. I meant that I would ride to Bradwen. I did not know that I was riding to Cattraeth. Gelorwid was right. It was our fate.

CHAPTER TWO

Gredyf gwr oed gwas
Gwrhyt am dias
Mierch mwth myngvras
A dan vordwyt megyrwas
Ysgwyt Ysgauyn lledan
Ar bedrein mein vuan
Kledyuawr glas glan
Ethy eur aphan

He was a man in mind, in years of youth,
And gallant in the din of war:
Fleet, thick-maned chargers
Were ridden by the illustrious hero.
A shield, light and broad,
On the flank of his swift slender steed.
His sword was blue and gleaming,
His spurs were of gold.

It was three days riding from Dumbarton to Eiddin, across the lowlands. It was the first riding I had done for more than a year. I rode the brown gelding that Evrog had given me, a good enough horse, not perhaps the best in his stable, but a steady beast under me as if he had sympathy with me. It did not hurt as much to sit astride him as I feared.

There were nine young men, beside Precent and myself. We did not ride, only, because we led the rest of the forty horses Evrog sent. Three horses to a man is not too great an allowance for a campaign. There would be none to steal from the Savages, because they find it hard enough to manage oxen – even oxen can escape them. Even Arthur could not have defeated them had they been mounted, because they came about him as lice about a hairy dog.

The horses carried the iron rods and bars, ready for the smith to hammer out into spear-points. Axes and swords with their edges sharp to cut a wisp of lamb's wool, they are different. You have to get a real smith to beat out those, who has served his seven years of apprenticeship and has learned to make the edge straight and beat in the charcoal to the spongy iron they bring us from the bogs of Shetland.

Swords are work for craftsmen, as are songs. They are not made by brawn and the hard striking of the great hammer, any more than by a sweet voice or the oft repeating of rhymes. In each the skill is knowing what to say, where to strike. Any man could beat out here the strips of iron that make the rim of a helmet and the arches to frame the hard leather cap. But sending iron for swords would be no use if Mynydog had no swordsmiths, and the likelihood was he had too few workers even to use the iron Evrog had sent him. So swords Evrog sent too, long horsemen's swords of blue smooth iron, to give reach to a man who leans forward to strike at an enemy below.

Lighter than the swords and the iron bars were the shields. A shield-frame is not difficult to make, but it takes time to weave the great oval basket, lightly dished, and time Mynydog did not have. The frames were covered with leather, but unpainted. A man must decide for himself what

24

he wants painted on his shield, and if he can get the iron, whether he wants it rimmed or not; most of us did not want iron on our shields, to tire our arms.

Swords take skill to make, and shields take time. Mail takes both. A mail shirt is not made in a hurry for one campaign. More jeweller's work it is than smith's. You hammer out the iron bars into long wires, a little thicker than oatstraws. Each ring has four more rings linked through it, and each of these into four more. A thousand rings are so linked and you have a little sheet like knitted wool, large enough to shield a man's breast from the flight of an arrow. So weeks and weeks of work will make at last a strip of fabric iron, and if you fold it you have a sleeve. A shirt has two sleeves, and the body will take as much work as a dozen sleeves. Then after a year, a smith, working small and quiet, ring after monotonous ring, may have enough mail to clothe a man for war. And all that time, the smith must be fed.

A mailed shirt is a precious thing, not easily or cheaply bought, and I did not think that all the Kingdoms of the North could muster five hundred. Yet Evrog had been better than his promise, and had sent forty of them, each worth the purchase of a man's life. I knew, we all knew, how bare he left his own armoury, with the Scots at his gate. These shirts he sent to Mynydog's men for this campaign, then Mynydog must give them their arms. To Mynydog of Eiddin they went: I went to Bradwen in Eiddin.

We rode under the rock of Eiddin, beneath the steep North Face that rises sheer from the meadows and the marshes, a mile from the Forth. The watchers on the walls of the Dun, at the western end of Eiddin, turned their eyes from the fishing boats to watch us come and try to count us and guess who we were and where we came from. When they recognized the squat figure of Precent, never graceful on a horse, they began to wave and to shout at us, and we waved back.

By the time we had reached the eastern end of Eiddin, and turned south between it and the Giant's Throne, as we called it then, to ride up the long slope to the village beneath the rampart, they were all out, women and children, shouting to Precent, throwing flowers at him, and beneath his horse's hooves. The children fed the tired beast with handfuls of grass, and the smallest ones pulled at his stirrups and at his heels, and called him to look at them; and when he did, they were overcome with shyness and hid their faces or turned away.

They were all glad to see Precent. Nobody looked at the rest of us. It was plain that young men on horses came in every day, always fresh men, every draft like the last. There was no novelty in that, in men they had never seen before. But Precent coming home, Precent himself, oh, that was different, even if he had been gone only a week from Eiddin. Precent coming home, now, that was something to sing about. So they sang, and our young men sang too with them. I did not sing. I did nothing. I did not even hide my face. No one looked at me.

We turned in between the two rows of little houses that edge the last mile of the path to the Dun, the King's mile from his Hall to his farm. We heard a horn blow, Gwanar's horn, I knew, who had succeeded Precent at the gate. It was noon, Mynydog would be sitting on his Mound of Judgement, before the gate of the Dun. Now any of his people, any free man of the Isle of Britain, could come to him where he sat with Clydno his Judge by his side to tell him what was true law and what was not. Every day he sat, like every King, to hear complaints of one man against another, or against the King, and do justice, in the Roman manner.

Precent led the file of men and horses up the slope. I dismounted, and let a small boy hold the reins of my brown gelding. This entrance had nothing to do with me. I would not ride up the slope behind Precent. I would not be his gift to Mynydog. I had as much right in Eiddin as any man, as much right as Mynydog himself. I was a freeman of the Isle of Britain, and I would give myself where I wished. I would give myself to Bradwen, and what she told me I would do. I let Precent ride on.

26

I looked about Eiddin from under my hood. It had altered little in the winter I had been away. But it had altered. The houses were the same. The people were the same, the women as talkative, the children as shrill, the men as silent, as they had been a year ago; only all a year older. A year makes a great difference to a child. You do not recognize a child you knew a year ago, he has changed; and he will not recognize you – he has more important things to fill his mind than the coming of grown-ups. But apart from the people, Eiddin had changed. Every other house was now a smithy, with men beating out spear- and arrowheads, and strips of iron for helmet-brims and shield-rims and for bits and stirrups. You cannot expect a smith who works on his farm and only lights his forge once a week, if that, and then only to straighten a bent ploughshare or edge a wooden spade – you cannot expect him to think of welding mail rings or beating the edge of a sword.

But busy they all were. They were men from the South, from the border of Mordei, from Mordei itself and even from Bemicia. Their own smithies the Savages had burnt, and they had fled north to Eiddin, to the only King who seemed strong and determined enough to promise that one day they would return to the lost lands. These smiths from the South sweated the bitterness of defeat into their weapons: their fires smelt of revenge. I watched their work. I had no feeling whatsoever. It was one thing to think of war by the candlelight of Evrog's Hall. It was different here, in the clear light of day, in a place so well known. It was different here, where Bradwen lived.

At the bottom of the hill was Mynydog's farm. It was a cluster of barns and stables and pigsties, and a fold for the lambing. There was another smithy there, with men who could have made mail, because they were skilful enough, but they had enough work of their own. There was also a wheelwright's shop and a waggoner's yard. All the carts of the Kingdom were made there. Mynydog lived well on his carts. And between the farm and the slopes and steeps of the Giant's Throne and the river, stretched the fields where

Mynydog ran his horses as my father did in the pastures of Cae'r Ebolion before Aber-Arth.

Now, though, there were more barns than I could remember, many more, great longhouses. Some of them were well thatched and all the cracks in their walls sealed, and they had stood the winds of winter as I could see from their colour. Others were new, their timbers still showing white from the axe, and their roofs hardly thatched, but covered hurriedly with leafy boughs, not enough to keep out the summer showers, let alone the drenching rains of autumn. These would not last. They were no more substantial than the booths we used to build when we were young, to sleep in through the summer nights when we were herding the sheep out on the high moors.

But they were not shepherds who slept in these huts. With the older barns, there would be room for two hundred, or more. A young man on campaign does not look for comfort in space. The nearer he sleeps to his comrades, the warmer he lies and the safer he feels. And there were more than two hundred. I could see them out on the meadows, forming into three lines, fifty yards apart, in the true Roman way. Far away they were, too far to see any one man clearly, to make out more than that they were horsemen, drilling.

Someone then, was drilling the King's Household like a regiment of cavalry, real cavalry like they have in the Empire, mail-clad from head to foot, fit to face the Goths. Yes, you could see the sheen of their helmets, and above them a long shimmer of red, a glowing streak across the top of each line.

I had been standing long enough. By now Precent would have spoken to Mynydog. What he said did not matter. Aneirin did not depend on any man's words. Somewhere past the Judgement Mound, Bradwen would be waiting for me. I walked towards her, up the long gentle hill to the gate of the Dun.

Before the gate, long ago, earth was heaped up to form the Mound, and the grass was green on it. Mynydog's

28

throne was set on the mound, so that seated his shoulders were above the heads of standing men. He wore the scarlet robe of state that his father had received from Vortigern the Good, who was King of all Romans on the Isle of Britain, before the Savages came and Hengist struck him dead at his own board. Across Mynydog's knees lays unsheathed the sword of the Kings of Eiddin, an old blade, made by magicians, the hilt of bronze stretched out in two wide horns above the pommel.

On his head, Mynydog wore the Crown of the House of Gododdin. Precious beyond belief, it was all of silver and covered with a film of gold, so that it sparkled to strike awe into all who saw it. There is a cross of gold on the summit, and the rim is set with precious stones of great value, garnets and amethysts and fine crystal won in battle from the Picts and the Irish Scots long ago before the Wall was made.

There were a great number of people about the King. Beside him stood Clydno the Judge, his ivory staff tipped and bound with silver, his robe bound with ermine like a King's and his head bare, to show that even a Judge goes in subjection to a King, though the King obeys the law.

Clydno's face was still glowing with the pleasure of seeing his son again after three years. Cynon stood at the foot of the Mound, with Precent. As I went up the hill, and saw the Mound ahead, so Aidan came down, and Morien, Gelorwid and Peredur Ironarms. Mynydog, I saw, had not waited, nor had he been niggardly with Evrog's gift. They came armed in mail and helm and unpainted shield, and each had a sword. Only a King may grant arms, and only to his own followers. A young man I used to know, called Gwion Catseyes, led them down to the huts in the King's farmyard. They did not notice me, or see me, not even Gwion. They were too happy, they were now men, and warriors.

I came nearer to the Judgement Mound. I had to push my way through the crowd. Nobody recognized me. They were not expecting me. Nobody, I thought, would know me unprompted. Nobody will be glad that I have

29

returned, except Bradwen. Bradwen will be glad to see me, however old and weak I have come to look, however long I have been away, whether I make songs or not. Bradwen will know me, she will be glad to see me come home. For Eiddin is my home, now that Eudav's Hall is burnt. I will not ride out, whatever Precent may think I meant at Evrog's table. I said nothing there. I only said that I would return to Eiddin. I meant that I would return to Bradwen. I did not promise to go to Mynydog's war, whoever is the Captain of the Household. I will sit here in Eiddin, and watch the armies ride out, and then I will have some peace, with Bradwen, and perhaps I may even learn to sing again.

I came to the front of the crowd, and all at once there was someone who knew me. Mynydog's little nephew was there, four years old, or perhaps just turned five, I can't remember, son of Mynydog's sister Ygraine, though who his father was, whether her husband Gorlois or someone else, was more than anyone liked to guess at. He had been sent here to be fostered in the North as I had been, and for the same reasons, first that it was safe here, and second that nobody seemed to care what became of him. His half-sister Gwenllian had come with him, fourteen years old then when she carried the baby into Eiddin in her arms.

The little boy was Mynydog's only nephew, and the King was very fond of him, as indeed everyone was in Eiddin. You would have expected him to be quite spoiled, but in spite of all the fuss and petting he was still the most loving and patient child you ever heard of. Perhaps it was his sweet and equable temper and his feeling for justice, even at that age. Of course, he had his favourites, and I, once, had been one. He was sitting on his little stool at the foot of the throne, as he had already started to do the year before. He was very good, for only four, an age when it is a penance to sit still for any time at all. But still he sat, his palms on his knees, and listened to every case.

I came forward then, towards the foot of the mound,

and I did not know if Cynon had been as free with his tongue as in Dumbarton, or if Precent had listened to what I told him. You could never keep Precent quiet in the old days. I did not know if I were expected or unexpected, a surprise to the King or one awaited and prepared for. I never found that out. As soon as I came out to the front of the crowd, it was the little boy who saw me and remembered me. Yes, at four years old, after a whole year, and that is a very long time in a child's life, a quarter of it, he remembered me, and that shows how marvellous he was, even as a child. He stood up and shouted.

''neirin! 'neirin! Look what I got! I got a sword, a real sword. Arthgi made it.'

And it was a real sword, only of wood, of course, just right for his size, and Arthgi had taken some care in the carving and in making the little scabbard of leather that the child was so proud to wear at his belt. He waved it at me, and the whole crowd turned to look at me, the King and all his officers. I stood there silent, and they too were all silent, and even the little boy stopped shouting, and looked about him guiltily for a moment as if he had done something to be blamed for, although that would have been impossible for him in Eiddin, even when he was little. And still is. But the silence was only for a moment.

Mynydog rose from his throne and came down the Mound of Judgement. I know that you will say that it is not much for a Poet to boast about, that a King embraced him; rather, it is for a King to boast that a Poet allowed his embraces. A King's embrace is not an honour: it is what you might expect if you have a mastery of language and can make songs and satires and hymns of praise, and if you can hold in your tongue the fame of every man you meet, and can determine how even the greatest king will be remembered. By the Poets who sat in his Hall is a King's greatness judged. Mynydog was a great King, great as Vortigern the Wise. Even Arthur will depend on the Poets to be remembered.

But for Mynydog to embrace me was different. We

embraced, as two men, one old, one young, as two close, too close kinsmen. Whatever had happened, it was meaningless compared to the bonds that held us together, that still drew us together till he died, whenever he died, because I never knew. Or how.

'Welcome again, Bard of the Island of the Mighty,' was what he said. I answered, 'I am no longer a Poet.'

I did not have to talk to him as simply as I did to Evrog, explaining or hiding things that could not easily be explained. Mynydog was wiser than his own Judge and cleverer than his own Fool, and he could foretell the future better than his own Astronomer, and he could do that as well by firelight as by starlight, and as well in daylight as in the dark. He knew what I meant. He did not need to be persuaded. He only repeated, 'Welcome, well come again into Eiddin, Aneirin of the Gododdin.' He looked round at his people. He asked, as always at the end of the hour of Judgement, 'Is there peace?'

We all answered, 'There is peace.'

Mynydog sheathed the sword of the House. Gwanar, as always at Clydno's elbow, his axe in his belt, raised his trumpet and blew the horn for the ending of the Court. The people who had come to seek justice or to see justice done to others went back each to his own village in Eiddin or Alban or the edge of Mordei. They would have justice. With Mynydog to proclaim the law, and Clydno to tell it, and Gwanar to execute it, there was always justice in Eiddin. Mynydog with his left hand took my arm, and the little boy, shy now, sensing only that something had happened to mar the happiness of those whose only care for most of his life had been for his happiness from minute to minute, he put his hand into my other hand and pressed himself close to my thigh, rubbing against me as we walked like a cat.

In silence we walked to the gate of the Dun, and nobles of the Court walked behind. Just before the Gate they broke off, and went to their own houses within the Dun or outside it. I thought, soon, in a moment, in the courtyard beyond the gate or in the doorway of the Hall, I will see Bradwen. Then I will be well come indeed. Once I see her, it will all be over and my journey will be at an end. She will heal everything. But I did not know that my journey was already to Cattraeth, and there would be no returning. For the King stopped in the gate and said, 'Let us wait here. Someone is coming up the hill whom you must meet.'

I looked towards the village The Horsemen were dismounting in the farmyard and breaking into little knots, unsaddling their horses and rubbing them down with handfuls of grass and throwing blankets over them. That I could guess, even though I could see only a little at that distance. My sight was keener then than it is now. Only one man out of all that host was riding between the houses now. We waited for him.

This then must be the man Mynydog had chosen out of all the men he knew to lead his army into the Mordei, and farther South. Who was it? Who was the man whom Precent had refused to name? Who had been chosen before Precent to be Captain of the Household of Eiddin, whom Precent was willing to follow? No one, I was sure, out of the Kingdom of the Gododdin. But from farther away? Who could have come to Eiddin across the lands and seas that the Savages and the Irish ravished? Were there heroes from among the South Britons, or from the other Romans of Gaul and Italy, of whom I had not heard? I waited and I watched. Mynydog and I did not speak. We knew each other too well. We stood, and half my mind was on the scene before me, and half was on Bradwen, and surer and surer was I that when I saw her, it would make all well.

The rider came nearer, walking his weary beast up the slope, his greyhounds trotting behind. And then, when he dismounted and let a groom take horse and dogs, I saw the Ravens on his shield and I knew, before Mynydog said, 'Now we see the long awaited meeting, between the two greatest men of all the Isle of Britain, between Aneirin the Pre-eminent Bard, and Owain, son of Mark.'

33

Yes, this was Owain, King Mark of Cornwall's son, Tristram's brother. There has been trouble there, and it would not have happened had not Owain come to Eiddin, to ride with us all to Cattraeth. But Owain *had* come North, flaunting his Ravens, at Mynydog's call, as if they alone would clear the Savages out of the Eastern coasts, and peck the Loegrians clear out of the Island. (Ravens we said they were. He said no, they were a smaller bird, a chough, that lives in the sea-cliffs of Cornwall, but they looked like Ravens to us, and the Ravens we called them always.)

It was this Raven flag and this Raven shield that men would follow: they had all heard of them. Oh, I thought, this is a shrewd move, to bring in from outside *this* man to lead us, the men of Eiddin, mingled as we were already with men from other kingdoms of the North, and with men dispossessed from lands south of the Wall. There would be no favourites, with this foreigner to lead us, a man of blood as good as any among us, and better. To lead us, I asked myself? No, to lead them. My business was not with Owain, but with Bradwen.

A big man, Owain, seventeen hands high and a half. You will not find his match for strength today among the nobles who follow Arthur. It would have been no trouble for Owain to have killed Bladulf – he could have done it in his sleep. It would have been no trouble for Owain to have killed a thousand Savages, if he had met them in fair fight. They could never have overcome him except by treachery. No, not Owain.

But it was not strength alone that drew us to Owain. Handsome he was, more handsome than any man who has ever lived. I have never seen Arthur in his manhood, but I am sure he is never as handsome as Owain. Corn was the colour of his hair, corn with the touch of gold that gives it life, not the dull yellow tow of the Savages. And his eyes were of that light ice-blue, cold and flaming by turns. Only to look into his eyes while he spoke, and it was no trouble to believe what he said, if he told you that

34

black was white, and no danger to obey him though he told you to leap into a blazing fire. And it was that he had us do in the end, and worse: and gladly we did it. It was his beauty that struck me in that moment of meeting, and his strength, as he ran the last furlong of the way to us, uphill, and in his mail, faster than many a man can run fresh and unladen on level ground.

He knew of me too. He had heard my verses often, and I had heard his praises sung. He looked me in the eye as he heard my name, and I knew what he thought. He asked himself if I were more than a witless minstrel who can string words together for a bed or a meal, but can no more understand the real meaning of the line he sings or guess what the sounds rouse in his hearers' souls than the smith can swing the sword he forges or feel the terror that comes to the beaten warrior who sees the iron shear down at him for the last time.

'Well?' he asked. He made no ceremony of greeting. Kings in the South are different, I suppose, or at least their sons are. 'Are you come to fight, or are you only going to sing about us who do?'

I refused to be riled, or drawn into a false move.

'I have come here to decide how to spend a spoilt life.'

'There is no better way to forget that than in spoiling other lives,' he told me. It is easy to speak like that if you do not know the meaning of spoiling. In any case, I thought, I will soon see Bradwen. Then there will be no more talk of spoilt lives. Then my life will be complete again. The nearer I came to meeting her, the plainer it was for me to see, that all the strange thoughts I had in those days, of being a Judge in the North the rest of my days, or of going down south to my father's people, or into Ireland to my mother's family or farther still into Little Britain or Gaul, or into Africa, anywhere I was not known, or even, the maddest thought of all, going on this campaign, or any campaign – these were all empty air and froth. Bradwen would take me to her and comfort me, and make me whole again. With Bradwen nothing changed. I was so near her, she so near me, and yet I had for form's sake to stand here and fence in words with this big foreign man.

'There have been lives enough spoilt already,' I said. 'For most of them, there is no asking anybody now to repair the damage. Not all the wars that you can wage in a lifetime will put one head back again on its shoulders once levelled or make one maimed body fruitful. You may lead your army where you will, there will be no end to blood. Why don't you live out your own life in peace on some cliff-top farm and be thankful that you yourself have not suffered.'

'And that from you, Aneirin?' He seemed genuinely surprised. 'You've got more cause for vengeance than any man alive. I offer you the chance to shed blood for blood and chain men who chained you. How delightful it will be when we lead Bladulf through the gates of Eiddin with his hands tied behind his back! When we do that, he will be the last Savage left alive in the Isle of Britain. Then we can put all our strength against the real enemy – the Irish. But what shall we do with Bladulf when we catch him? Shall we blind him and set him to grind oat-flour for the rest of his days to spare women's hands? Shall we set him loose on the sea in a boat to die of thirst? Shall we sink him to his neck in a manure heap to cook to death? You shall choose, Aneirin. It's only fair, you have suffered more from the Savages than any man alive. How they must have rejoiced to have the Pre-eminent Chief Bard of all the Island in their hands—'

'It made no difference,' I corrected him. 'They had no Poets, and certainly would take no notice of them if they had. They aren't like us. For us poetry is the whole reason why men live. Not for them. Besides, they don't know one Briton from another. I was nothing more than another pair of arms and legs that might have their uses on the farm.'

What uses, I did not tell him. It would have been too shameful, there in the open gate. Besides, he knew it without my telling. I could see it in his eyes, so full of pity and of angry pride that such a poet should have lived in our nation.

I did not tell him that they had shackled me up to the plough-beam with the ox, and whipped me to break the stubborn land – our land. With the ox, I had pulled the heavy cart of stones picked from the cornfield. With the ox, loaded and goaded, I had walked the weary round to tread the wheat from the ear. And if Precent had not come, then I would have ended up like the old ox, they would have killed me at the end of the summer, and on the night of the Holy Souls they would have fed my worn-out body to the dogs. Was there anyone here who knew the whole truth of it, the truth I would not be even able to tell Bradwen?

There was nobody who could know, and yet, I felt, Owain did know. That was how he led us. He could always make it plain that he knew how you suffered and how you felt, whoever you were, whatever you had been. A man like that you can follow and feel no shame, even if you are as noble as he is, and though you know that you can surpass him in a dozen ways. And there was no way in which any of us could surpass Owain.

'That is all I ask of you,' he answered. 'All I need is another pair of arms and legs to ride with me into the South. Another pair of thighs to grip a horse, and another right arm to cast a spear, and another head to wear a helm. Look, I have had all our helmets set with red feathers, as great generals did in the days of the Legions.'

He was like any soldier, he thought that things of this kind, red feathers and shining helmets were important. And yet, though I knew this was all nonsense, for a moment I wavered, I was on the point of saying yes. I almost answered, 'Yes, I will come with you as a soldier against the Savages, I will add another head of red plumes for the Savages to count. I will do this even though I know that I will be cutting myself off for ever from the company of the Bards of the Island, that by

37

delivering the stroke of Justice I disqualify myself for ever from Judgement.'

I was on the very point of saying all that, and of a sudden I thought of Bradwen, and I knew that I could not go. She would never have me go, she would never let me leave her, now I had come back to Eiddin. She would know what to think of all this talk of glory and revenge. Bradwen the Wise Maiden men called her; cool and clear-thinking she was. She would have made a good poet, if it were lawful for a woman to make verses. It is only emotion that stands between a woman and the Muse. Any man who can look at life clear and cold and bleak, as it is, and not be deceived by his own desires and fears, can be a poet. The rest is a mere matter of words and metres: the rest is only a game of sounds. So I replied to Owain instead, 'There are plenty of heads in the lowlands, and in the mountains too, who would be glad to wear your pretty feathers. For every man Precent brought from Dumbarton, he turned back nine, because this one was too old, or this one too young, here a married man and here an only son, and there a man who limped but not enough to stop him doing a hard day's work behind the plough or in a boat. Take them, Owain, hard men used to war, and they will help you more than a hundred poets.'

I expected to hear him tell me they would not do because they were too valuable, but that my useless arm would stop a blow as well as any. In any army, there are only two or three men who kill the enemy, the rest cluster around to shield the champion from the blows of the enemy champions. But what Owain said now was, 'Empty heads, Aneirin, empty heads. In such a campaign, as we go on, there is too much work for me to do myself. In a host like this, I will need a Judge, Aneirin, to tell the law and judge our disputes. You know all the laws of the Island, of every part of the land, and you can help me make this Household of Mynydog's into one army.'

'But Cynon is going with you, and he knows enough law for your purpose. He has learnt it from his father.'

38

'If that were all the law I needed, I would not worry. I have Cynrig of Aeron with me, too, but I need more law than he knows.'

This was something to hear. Cynrig was a prince of Aeron, but not heir to the Kingdom, because he was a second son. Now, to be thought superior as a Judge to this Cardi man was something. Owain added, 'But he cannot be my Judge, because when he came, first his elder brother Cynddelig followed, out of jealousy. And then the younger brother came, Cynrain, to keep the peace between them, and they do not thank him for it. And that, Aneirin, is why I need a wiser Judge than Cynon, and one whose reputation is wider.'

That I could understand. But still I told him, 'I do not think myself wise enough yet for that.'

Owain did not try to rebut this argument, or any I ever used. He neither quarrelled with men, nor set up counter-arguments. Instead, he would always find another way to put his case. If only he had acted in war as he did in peace, and shown the same maturity in the face of steel!

'These Savages you have up here in the East, they are a funny people. I've never met them before. I've had enough to do, fighting the Irish.'

This was how he got his reputation, at war with the Irish who came by sea all along the Western coasts. Down in Demetia, they had even begun to settle and till the soil and build villages, dispossessing the Romans they found living there, as the Savages had done in Bernicia and were trying to do in the debatable land of Mordei. It was the Irish who were the enemy in the land. Now Arthur has utterly destroyed the Savages, he must show his real quality by beating the Irish. If they are not stopped they will first conquer this land, and then cross the seas and bring all the Empire under their rule, as far as Byzantium.

'Yet,' Owain went on, 'the Irish are not so different although they have their own uncouth language. They worship the Virgin, and obey laws like ours, and they know that the true aim of a kingdom is to nurture poets.

39

And there is no shame in marrying them.' He knew, and I knew, that each of us was born of the lawful union of a Royal House of the Roman Island of Britain with a Royal House of the Island of the Blessed. He could not speak scornfully about the Irish for his own sake, let alone for mine.

'But these Savages. They are something quite outside the whole range of humanity. The Church has no doubt that they are not men but devils. It is forbidden to speak of holy things to them, and we all agree that they are no more capable of baptism than my dog. And I have had some very reasonable and cultured dogs in my time.'

He laughed, and I had to laugh with him. That was another thing about Owain, that helped men to obey him, against their inclinations. He could destroy the tension of an embarrassing moment, not to flee the judgement point, you understand, but to step back and approach in another way. Even his laugh was an argument. Nothing was wasted. Once he had taken on himself a task, then everything he did and said was part of that task. He went on, still smiling.

'But these Savages, lack of Baptism is no penance to them. They do not know what God is, and they worship nothing.'

I could not understand how a man could be so wise and yet so ignorant. I corrected him.

'They worship demons. They have a wind demon, called Odin, and they can sail to us only when he favours them. And they have a fire demon called Thor, and it is his magic which gives them those terrible swords which cut through three thicknesses of mail. And another demon called Baldur who makes their wheat grow. All these they worship. They make offerings to them under trees.'

'Do they, indeed. You learned all this when you were a prisoner. All just by watching them?'

'No, they told me about it, boasting of how the demons would overthrow and eat up the Virgin and the Saints.'

40

'They spoke our language to you, then, did they?'

'Oh, no, they cannot speak the tongue of the Angels like us, not Latin, because their tongues are too short.'

'Then how did you learn this?'

'Oh, I had to learn their language, enough at least to speak a little to answer when they taunted me, and to obey the orders they gave me.'

'So you speak their language. And you know their ways.'

I did not see the trap Owain had set, and I boasted, though the Virgin knows that all I said was the truth.

'As well as any man. I know how they dress, and how they make that wheat bread, and how they sit to eat; all this by watching, because they fed me with the dogs.'

Owain sprung his trap. 'Think, Aneirin, how few men there are in all the earth who know the Savages' tongue. Can you name another? Even one other? Think of it, Aneirin. We have come together to fight these people, and we know no more about them than if they lived on the other side of the Ocean. Should we hunt them like deer, lying out on the high moors and crawling on our bellies till we can shoot them with the crossbow? Or ought we to wait till winter and then poke them out of their lairs like bears, with long poles and fire? As long as we don't know anything about them, they'll continue to settle and breed till they outnumber us. I don't want you with us for the sake of your arms, Aneirin, not even for your skill with the crossbow, which we have all heard about. I want you to come because you only can tell us about our enemies and guess what they are going to do.'

I saw what he meant, and what he wanted. For another moment I was on the point of agreeing. Then I thought of Bradwen. I had not seen her yet, though a number of Mynydog's people had come out of the houses in the Dun and stood about at a distance to watch the first meeting of Owain and Aneirin. I had not seen Bradwen among them, I had not even heard her voice. I only half listened to Owain, I had most of my attention on the sounds from the

Hall, in the hopes of hearing at last the long-loved tones. I thought of Bradwen and of how she would welcome me, and I answered – and I was quite sincere in this, it was what I felt, it was not a mere excuse:

'I have been a winter as a Judge. Before that I was a Poet. I have had enough of telling other people what they ought to do, and letting them do it by themselves. I have had seven years in which I have taken part in no action. If I were to come with you, I would not come as a mere adviser. I would want a more active part. But there's no need for me to come with you for that. I can tell you all I know before you set out for the campaign, and even teach half your soldiers enough of the Savages' tongue for all your needs. But I will not come. I have had enough of wandering. I will stay here in Eiddin.'

Mynydog the King, who had been standing by all this time, listening and not saying anything, now spoke.

'If it is an active part you want, Aneirin, then I can help you to one. I will give you arms. You can have my own shirt of mail, that I brought back from the South, when I rode in the Household of Vortigern the Handsome. And I have a helmet, too, I picked up after a battle against the Irish – oh, a bloody day that was, for we killed twenty-seven of them and lost seventeen men ourselves. Was ever such carnage seen in the Island? They will keep your head safe, and turn a spear. And a shield-frame and leather I can give you, to paint for yourself.'

I wondered a moment what I should paint on my shield. A wolf? An eagle? But why wonder. I would never paint a shield, nor carry one. I would spend the summer, all the campaigning time, here in Eiddin with Bradwen. She would be glad to have me here, whatever had happened to me, whatever other men did, whatever other men said. This offer of Mynydog's was a trick, to make me feel a coward that I did not go. I told the King, 'I will not take your arms. I have been a Bard too long to think of breaking what I have always preserved. Find some greater hero to wear your arms, King Mynydog.'

'That is a pity,' Owain came in. 'I would have liked you to come with me. I know who I would rather take to war, if I had the choice – a clever man who is not used to fighting or a stupid man who is. I would take the clever man because . . .'

His voice went on. I did not listen. I looked beyond him, across the courtyard. Bradwen came from the Hall. She wore a dress of red, the colour she always liked. At the hem her feet twinkled in their shoes of red and yellow, leather of Cordoba, paid for with their weight in silver. She had a chain about her neck, that I had once given her, made of silver with an amethyst hanging from it, and I had had it from a Pictish Lord far in the North, on the shore opposite Orkney, for singing him a satire on the Lord of Orkney who was, let us not say his enemy because there are no enemies among Romans, but, at least let us say, not his best friend. She wore it still.

The bracelets on her wrists Precent had given her, bronze patterned with red enamel and set with garnets and precious red glass. He had taken them from an Irishman who had come East under the Wall to the boundaries of Mynydog's Kingdom. He ought not to have come so far from his ships. Precent had caught him and left few of his men alive. These armlets were the best the Irish had, and they were voted to Precent as the bravest of the Household that Mynydog had sent. He had come straight back to Eudav's Hall and given them to Bradwen. That was what she was to me, even to men brought up with her as brothers.

She came down the steps towards us, her blue eyes shining with love and anticipation, her black curls blowing in the breeze as they always did, for gales haunt the crest of Eiddin. She came to us, stately and dignified, standing as she did only half a head shorter than me, and taller than Precent. Oh, she would have been a Queen in any Kingdom, she would have been the greatest lady in any Court, Caerleon or Camelot or Byzantium itself. This, I thought, is what I have been longing for, all this time in

43

the North by the bitter sea. I had been ashamed to come and face her when they had brought me home from my prison among the Savages. But now, just to see her again was enough to show me that all I dreaded, all that made me afraid to look her in the face, all the pain and grief I suffered was only a construction of my own mind. It was a fiction of the Poet's thoughts, that will seek out the complete and hidden meaning of any action, and find significance where there is none. She will welcome me, I thought, she who has been longing for me to return, thinking of me all through the winter, as she used to do, she said, in the old days when I wandered the length of the Isle of Britain, north of the Wall. Now, I could tell her what she meant to me, of how I too had been thinking of her and longing for my return. And I watched her come to me.

Bradwen did not see me. She reached out and took Owain's arm. With the merest gesture of formal courtesy to the King, she drew away from him the Son of Mark, the Raven Shielded, the Glorious, the Supreme Warrior in his armour, his plumed helm in the crook of his other arm. She led off from us the Victor over the Irish, the Deliverer of the Kingdom of Eiddin. Together they walked away from us.

I said to Mynydog, 'Grant me thy arms, my Uncle and my King.'

CHAPTER THREE

> Gwyr a aeth gatraeth oed fraeth eu llu
> Glasved eu hancwyn a gwenwyn vu

> Men went to Cattraeth, talkative was the host,
> Blue mead was their liquor, and it proved their poison.

So I came home to Mynydog's Household. Oh, it was a fine life in the King's Hall. As one of the family, I slept in the Hall, where I had always been used to sleep: in a wall bed, on the North side, that they had kept empty all through the winter in case I should come back without warning. The new straw was clean and dry, the old being turned out onto the floor.

I know that a King's Hall in the North is not like one in the South, in the twenty-eight cities of the Island; there were only twenty-six we counted in those days, because the Savages had slighted Carlisle. And they had taken York and burnt it, they had destroyed its Palaces and Churches, and pulled down the walls, and that they were to regret when Uther came against them: but that was later. Down there, in the Halls of common Kings, the roof-columns are of marble, all streaked in bright colours, and in the Hall of the Emperor in Byzantium the pillars are of gold, and in his private rooms they are of precious stones, garnet and diamond, ruby and pearl, sardonyx and opal, as is said in the book of the Blessed John which I have heard read. And the walls are painted with strange scenes, so that a man might think that there were no walls at all, but that he looked straight out into the woods and the pastures.

The pillars of Mynydog's Hall were of pinewood, holding the stout oak roof-tree. The walls were of oak frames and willow withies woven tight, and the chinks well packed with clay. They were hung with red cloth, and every pillar gleamed with mail and blades, helmets and bright-painted shields. Mine among them. Not perhaps that fine mail the Legions wear at Byzantium, fine as knitted wool and so light – in a coat of that mail, a man may run a whole day's journey, and fight at the end of it, and pursue through the next day, and at the end be no more tired than if he wore a linen shirt over his skin. Our mail was heavier: but it served.

The walls of Mynydog's Dun served us, too. They were not like the walls of the cities in the South. Camelot, they say, is a splendid place, and what is Camelot beside Cardigan, or Kenfig? Caerwent, I have heard about. It is only the port of Camelot, and yet there are walls about it seven times the height of a man, and as thick as they are high. The great bastions that look out over the Severn Sea are as high again as the walls. So great is Caerwent that a man may come into it by the North Gate and walk south. For a day he will walk through the entry of the city, and for a day he will cross the centre of the city, and on the evening of the third day, if he walk straight ahead all the time and never turn out of his way, he may reach the South Gate and go down to the water and get into his skin boat and sail away. From the water, he may turn and look back at the city, as we may look back at Eiddin from the Forth. The roofs of the houses are covered with tiles of shining gold, not the oatstraw we grow for thatch, and fixed with nails of silver, not weighted down with stones and ropes.

Eiddin was not a rich town like that, but a little huddle of houses on the hilltop. We heard of the great cities from men who came to us from the South, Cardi men who came with Cynrig, thin slight men with delicate small feet, used to treading daintily on the marshy mountain-tops where there is barely a fingernail's depth of the soil on the hard and barren rock. They live nearest to the Irish and suffer from them most. They dare not leave a pin outside their house at night in case some roving sea thief leaps ashore to take it, smelling the slightest booty from the further shore. Saving and careful they have to be, from their poor land and their uncertain tenure, and so they have a reputation for meanness, for demanding full value for anything they give. But they give full value, too, let the dead testify.

The men who had come with Owain from Cornwall were different again, and you could tell them by seeing them before you heard them talk. They were as fond of cream as the Cardi men of cheese, and they were the ones to ask for lobsters since they had supernatural skill in catching them, knowing where to put the pots even on this strange shore. To mead they preferred a hard strong

47

cider made from the juicy apples they grow down there in the far South, where, they told us, there is never snow or frost, and the summer days are always sunny and the winter nights are short. They told us true, and so did the men who came from Little Britain.

Most of the Household, for all that, came from Mynydog's own Kingdom. Some were from Eiddin, the centre of the Kingdom, around the rock itself, south of the Forth. Others came from Mordei, the debatable land, that lay south of Eiddin and north of the Wall, north of the Wood of Celidon. Here waves of Savages came and went like the tide, and every sweep, like the tide, they receded a little less, and so they ate the Kingdom away. Men were still willing to talk of fighting for Mordei. None, until Owain, talked of fighting for Bernicia.

There were men in the Household who counted themselves as Bernician by descent. They were not born there, but anywhere in Eiddin, or north of the Forth in Alban to the borders of the Picts. At least they remembered the names of the farms their grandfathers had in Bernicia, or at most where those farms had been. The land was lost. The Savages had settled there, from the Wall as far as the Humber. It was a generation since they had laid waste York. They blocked the road that ran south from Eiddin, through the Wall, past Cattraeth and York, to Lincoln and the Romans of Elmet. And once, they said, it had even been safe for a woman to travel all along that road, with no more than a dozen armed men for an escort. That was the road we now had to open. We still told of the great feat of Cynon, four years before, when he had returned from the South, all the way by land, bringing Gwenllian out of Uther's Camelot, clutching her half-brother to her, a tiny baby. Now he was the thriving boy we all loved. Then there were still Romans living in Carlisle, but the Savages burnt the place hardly a month after Cynon had passed. Now it was only safe for single men, or parties of not more than two or three, to travel up the west coast in skin boats, looking out for the Savages on land and the Irish by sea, making a detour around the lost shore to come from Mona to Strathclyde. But the Household would now regain Bernicia, and perhaps even Deira too, between us and Elmet. And then the road would run from Eiddin to Camelot itself.

No men came to join the Household from Elmet. Elmet men had enough to do.

Each Squadron had men from all these regions, all mixed together. Never before had any King raised such a Household, bringing in riders from all over the Island, and beyond. The most any King had done before was, perhaps, to have a man from a kingdom near by to be Captain of his Household, as Evrog had kept Cynon. Now we had so many different Kingdoms together, Owain insisted that each Squadron should include men from each region, all mixed up together.

'If a Squadron come all from one place,' he used to say, 'then it will be full of relations. It won't be long before we have Squadrons fighting each other instead of the Savages. We must learn to trust each other in war and peace. Quarrels between kinsmen are the curse of the Roman race and the downfall of the Island.' So he said, glaring at Cynddelig and Cynrig. Owain was Tristram's brother, King Mark's son.

Because of this idea of his, Owain would frequently change us around in Squadrons, taking whole sections of ten men from one Squadron and putting them into another, even in the middle of the day's exercise.

'In the middle of a battle,' he would say, teaching us quietly and patiently, but never leaving us without the conviction that it was he who understood it all better than we did, 'Squadrons break up, and men rally about whatever centre offers. You must always be able to depend on your neighbour in the line to do the right thing, even if you have never seen him before, and this is quite possible in such a huge army as this. Who ever saw three hundred and fifty men mounted in the field before?'

We always rode in pairs, of course. Usually I had Aidan

with me, to keep my back, but Owain often had us change our riding partners.

The most noble of us all had command of the Squadrons. There were more of them than there were Squadrons, and they too took it in turns, by Owain's order, to lead. At the beginning of each day in the field, I, as Judge of the Household, would draw tokens out of a helmet to see who should command that day and who should obey. So, not only did we all get used to the voices of different commanders, but we all of us, however noble, became used to obeying. Even Cynddelig, on occasion, served under Cynrig: but it took all Owain's arts to bring that to pass.

Always, Owain led the seven Squadrons together. No one ever took Owain's place. Sometimes Precent or Cynddelig would exercise two or three Squadrons together, but never all seven. It was Owain who was Captain of the Household.

And then, after the heat of the field, after the confusion of the exercise through the morning, after the quiet of the afternoon when we sit and mend our harness or our armour or hone our sword-edges, or just sit and watch the birds in the sky, then would come the feast in Mynydog's Hall. That Hall was a vast building, as big, I am sure, as any Arthur has in Camelot. Seventy of us could eat there, sitting at the tables or perched on the beds fixed against the wall. Woe betide any warrior who spilt mead on my pillow. I have satirized men for less.

A whole Squadron, fifty men, would eat in the Hall each night. The other Squadrons would eat in the houses where they slept, or outside on the grass. They had as much meat as they could eat there, served on platters of oatcake, and mead to swim in. They did not cook for themselves, or serve themselves. A crowd of young men like that, all unmarried, to look after themselves when they were just about to go off to the wars? Never! Every girl in the Kingdom came drifting down to the Rock of Eiddin, sooner or later, to hang round the huts trying to

50

get herself a soldier. So, anything one of our lads wanted done, the girls would do for him. They'd mend shirts, sew up leather seams, wash clothes. If you walked down between the huts any summer evening before supper, you fell over men everywhere, lying with their heads in the laps of the girls combing out their long hair for lice.

Then, after supper, the stars would come out in the clear sky, and even in summer darkness is cool and the dew is wet. The Household had their long houses to sleep in, that Mynydog had built for them so that they would not catch cold. But as for the poor motherless girls, so far from home, who cared where they slept? Who cared, indeed? Why, the Household cared, they cared all right. Out of charity, they took them in, they sheltered them, they lavished on them all the affection of which, obviously, their mothers had deprived them. If they were not deprived, what were they doing here? Why else would they have come down, relay after relay of them, walking purposefully down from the hills and over the river. And then they would, after three days, or a month, go walking for days home again, back to the farms they came from. There they could boast to the boys who were left of how they had seen the Household of Mynydog, now they had seen for themselves what *men* were like. They might boast to their mothers, or even to their fathers, though this last is doubtful. But as they walked back they would certainly boast to the other girls they passed, latecomers, hurrying down to the rock of Eiddin, all haste and anxiety to reach the huts before the Household rode out against the Savages.

Oh, yes, it was a fine life in King Mynydog's Household, a fine life indeed. Many of the young men had been there since the year previous, coming in for the barley harvest or just after it. Life was a perpetual feast, night after night. They said that the best girls had been the ones who came down in the early days, when the Household was new and small, and there were only a few men to work themselves to death lavishing love and affection on

51

the poor things and run off their feet to do it. Oh, those were the days, Graid and Hoegi told me, cherishing the memory, licking their lips.

And for all this fine living, what in return? Nothing very much, riding on fine horses, hunting in the hills, always hunting. Because at the end of the year, on top of all this good treatment, all these luxuries, they would have the honour and glory of a battle, and the name of the men who had driven the Savages out of the Island of Britain. Mead, Mynydog gave his Household, and we in our turn would give him our strength and our glory, so that his name would live for ever, and ours with his because we were *his* Household.

So we hunted. We hunted, day after day, because Owain said we should.

'This is how we will fight them,' he told us. 'We will round them up like deer on the high moors and hunt them down, throwing our spears at them. There will be no difficulty.'

'But it won't be like that,' I objected at last. 'They don't live up there on the high moors. They stay close around their farms. If we meet them, they will be in large bodies. They will stand and form a shield-wall.'

'So ` perhaps they did when you saw them,' Owain corrected me. 'But then they were attacking, banding together to make war on us. We will catch them when they are not ready to fight.'

'But you will need infantry to break these shield-walls,' I persisted.

'We will have infantry for all the good they are,' sneered Owain, and everyone within earshot laughed at men who fought on foot like Savages. 'They will do for mopping up and consolidating afterwards, or for holding the spare horses. You can fight with them if you prefer, Aneirin.'

I held my peace. It was always the same in the Hall, too, where I dined every night, being of the Family, as did those of Royal blood. The other warriors dined each once a week, so that every man could say of his King that he was on dining terms with him. Some, of course, were used to dining in a Royal Hall. Others had won their way into the Household by their own skill and strength, as had Morien the Charcoal-burner, and nobody knew who his father was. And it was a question even as to whether he was more use back in the woods than in the Household. To make a sword from the bars Evrog had sent would take the weight of two sheep in charcoal: and ten times as much to caseharden the bars beforehand, and twenty times as much to smelt the ore before that again. Still, he was admitted of the Household and was honoured by eating with the King and being called by name in the Hall.

Most men would wash and put on their clean shirts for this day in the week, but we who dined in the Hall every night did not take so much trouble. Except Cynrig of Aeron, who was always dainty, cleaning his nails always with his knife before he cut his meat. He washed his arms and feet almost every day, and would often put on a clean shirt for no reason at all but that he had slipped in the mud or put his elbow into a pile of horse-dung. Or if he had tumbled in the marsh and the shirt was wet through and spattered with slime, instead of drying it by the fire and putting it on again like any ordinary man, he would not be satisfied if he could not have a clean shirt to wear and persuade someone else to wash the old one. He was quite shameless about that, and would even, if he could find no one else, try to coax Gwenllian to wash it for him. But she never would. She always washed mine, every week, and said that was enough for her, taken up as she was with looking after her half-brother. But Cynrig had plenty of shirts, being a wealthy prince, and he could afford it.

Oh, they were fine evenings in Mynydog's Hall. Every evening was a Whitsun Day. The King would have them light as many rush dips as did Evrog the Wealthy, and on Sundays or on Ascension Day he would have lit candles of wax and tallow all around, so that the light should be clear and steady. The clear gleam lightened the hangings on the walls, so that they seemed to float above us like clouds, or close us in like shimmering mists; and through the mists the armour glittered like lightning on the mountains. By that light we could eat and drink, and Mynydog could see how each man behaved himself when the mead was set before him, a cup when he sat down, and a cup when the meat was set before us, and a cup when the platters were cleared away and the singing and the story-telling began. For every man, sometime in that year, spoke or sang in the Hall, so that we should learn all the songs of the Island and understand that all of us who speak the tongue of the Angels are one nation.

Bradwen always sat at Mynydog's table and poured the mead first for the Captain of the Household and then for the King, Mynydog's Queen long being dead. Yet I thought it was Gwenllian's duty by right, since she and not Bradwen was of Royal blood. Perhaps she was ignored because she had come among us from the South as almost a child, and it was as a child that people still treated her, out of habit. Only I, who had been away so long, saw that she was now a woman.

She still behaved, often, like a child, standing back timidly to let an older man go first, not taking her proper precedence like a lady of rank. She was always surprised to see a warrior stand back and let her pass. She was still very shy of strangers, however familiar they showed themselves with the court – or with her. She always came running into the Hall late, from putting her little brother to bed in the house on the north side of the court where they slept. Sometimes, even, the little rascal would not settle but would evade the maidservant who minded him and come creeping himself into the Hall and insinuate himself onto her knee, or even onto mine, because I always sat next to her.

She would sit by me till late. If the little boy had come sliding out to listen to the stories and the songs, she would wait till he fell asleep on her lap or mine, and then slip off with him to his bed and come back to me again. After the third cup had been poured, the Household would drift away from the Hall, each man coming up to bid the King good night and receive from the Royal Hands a jug of the King's own mead, made from the heather honey with a taste of its own. We older men would stay, those sitting lower in the Hall moving up to it on the lower side of the high table, opposite the King, so that we formed a ring. Bradwen would stay with us, and talk. And Gwenllian would stay, too, watching Bradwen.

We would all listen to Bradwen. Wise as a man, Bradwen would talk like a man and help us to plan the war, where we who were princes and nobles sat with the King and with Diarmaid, the Irishman, the wild man, who alone was able to pass between the King of Eiddin and the King of Elmet in Lincoln, crossing the Irish Sea twice to avoid the Savages. This man was a close friend of Cynddelig, riding and talking with him a great deal in those days. He knew the King's plans as well as any of us. Mynydog would tell us again and again what he wanted us to do, how we should strike south while the host of Elmet came north.

'We will have them,' he would say, 'like a horseshoe, between hammer and anvil.'

'I have never seen the horseshoe move on the anvil,' I told the King at last one night, when we were all there. 'The Savages will move. They won't stay to be attacked.'

'They won't realize what is happening,' Bradwen told me at once. 'We will be too fast for them. The news will spread only slowly from farm to farm, not as fast as we will move.'

'It's not a matter of news spreading,' I objected. 'They have a King, Bladulf, to call them together.'

'All the better,' said Owain. 'If they were to come together, then the first army to attack will hold them so tight that the late comers, whether they be Elmet or Eiddin, will take them by surprise from behind. Then they will run.'

'They won't run,' I warned him.

'They will. It's only in fables that Savages will stand in line to fight. Who ever heard of it in real life?'

'Who ever heard of a real battle in this Island?' I retorted.

'There have been raids, of the Savages on us or of us on the Savages. But never a full battle with one army drawn up against another in open field. That is what we must – no, not expect, this is not a foreboding I have – what we must bring about, somehow. If we cannot bring their men together in such a battle, then we cannot destroy them.'

'They'll never come together,' Owain insisted.

'They will. I know, I have lived with them.'

'Oh, you have only lived in one place. Perhaps you only met the boastful ones. They won't come together to face us. You'll see. I've had more wars than you have had hot dinners. You come along and see what really happens, and then you can start to sing again, and sing about that. That's your trade.'

He laughed. Bradwen laughed too. Precent grinned. There was laughter everywhere after so much mead. Why did I not argue on, insist, bellow at him, 'But that's why you wanted me to join you, to tell you what they were like, to tell you the difference between these Savages and the Irish you are used to fighting'? Because it was Owain who spoke to me, and there was nothing Owain said that I could not believe, did not believe even against the evidence of my own senses and my memory.

Only Gwenllian did not laugh at me.

CHAPTER FOUR

An gelwir mor a chynnwr ym plymnwyt
Yn tryvrwyt peleidyr peleidyr gogymwyt

We are called! The sea and the borders are in conflict,
Spears are mutually darting, spears equally destructive.

When we were ready, we went on Patrol, Squadron by Squadron, down the coast from Eiddin. I went under Cynon, whether to give Cynon practice in Command or to give us practice in obeying Cynon I was not quite sure. The decision was Owain's. On this ride, Cynrig, like me, obeyed Cynon.

We rode easy, unworried. On this ride we stayed within Mynydog's Kingdom, where no Savages had settled, and where they raided little. It was good practice in itself for the great journey. We rode in the Roman fashion. Owain had drilled us again and again in riding abreast, in a long line, in walking or trotting or galloping together with no man falling far behind the line or pushing ahead. But on the march we went in Roman fashion, in column, always riding in pairs, to guard each others' backs. Aidan always rode with me on this journey, since he knew me best of all.

We slept each night at farms. Fifty strong, no more, we could always find room to sleep in the stables and the barns. Roofs were not absolutely necessary that summer. It was a long, fine, hot summer, a better summer than any I have seen since. The people were glad to see us. We showed at least that Mynydog was willing to help them guard their fields from the Savages. It was not merely a matter of the King demanding things from them, though he demanded enough, and all Kings did that. He would guard them in return, and there were few Kings to do that.

We did not need to carry food with us. We hunted the high moorlands inland of the farms, and most days we could count on sighting deer, and then we would ride out in two long wings, one starting the deer into the other, so that we could thin out a few of the bucks. Other times we could loose our greyhounds at hares, or fly our hawks at grouse or duck or a variety of other birds, all good eating. The barley harvest had started, and the people on the farms had no time to hunt, so they were glad to have the fresh meat we brought them. They gave us oat cakes and lettuces, onions and radishes to go with the meat. And they would always be ready to roast us a sheep or three, or bring out the great cauldrons for a mutton stew, to put new life into dead men. You need a hot meal after a day in the saddle, however hot a day it has been already. It is dusty on the road in summer, but when you dismount, and the sun is beginning to go down, you remember now that you have been sweating all day into your flannel shirt, and the cold and the shivers grip you. That's when you need the hot soup and the meat in it, and the fine sharp taste of onions. We would be so eager for it we would hardly strip off our mail: we always rode fully armed, so that our horses, as well as we, could get used to the weight.

What we did not eat hot in the night, we took away with us cold in the morning. In the middle of the day, with four hours riding behind you, and another four hours ahead, there is nothing to keep your heart up like a slab of cold roast mutton, with the crisp white fat in it, firmly breaking between your teeth. They were wonderful days, that summer. We would sit out in the noon sun to eat, the hobbled horses grazing around us. We lay on our backs, and watched the high clouds over us. We played 'She loves me – she loves me not' with the daisy flowers, and blew dandelion fluff into other men's faces, and covered our friends' backs with the bared seedheads of the grass. We would practise the songs we knew, and dance, men with men, the dances of every Kingdom in the Island of Britain. For songs are the same everywhere, since we speak the same language, from Wick to Cornwall, but every Kingdom has its own dances.

They were peaceful days, and we were all friends. I had little work as a judge, because there were no disputes. You may find it difficult, nowadays, hearing of all the quarrels and rivalry of Arthur's Household, to believe that there were no quarrels ever in the Household of Eiddin: but it is true. It is easy enough to keep from quarrelling, when there are enough girls to go round, and meat for everybody, and enough mead but not too much. Sometimes there were arguments about precedence of families or the pride of pedigrees, and it was then that I had to work my memory to bring back the order of the Houses of the Island. But above all, what kept us from quarrelling was the thought, always, that we were the greatest Household that any King had ever raised, and that it was our destiny to ride South and deliver all the Island from the Savages. And if that was our aim, then why should we quarrel over lesser things? We were consecrated, set aside, for this great enterprise and for this holy aim. The Virgin kept us in peace.

What we practised thus in harmony in the day, we sang and danced in earnest at night, in the fenced farmyards with the girls around us to join in, to learn the new choruses we brought them, and to make themselves perfect in the new steps and unfamiliar rhythms of Gwent or Little Britain. Oh, they were merry nights indeed, around the big fires the people lit for us, coming in from three or four miles away, from their own farms to the places where we slept.

Yes, the nights were merry, and the farmers poured out the mead for us, what mead they had left, and they gave it willingly. They had paid, already, that year, a treble tax of mead to Mynydog, and a treble tax of grain for three years, and of wool the same. This had fed and clothed the whole Household for one year, giving each man his feasts, and his three shirts and his saddlecloth and his red cloak. And mutton, too, besides wool: they had sent their sheep in to mix with the game we hunted for ourselves. They had thinned their flocks for the Household, and never grudged it.

Besides the meat and the wool, there was the leather too. The mail of a coat will keep the edge or the point from tearing the skin. It will not stop the force of a blow. A good stroke with an axe, or even with a staff or an iron bar, landing on a body protected only by iron, will break a bone. You see men, too, dying slowly from a ruptured spleen after a blow in the back, or coughing up frothy blood with their ribs splintered into their lungs, and dying just the same, and even men with their backbones

60

broken, who live, may live a long time, but cannot move. And sometimes a blow will not itself break the skin, but forces the broken ends of the bone out into the air of day.

So when the smiths have made you a mail shirt, you must stitch it to a lining of boiled leather, stiff and unyielding. Always remember to have five or six more layers of boiled oxhide over the shoulder. This will save you from a downward stroke to break the collarbone: also, it stops you raising your arm too high in excitement, and taking a point in the armpit. The farmers all down the coast, now, went without shoes, and they guided their horses with ropes of straw, because for three years they had sent all their ox-hides to Mynydog. All this had stiffened our mail: because of this we could afford, every man of us, to ride in high leather boots, and tuck into them breeches of two thicknesses of leather to keep our shins safe in battle or in the briars.

But you need more padding than this. Stiff leather does little more than muffle the blow and spread it over your whole trunk rather than on a narrow line. Even then, a well-placed stroke might leave you winded, rolling and gasping on the ground, and hoping in your agony that some of your comrades would come up and stand over you. What we used to do was to wear two sheepskin jerkins under the mail, one with the fleece outside, the other with the fleece next to the body to soak up the sweat. You did sweat under all that, and when your shirt dried at night, you would find it in the morning white and stiff with the salt, to stop a blow on its own. I had to wash my shirt at the end of every week, and that is why Mynydog had given us so many. It was the fashion, too, to wear scarves around the neck, if you could get them, to stop the armour chafing as well as to soak up the sweat, and at the end of the day's ride it was nothing for a man to take his scarf off and wring it out and see a stream of water pour from it to make a puddle at his feet. Men would get their sweethearts to make them scarves in the colours of their families or their kings. So because of the shirts we

61

wore, and the sheepskins we had under the mail, and the saddlecloths we sat on, and the leather jerkins they made for the infantry, the farmers down the coast and up into the hills had all to make do with their old coats a year longer, through the rain and the snow, or lie a layer colder in their winter beds.

These were the people who had paid for the Household. They had done it all with poor tools, and not enough. A year earlier, even before they had ridden down to rescue me and avenge Eudav, when Mynydog was still only planning this campaign in secret in his own mind, Precent and Gwanar had ridden around every farm in the Kingdom, looking for iron, taking away all the metal the farmers could spare, and some they could not. Precent picked up any old spade, or fork with broken tines: or if there were a farm cart that nobody was actually using at the time, and Gwanar could attract all the attention his way, then Precent would take the iron tyres and the chains and the swingle-rings. A broken ploughshare was a great find, and the nails out of a pair of shoes not too little to take. These farmers had paid, then, in iron as well as in labour. Later in the summer they would be ready, many of them, to pay in time, and in blood, because they were willing to march as infantry with the Household down to the South. They had paid all that the Household had cost, these farmers, and when we came riding by they were pleased to see how all their goods had been spent.

They *were* glad to see us. They had paid, they saw, for an army gathered from all the Kingdoms of Britain, and farther, because we had those men from Little Britain across the sea. They saw our army with their own eyes, riding up and down the coast as far as the edge of Mordei, to press back the Savages, however they came, by land or sea. This was what they wanted. Mynydog had not wasted all the taxes they had sent him, and they were satisfied, and more than satisfied, to see us. We meant to them freedom from fear and anxiety. So nothing was too good for us, who had come to fight for them, nothing too lavish even though they starved themselves. Just to see men who had come such immense distances, from Orkney or from Cornwall even, places they had only heard of from wandering poets like me, come just to defend them, why, it made them sing all night, even sober.

We rode an easy way, east and south, under the blue sky of a hot June, looking out over the blue seas, at a few white clouds, at a little white foam. The wind blew, lightly, from west of south. When at last we came to the end of our ride, the border of Mordei, the debatable land, we saw smoke blown out over the sea.

We looked south, across the empty country where no one lived any more. The stone castles that our fathers had built were empty. Those walls can keep out the Savages all right, because they do not know how to attack them, or how to build them, and they are afraid of what they do not understand, instead of wanting to understand it and conquer it like a civilized man: but how can a man live in a castle when he dares not walk as far as his own cabbage-patch, let alone ride his sheep-walks, for fear of being killed without warning by men who sit all the time motionless in the woods, watching him. Nobody lived in Mordei, not our people, not the Savages. But somewhere down there, perhaps as far south as the border between Mordei and Bernicia, there was a fire, so huge a fire that though it was too far to see flames, we could watch the smudge of dirty smoke rising high in the air and drifting out to sea.

'What is it?' Aidan asked. 'Are they burning up all the world?'

'They would if they could,' I answered him. 'They have powerful wizards, who make their strong swords. I have heard it said that there is an Island in the northern seas where their demons have set the mountains on fire.'

'It's evil, whatever it is,' Cynrig agreed. He never liked to talk about magic. Perhaps he was too ashamed of his family who had their own dealings with the Little People who live under the sea near Cardigan. He turned away from us on the hillcrest, and shouted to the rest of the

Squadron who had not thought it worth the effort to climb with us, and were grazing their horses in the dead ground behind us.

'Come up here! All of you, come on! Come and see the evil these Savages are bringing on us. They say you can burn the stones in Bernicia, and that is how the legions held the country. I think that this is what the Savages are doing, burning the land itself to spoil it for us.'

The men strolled up the rise to look, chatting as they came and falling silent as they saw the smoke.

'Burn all the Isle of Britain, they will,' breathed Aidan, full of a kind of pride at having been the first to see it. 'Demons they are, indeed. What do they look like? Do they look anything like men?'

'Never seen one, boy?' Cynon smiled at him. 'Like men, they are, only horns they do have, or so they say who never saw any, let alone killed any. And watch out for the females, they're worse. You'll see them, soon enough, horns and all. Come on, then, if you've all had a good look. We don't want to spend too much time watching here for nothing to come. Cynrig, you get them mounted again.'

We straggled down the slope. Morien stayed longest, looking fascinated at the smoke till the last. We laughed at him. He looked seriously at me.

'Burn the whole country,' he breathed. 'Aye, that would be a fine thing to do. Scorch them out of the way, I'd like to do that. And I will, too. You wait.'

We laughed at him the more. I pulled myself up onto my horse, a brown gelding that I had broken myself three years before and Eudav had given me, and Mynydog had kept for me. I walked out to my place, right marker, and waited while the others finished fussing over their harnesses and got themselves up into their saddles. Then Cynrig bellowed the orders like a true Roman, as Owain had taught him, trying to sound like Owain – we all tried to sound like Owain in those days:

'On your marker, into line . . . walk! Right . . . turn! In

extended column of pairs . . . walk! . . . *March!'*

Going north, for the first hour, I rode as Scout, Aidan as always by me.

'No, never seen any of these Savages, I haven't,' he told me. 'Have they *got* tails, then? Really? Have they really got tails?'

'It all depends. If you are frightened of them, then you'll see tails on them, if they've got them or not.'

'And horns?'

'Oh, yes, horns, of course.' I smiled at him, smiled, not laughed. 'And so have some of us. Why, Aidan, you're a horned man yourself.'

He looked at me suspiciously, puzzled, while we rode a few paces. Then he began to grin.

'Horns? On my helmet, you mean?'

'Yes, on your helmet. And so do they on theirs. But we put whatever we like on our helmets, horns and wings and wheels and moons and stars. They always put horns.'

'But . . . Aneirin, is it true that they boil living men in their big pots and eat them?'

'Nonsense! Even Savages aren't as bad as that. The Picts used to do that, once upon a time, but you've never seen Precent eat anybody, have you? And, anyway, who ever saw a pot big enough to boil a whole man in. You could never make one, not even out of iron.'

'But they used to have them in Ireland. Everybody knows that. The old Kings used to keep them, and they used to boil their dead soldiers to life again after battles.'

'Tales, Aidan, tales. Men like me make them up.'

'But you haven't been in Ireland, have you, to see? I know people who have been, and they've told me about it. I hope the Savages haven't got one of those Irish cauldrons. Still I hope too I get a chance to see one of those Savages alive before we start killing them. Just to tell about after, like.'

'Little chance of that,' I told him. But even so, he was the first, a few steps later, to see the ship, and the Savages in it. We had come to the head of a steep path winding

65

down the face of the cliff into the bay. It was too steep for a horse, but farther on, between the rocky headland where we stood and the more northern spur of rock, both jutting out into the sea, with the waves breaking at their feet over the cruel stones, sand-dunes ran down to the water's edge. From the cliff, we could look down into the ship, drifting in gently against the light wind, on the last hour of the rising tide, between the horns of the cliff its own dragon head horned.

It was a Savage ship, I could see that. It was bigger than any vessel we Romans build, huge, immense, fifteen or twenty paces long at least. They have wizards to conjure these ships together, making the sides firm with planks of oak because they have not the wisdom to sew leather as civilized people do. They glue the planks together with Roman blood, and sew them with the sinews of Christians.

Aidan, riding ahead, saw it first, and called me to look. He was amazed, saying it was some King's Hall that had fallen into the water. He was more alarmed when he heard it was a ship. I shouted back to Cynrig, but he, leading the main body, was too far back to hear. I told Aidan, 'You ride back and tell Cynon. I'll go on, and find an easy way down there. I think we can ride over the dunes to meet it.'

'Don't go by yourself down there, not by yourself!' Aidan was terrified. 'They'll bewitch you.'

'Better they bewitch one than two,' I laughed at him. 'I'll sing them a satire.' But when he was gone, I remembered that I would sing no more satires. Yet, as I rode down to the beach among the marram and the sea holly, I thought what satire I would have sung, and what the rhyme structure would have been, and what pattern of alliteration would have been most effective in quelling a wizard.

When I had found a smooth way down through the dunes, firm for the horse's feet, the ship had already grounded, some way out, stuck on a sandbank, with the water still all around her. The tide was near its peak, and soon would be hanging, as it does, for an hour. I watched the ship, leaning over on its side, till the leading riders, Aidan leading Cynon and Cynrig and a score of others, came galloping over the sand to me, screaming and shouting as if they were going into battle or driving deer into the nets. I shouted back at them to be quiet, and they settled down, some of them sitting with us and others wandering about up and down the beach on foot. They poked in the seaweed and driftwood, and filled their helmets with mussels and winkles. Caso spread out his red cloak on the sand and went to sleep in the sun. At least, they were quiet, and let us alone to listen for any voices out of the ship.

'*Is* there anyone in it?' Cynon asked, when for a long time we had heard and seen nothing.

'There must be,' I answered. 'I think I saw something from the cliff. Yes, I am sure that I saw people in it.'

'How many were there?'

'I do not know.'

'Think! Were they men or women? Or both? Were they armed? Did you see their weapons shine? Did they move about? Did they look up at you, or wave?'

'I do not know. I cannot remember.'

'Did you not try to count them?'

'I never thought.'

'Then what did you think?'

'I remember that. I looked down from the cliff, and I saw the water so blue, against the rocks so grey like shining iron, and spattered with the white foam so clean. And on that pure sea, the ship lay dirty brown, like a . . . like a turd, come floating in to foul our pure sand.'

'Oh, a nice poetic thought that was, to be sure. But it's with a soldier's eye you've got to be looking at things now. Fine verse it would make, to be sure, but it don't help the first boys to go up there, now, do it? How do we know what's waiting for them?'

'All right,' I said shortly. I was nettled by Cynon's sneering, his blunt words. It was more like Precent. It was Owain we tried to be like; but in stress and action, it was Precent we imitated. 'I'm going up first.'

'Oh, no you're not,' Cynrig told me. 'We're not losing our Judge so early. I'm going into it first, I and . . . Caso. Caso! *Caso!* Kick him awake, somebody. Come here, boy, and bring your sword. Now, who else would—'

But at that moment the noise started, a blurred indistinct half-moan, half-grumble, from inside the ship. Then a head appeared over the bulwarks, two feet above our faces, and looked down at us. It was a man. At least, it had once been a man and not a woman. He was old, in his forties at least. His hair and his uncut beard were turning from yellow to grey in themselves, but over this they were streaked with white with sea salt from the dried foam. The salt was encrusted too on his face, clinging in the layer of grease with which he had tried to protect his skin from the drying wind and the sun. He hung there, his face just above the gunwale, and croaked at us, and croaked, and croaked. It was difficult, but at last I could tell Cynon, 'He's asking for water.'

'Oh, it's water he wants, is it? All right, boys, let him have his water.'

Cynrig and Caso rode out into the sea, as far as the ship. Mounted, they could have leant over the bulwarks. They did not go as near as that, only close enough to catch the old man by the arms and drag him over the side, to drop him, face down, into the salt waves. He rolled over, spluttering and retching, trying to hold his head out of the water, which was only ankle deep. Everybody laughed. He got up onto his hands and knees, and crawled a little of the way towards the land. Then he collapsed again. Aidan ran barefooted into the little waves and, catching him by the legs, dragged him backward onto the dry shore. Then Aidan poured some water from his flask into the dry mouth.

'Clean that bottle well after him, lad,' Cynon advised him. Cynrig, dismounting by Aidan, asked me, 'What's he trying to say now?'

Even after drinking, when I was kneeling by him, the old man was difficult to follow. I was able, at last, to say,

'An ox, he seems to be talking about an ox. He wants us to take care of an ox.'

'Got an ox, then, have they?' asked Cynon. 'Have a look, boys!'

There were at least a dozen men now who had ridden or waded out to the ship. At Cynon's word, they gingerly heaved themselves up to look into the ship. They began jumping in with shouts of discovery.

They were very gentle with the ox. First of all, Hoegi passed his helmet full of water up into the ship for it. Then they hoisted it out and down into the knee-deep water. It could hardly walk, but they urged it up the sand, to where Morein had lit a fire of brushwood. They brought out, too, three young pigs, and these men had to carry.

'Anything more?' Cynon shouted.

'Lots of iron,' Caso replied. There was, too, a great deal. Six or eight of the curved knives they used for wood-splitting or fighting came first, a little longer than a man's forearm, single-edged and curved. Then there was a bay-fork, two wooden spades edged with iron, three axes, a hammer, two sickles and a scythe. A whetstone Caso thrust through his belt. There was a quern, which they threw into the water. Against it, our men broke a large number of pots and dishes, coarse and clumsy, and bad in colour. Hoegi cut the stays, and then Caso beat the tabernacle to pieces with his axe, so that the mast and yard, with the tatters of sail, fell over the side to be dragged to the shore.

'Any people there?' Cynon asked.

'No, no people at all,' Caso replied. 'Some Savages, though.'

'How many? Dead or alive.'

'Some dead, some alive. Most betwixt and between.'

'But how many?' Cynon asked again.

'How many?' I asked the old man.

'We were thirty,' he answered.

'Fifteen up here,' Caso shouted. But Cynon looked down at the old man and snarled. 'Tell us more!'

'Tell us more!' I repeated in his language. He shut his mouth, firmly, defiantly in a straight line.

'All right, then, hold your tongue if you want to,' Cynon shouted at him, and from the saddle kicked the old man in the back so that he fell forward again on his face in the sand. Meanwhile, men were bringing clothes out of the ship, and bags of household stuffs that they spread out on the beach for us to share out. There were cloaks and shirts, and instead of the togas we wear kilted around our bodies down to our knees the Savages use trousers of cloth to walk about in, as we wear leather breeches to ride. There were some pieces of jewellery in the bags, and I managed to snatch a ring with a stone in it, though what the stone was, and whether it was brass or gold or even bronze the ring was made of, I had not time to see.

Then the soldiers lifted out of the ship, with difficulty, two big leather bags, full to bursting with something that squeezed and shifted. They balanced the sacks on the gunwhale, and Caso slashed one of them with his sword, bringing out a handful of grain which he passed over to me.

'Seed corn,' I told him. 'For wheat.'

'Let it grow in the sand!' laughed Cynon. The old man watched as we emptied both sacks into the water. The grain floated, a scum on the surface, spreading out to hide the blue of a wide stretch of the shallow sea, dirtying it, stealing its beauty from us, just like the Savages who brought it.

Last of all, we could see half a dozen of our men heaving and straining till something of great weight fell over the side and splashed into the water. And there it sank into the soft sand, and proved very troublesome to those who tried to bring it out onto the firmer beach. But they did it, and pulled the heavy thing up the beach to the fire. It was a Savage plough, with a beam of oak as thick as a man's body, and a pole of ash: the wheels were iron-tyred, and the share of iron, too, three times the size of a real civilized share. It was built to cut deep furrows in the clay, so that the Savages could plant wheat, that evil plant, which grows in the bad soils where oats run rank and thick. It was too heavy for a horse: it was what the ox was for.

The old man followed us with his eyes as we pulled the plough towards the fire. When he looked up the beach, he gave a wail at what he saw. There they were butchering the ox, and getting the joints ready to roast on a spit that Morien the forest man had made out of the poles of the mast and the yard. Cynon dismounted and shook the old Savage.

'Talk!' he said fiercely. Like so many Eiddin men, he had a few words of the Savages' tongue, not enough to carry on a conversation, but enough to follow, vaguely, what was said in common talk. 'Talk! Where from?'

The old man looked blankly at him. It was wilful insolence, he must have understood Cynon, he had shouted loud enough.

'It's no good,' I told Cynon. 'He *won't* talk, he just won't.'

'Won't he then?' growled Morien. He and Caso grasped the old man under the armpits and dragged him to the fire. Morien took hold of his foot and held it close to the flames, till the filthy cloths in which he wrapped his legs began to char and the leather in his bursting shoes, salt-soaked, curled back and steamed.

'Talk!' ordered Cynon. 'Here, push it right in! Talk! There, that's loosened him. Give him some water, somebody, or Aneirin won't be able to hear him. Now, then, what's he got to say?'

'He says they come from far across the sea, very far,' I explained to my comrades. 'They used to live in a very flat lowland, on the edge of the sea, by marshes and lagoons. He says it is not good land for men to live in. They cannot grow much wheat, and have to kill birds and animals for food. The water is rising. Some of the marshes used to be fields when he was a boy. They can no longer grow enough wheat to live. They cannot go away inland, because they are afraid of the people who live there. So they have set out to sea to find a new land.'

'Then they had better think about another new land,'

71

ruled Cynon. 'They have no place in ours. Let them try Ireland.'

I listened to the rest of the old man's story, putting it as well as I could into the language of the Island of Britain. He said:

'We bought this ship from our chieftain. We gave him all the amber beads we had, and two pieces of gold that my mother's mother had stored away, and three silver buckles and a bronze pot. We were thirty in it, myself and my brother, our sons and their wives, and some children. We had never been on the sea before, any of us, ever, only on little boats in the marsh. We suffered on the first day, and some of us ever after, always being sick, spewing up what we had to eat, burning and blistering in the sun and the wind. We thought that it would be a short voyage, only three weeks, that is what they told us who had been here and come back, only three weeks to Britain with a good east wind. We thought we would have an east wind, because we had sacrificed to the Wind God a sow, and a white horse that we bought with our old ox and two cows. We drove them into the sea, and cut their throats so that the blood drifted out towards the West, and the way the ship would go, and we thought that would bring us an east wind and good luck in all the voyage.

'Then, as soon as the wind began to blow from the East, at the end of the spring, we set out to sea. Oh, we thought it was a great thing, to be out on the sea, just to point the ship before the wind and glide to a new land, with no work, no effort to move us on. At first, it was all a long feast: we ate and drank as much as we liked, even though it all went to waste over the side. But after a week, the wind changed, and began to blow from the West, and the ship went every-which-way whence and whither. Only sometimes at night could we make out the stars, and never in the day did we see the sun through the cloud, the thick cloud that never rained on us, so we never knew, in the end, which way we ought to go.

'And soon, there was no food. And after that, no water.

72

The little water we had, the last of it, we kept for the ox and the pigs. The children died first. Then the old. My brother died the first, and then his wife, and mine. But towards the end, it was the young men and women who began to fall away and dwindle. I was the only one who had still strength to look over the side when I heard you speak, and knew we were safe.

'Still, in spite of all, we had kept the ox alive. It was all we had to help us break the ground and grow food. We brought all the tools we had, so that we could clear the scrub and plant our wheat. We were not afraid of the hard work in clearing the forests, but at least we knew there would be plenty of empty land we could settle on. Nothing else in this Island, but enough land. It was late in the season, we knew, for setting out, but as long as we had the ox alive, and the seed corn, we would be able to grow enough to keep us through the winter and begin early next spring. That work we were prepared for, and starvation through next winter. But not the thirst on water: that was too much.'

'How then would you live through the summer, till your harvest was gathered?' I asked him. Oh, but I knew how they would live. We would see them all over the civilized land, little bands of them, sometimes only one or two men, sometimes whole families, in rags, drifting from door to door, begging for old clothes, for food, for drink, for anything. If there were children with them, oh, they were expert at pinching them to make them cry and draw pity from our women.

I had seen Bradwen herself feed them, a hundred times, down in Eudav's Hall, and at the end they had come back and burnt the Hall for her charity. That was what they wanted, to find a woman alone in a house, all the men out in the oat patches or farther out with the sheep. They would sit, all quiet and still, not saying a thing, watching her every move till her nerves began to shred. Then they would start, picking up a few things here and there, always with one eye for the men coming back so that they would have time to run into the woods. And if she protested, they would threaten her, and seize whatever else they could see, and if she did not protest they would take the same things, but more slowly. And at the end, if nobody came back in time to frighten them away, they would take her as well, raping her on her own hearth, often on her own bed, perhaps four or five of them in turn. Oh, yes, that was how we had seen the Savages live through the summer, before they went home to their own harvest of wheat in August. That was how this man was going to live, dress it up how he might.

'We would live somehow,' the old man told me. 'Somehow. There are some of our own people settled, they told us, almost everywhere along this coast, wherever we came ashore. We would go to the nearest chief, and ask him for protection and food, and promise him support in return – as we promise you our loyalty for the food you will give us. That will ensure us a little wheat, enough to keep us alive through the winter, just alive. But besides, there are the forests. Oh, yes, they are full of food for the taking, everybody knows that. There is fruit there, hanging from every tree, and honey, as much as any family can want. The pigs run where they wish in those woods, and belong to no one, and they will come to be killed when you call. And deer, too, so tame that you can catch them with your hands as you walk in the woods, and they would do, though there is no human being who would eat deer meat for choice. Nobody can starve in this great and empty land. It's fertile, too. It has never been tilled. A man has only to scratch a furrow with his plough, and plant six grains of wheat, and at the summer's end, even if it is a bad summer, he will have six bushels. We have heard all about it from men who have been here, and returned to bring over their sweethearts or their children or their parents. And the weather here, we know about that too. It is never bitter cold here, like it is in the homeland, and the snow never lies for weeks together, deep as a man's thigh. And there is never drought, never a lack of rain to swell the crop. Oh, this is a glorious land, a splendid land – and all empty.'

And then he turned angrily, sweeping us, myself, Cynon, Cynrig, Caso, Morien, with a furious look.

'And what have we done to you? What has changed? When first our people came here you welcomed us. Those first comers, you took them in, and fed them, and let them wander far into the country, up to the source of the great river in the South, till they found good clay land to plant their wheat. You were glad enough to have them then, to have more men in your empty Island. And they were no different from us, no better, no worse, three generations ago. I remember, myself, the talk about Hengist, how he sailed, in my grandfather's time. He came, and your Kings welcomed him, too, and made him a King like themselves. The poorest Prince in Jutland, he was, a laughing-stock all over the mainland, and yet you welcomed him and gave him a Kingdom. If you took men in before, why do you not now?'

'There is no room for you,' I told him. 'The land is full. There is no land to spare.'

'But no, but no! This island is empty. We know that. All the world knows it. All the Romans have gone. They went away, by tens of thousands, by tens of thousands, in our grandfathers' time, all of them streaming away across the narrow sea, back into Gaul to quarrel among themselves and fight the Franks and Goths. They left the Island empty. The Romans pulled down the walls of the cities, and stripped the gold from the roofs and the silver from the gates, and they sailed away with all their wealth. We have not come hoping to find the treasure to carry off ourselves; we know it is all gone. But the Romans left the land, they could not carry that off. We need the land to grow our food. Give us the land, so that our children will not starve, like those we left behind in Jutland. Why will you not give us the empty land the Romans left?'

It was Cynon who answered him. I translated as he spoke, even running on ahead, sometimes, because there was only one answer, whoever framed it.

'There is no empty land. The Romans have not left. *We*

75

are Romans.' He stood there, in his red cloak, the red feathers blowing in his helm, proud as Owain. 'The legions, yes, they left, and that was fifty, sixty years ago, to conquer all the world. What does that matter? What does it mean? North or south of the Wall, this Island is Roman. Roman it shall be. From Wick to Cornwall we keep the Roman faith, the Roman laws. We live and think as Romans. And this Roman land is not yours to settle in, nor ours to give you. It is a land we must keep for our children, so that they can live as Romans live. If we were not Romans, we would live like wild beasts, in the woods, as you do.'

The old man looked at us. At me, the go-between, still thin and frail after the year I had spent as the Savages' slave. At Cynrig, fastidiously picking the lice out of a Savage shirt, and flicking them into the fire. At Cynon, rock steady, his feet wide apart on the sand, one hand on his sword, the other holding the rib of beef from which he picked the meat with his strong even teeth. At the rest of the Squadron, eating beef around the fire, cooking mussels in a bucket, paddling in the sea, collecting more driftwood, or even just sleeping in the sun. In the heart of the fire, the ploughshare glowed red through and through.

He asked: 'What shall we do now? How shall we live? You have stripped the clothes from our backs. You have broken our plough, and killed the poor ox that was to pull it, that was dearer to us than our children, because we kept it alive though they died. You have scattered our seed corn into the sea, that we thought dearer than our own lives, because we starved rather than eat it. You cannot do all that to us, and not feed us. Let us have water, at least, just a little water – there are some still alive in the ship. Give them water! And then, food! You must give them food, you must let us have food. How else shall we live?'

I gave him Cynon's answer, before Cynon spoke it.

'We do not care how you live, so long as you do not live here.'

At Cynon's sign, Cynrig and Caso took the old man by the arms and dragged him down the beach again to the water. Those of us who were still awake followed, in a jeering, shouting, mocking throng. Some were on foot; others, like myself, rode. By the ship, now almost surrounded by wet sand, because it was a little past the ebb, we stopped. Four men took the old man by the arms and legs, and swung him back and fore, back and fore . . . and at last, they flung him high into the air. He fell limbs threshing, into the bottom of the ship, landing on the loose planks with a rattle and a crash, screaming in pain and then moaning.

'Push her off, boys!' Cynon shouted. Men crowded to put their shoulders to the sides and slide the vessel down off the sandbank into the water. I looked down from my horse into the ship. There was a huddle of bodies lying in the bottom, half in and half out of the bilge-water showing where our men had torn up the deck-planks in their search for treasure, or iron.

The Savages looked back at me. They did not move, they did not speak, they only looked at me with dying eyes that had little life left in them. One was a man of about my own age, hardly covered by a few rotten rags, his lips puffed and scarred, his body scattered with open sores and running boils. There was a girl of, perhaps, fifteen – it was hard to tell, she was so dried out, but I judged by the budding breasts under the strands of matted yellow hair. There was an old woman, with no teeth left. They were all starving, pot-bellied, their ribs showing, their skin hanging loose on bodies grown too small for it, and dried and shrivelled and peeling. They did not cry for help, or moan in their misery. They did not move even. Only the old man writhed on his broken bones, head lower than his feet. They just looked at me, all of them, with their great empty eyes, blue stones sunk in dark pits. There may have been fifteen: I did not count.

I dropped from my horse into the water. I linked arms with Aidan, and we too put our shoulders against the side of the ship to shove. She was moving already, but even though more and more men came down to help us, she was heavy, sinking into the soft sand. But the half liquid sand soon began to help as much as it hindered, and suddenly she began to feel lighter, to lift as she slid farther and farther off the sand and into the ebbing water that began to snatch her from us. She would drift away from us now, out to sea, out to the narrow gap between the two arms of the cliff which fell grinning into the waves. Pushing, we were up to our waists as we fell into the deeper water, and we laughed and splashed and ducked our friends' heads and played like children.

Then, as the ship began to pull out of our hands, so that not all our weight now could hold her straight, then, with a scream and a shout, Morien came riding down the beach and into the sea. He had rubbed his face with charcoal, so that he looked like a Pict. He flogged his mare into the waves; when the cold sea touched her belly she whinnied and voided herself. In his left hand, Morien whirled a torch, made of dry wood and wrapped round with some of the old rags out of the ship. He waved it violently to keep the flames alive. He flung it up high into the air, and we watched it circling and falling into the ship as it moved slowly out of our reach.

I stood with Cynon by the fire where the soldiers were now burning the offal and the bones and scraps, raising a stench and a cloud of black smoke. Cynon said, 'There was no need for what Morien did, no need at all.' He had grown up on this coast. 'Watch her go, now.'

We did watch her, as she spun slowly round in the ebb, the smoke rising from her steady and black in the air. There was no sound from her, not that we could hear from that distance, over the laughter of our men dancing on the sands. The ship was moving faster and faster, towards the gap between the cliffs, towards the open sea. Morien and Caso were using the poles that had once been the mast and yard to push the ploughshare out of the fire. The wood had all burnt away from it, leaving only the metal, a huge lump of red-hot iron for which our smiths would be glad. It, with the iron tyres, would make ten or twelve swords, or at least twice as many spear-heads. The ploughshare glared its heat into our faces, and the air danced between us and the ship, so that she seemed to shiver already on the calm water. Cynon murmured to me:

'Now, it takes her.'

We watched her, and it did take her. The current took her, and whirled her faster and faster, not out through the gap to the open sea, but towards the rocks, the fire racing down to the waterline with the draught her own motion made. Caso threw a bucket of water over the ploughshare to cool it to carry, spoiling its temper so that it would never now cut into our Roman land. The steam rose in front of us, hissing and whistling like mussels alive, stewing in their own juice in a bucket: for a moment it hid the ship from us completely. When it cleared, she had struck, on a rock still hidden by the tide, twenty paces from the foot of the cliff. She had struck hard, with the fire now down to the rubbing strake, and in an instant she had broken apart, and the fire quenched, and that steam, far from us, rose silent.

That was the end of the Savages, men, women, and, if there were any, children too, though I never heard one of them speak, or even saw them move, except the old man, and he was no loss to us. A meal we got out of it, a snack rather, for the noon halt, for a young ox, half starved, and three little pigs fed no better will hardly give a mouthful between fifty men. And we got out of it some iron, and the hide of the ox would cover a shield for someone, and the pigskin would give a pair of shoes for riding. And there was enough tallow for a night's candles in Mynydog's Hall, and clothes to give away to the farmers we passed on the way back. And best of all, the Savages were gone with the ebb, drowned, or burnt before, and not to come in again till the next high tide. But by then we would be gone, too, dancing around the fires in a farmyard, and flirting with the girls for whose safety we had gone to war. We at least left the beach clear, the ashes buried, the sand swept over all.

Other patrols found the same, almost every week now in the sailing season. That was the first duty of the Household, to scour the shore for the Savages. Cynddelig's Squadron found a big party of them, who had come ashore the winter before, and built themselves houses close to the sea, and hung on there unnoticed till they had seen their new-sown wheat break the soil. Cynddelig killed them, he and his Squadron, every one. He brought back iron and bronze and silver, clothes and ox-hides, more than we had found. Yet, however we kept the coast, the smoke still rose from Bernicia.

On all that, I might have made a satire, if I had still been a Poet, and this is the satire I would have sung though I could not:

'There is no more to power than wealth.
Wealth does not come to those without power,
Or power fall into the hands of the poor man,
Except he spend effort and blood and shame:
For no new wealth can ever be created
And Power is indivisible and single.
Those who have wealth have more heart to fight to
retain it,
Than those who have not to struggle to take it from
them.'

This was the satire I could have made. But whether I sang it or not, it was true. It was to keep our own wealth and power that we went to Cattraeth.

CHAPTER FIVE

Pan gryssei garadawc y gat
Mal baed coet trychwn trychyat

When Caradog rushed into battle,
It was like the tearing onset of the woodland boar.

It was not every day we drilled, or rode out to the coast. We did not drill on Sundays, or on Holy Days, or Feasts, or when we had worked very hard the day before. There were many days when the Household did nothing, or when those who felt like it would ride out to hunt, to get some venison to eke out our mutton and salmon.

I remember the last time I went hunting from Eiddin. I came from the Hall on a fine hot morning, for in that year every day of summer was fine and hot and dry. In the courtyard, Precent was talking sternly to Mynydog's nephew.

'So, as soon as anybody makes you a bow and arrow, *what* is it you said you were going to do?'

'I a hunter, I going to hunt the cat.'

'Oh, no! You mustn't hurt the poor cat, now, must you. What has the poor cat done to you?'

'But I a hunter, I shoot her.'

'Why don't you shoot a dog, instead? There's poor old Perro, here, why don't you shoot him?'

'He's too big. I a hunter, I shoot Pussy.'

'But it's the King's Cat, lad. You know what you'll have to do if you shoot the King's Cat? You have to pile corn over her till she's all covered up. Have you got enough corn to do that?'

'But I want to be a hunter. I want to go hunting. Men go hunting. I'm a man.' Satisfied with the logic of four years old, he turned and saw me. 'Aneirin! Will you take me hunting?'

I couldn't say no to him, not straight out. I couldn't offend him, and no more could Precent. So I answered, 'Go and ask Gwenllian if she'll come, and if she will, then you ask her to take you. But don't tell her I said so.'

Off he went, bubbling with it, and of course he told Gwenllian I said he could come hunting, which he had never seen before, and that I said Gwenllian was to bring him. She hunted sometimes, but not as often as Bradwen who hunted almost every day, as skilled as any man at it, and strong enough to stay out with us all day. But deceived by the little boy's joy, Gwenllian did come out, saying, 'Just to please him, let me ride along behind the main party with him on my saddle-bow, so he can see.'

So we were, literally, saddled with him for the day. We rode out a good strong party, led by Bradwen and Owain. Precent did not come, staying behind to drill one half of the Household. Still, there were nearly forty of us, with dogs, and we were ready to take anything we could find for our supper. We cast round to the south of the Giant's Seat, Gwenllian and I riding together at the rear of the party. As we went, I heard her singing to the little boy one hunting song after another, but the one he wanted to hear again and again, as children will, was one I had made for him myself, long ago, and I was surprised first that he, and then that Gwenllian, should remember it.

'What shall Daddy bring you back from the mountain,
What shall he bring you down from the glen?
He'll bring you a salmon, a wild boar, a roebuck,
Speckly eggs from the grey moorhen.

'Daddy will lay his spear on his shoulder,
Daddy will sling his bag on his back:
Through the deep forest and over the mountain,
Daddy will follow the old hunting-track.

'Daddy will take his net and crossbow,
Dogs Giff and Gaff will run at his side,
He'll go by the Ridgeway and under the waterfall,
The way he once went to bring back his bride.'

It was only doggerel, and I was ashamed of it, ashamed of having sung it first, ashamed that anyone else should remember it. I told Gwenllian so.

'Why, what is the matter with you, Aneirin? It is a very nice little song, and I am grateful to you for making it, because I can rely on it to get him to sleep when nothing else will. And here we are, on a fine July morning, and I still can't get a smile out of you, and I haven't done since you came home in May. What is it, now, what is it?'

83

I rode in silence. She waited a little, then again: 'What is the matter, Aneirin: It is plain to me, but it will not be plain to you until you speak about it.'

I looked around in the clear air, down to the level land below us, for we sat our horses on the lower slopes of the hill and watched the rest of the hunt spread out across the plain, colourful and clear and sparkling. I watched Bradwen pass out of sight behind a thicket, and then my eye was dazzled by the stone in Gwenllian's ring, the one out of the Savage ship, that I had given and that I hear she wears still at Arthur's court, an emerald they say it is, set in gold. I said:

> 'My love said farewell to me in May,
> With a greeting she bade me goodbye.
> Now conversation forbids communication,
> Courtesy tempers the violence of feeling,
> The clamour of passion is barred out by custom.
> A wall clear as glass she has built around her,
> And she has mewed herself with ravens, not with hawks.
> My love said farewell to me in May.'

'And you are no longer a poet?' she asked me. 'Is that why? Is it because of her that you no longer make concise sayings, that you no longer count the syllables and the feet, that you no longer balance opposites, compare white with black, contrast like with like?'

'No, it is—'

'Do not tell me. I know the laws, I know, I know, I know! But the laws never bade a man strain after what no one could reach. Go on, tell me that peace is always beyond a poet's reach. I think I understand it. You cannot sing unless you feel that you are badly treated. And now you have made yourself feel so badly treated that you dare not sing. What a song we shall have out of you in the end!'

'There will be no more poems.'

'And have you not just said me one? You must have been rankling over that one a long time, Aneirin, to have it out so perfect. It has spoiled you, being a poet, Aneirin, and such a great one. You have never known a failure till now. But do you think you are the only one to yearn after Bradwen? Why do you think that Cynon went away, so far away, first into the South, and then, after he brought me back, away again into Strathclyde, but because of her. If you had had to hear his lovesick yearning across the length of Britain as I had to, then you'd know that you weren't the only man who loved Bradwen. And why do you think that Gelorwid wants to be a hermit? He was up here with me last week, trying to choose a spot for his cell. This place was too cold, and that too windy, and another too damp, and another too close to the llan where Mynydog's down hermit lives already: but the main trouble with them all was that he wanted to have the best of both worlds, and to have a cell where he would see Bradwen. And Precent, why does he prefer to stay here and be Mynydog's gatekeeper, when he could rule his own Kingdom among the Picts?'

'But I had thought—'

'That she would have chosen the Pre-eminent Bard of the Island before them? But she did not, Aneirin. She knew you all as brothers, she did not think of you as suitors. But when the pre-eminent soldier of the Island came into the North—'

'Why, yes, then,' I finished for her. 'He did not come for the price, but he took the price eagerly, the price that Mynydog offered him, the price Bradwen was willing to pay, not the wide lands Eudav held by the Wall – what is that to a Prince of Cornwall? No, there was also Bradwen's white body to wallow in, in his bed.'

'And are there no other white bodies, Aneirin? And no other lands, no other homes? Will you waste yourself for ever because Bradwen loves, and not you?'

But before I could answer, we heard the horns close to us. The deer, flushed out, came past below. The little boy shouted in excitement, and waved the little spear Arthgi had made for him. Without a word spoken, Gwenllian and

I set in our heels, and swept down on a buck on the edge of the herd. I whistled, and old Perro, baying, cast round to the other side of the buck to head him into us, so that in a few strides we were running parallel with him, a few yards away. I held back till I heard Gwenllian give the word to her half-brother, and saw his toy spear flung – a miss, of course, but still he cast at a deer. I threw my own, straight to the heart – but there, I had had practice. The buck fell, and we pulled up our horses and dismounted.

Gwenllian caught Perro by the collar, and held him back, while I cut the buck's throat. The little boy wandered off a little to pick flowers, not having much taste to see me rip up the stomach to clean the carcase, pushing the steaming tripes away for the dog.

The horses stood still some paces away, as they had been trained. I knelt among the blood and ordure, my arms stained to the elbow. Gwenllian stood over me, and asked again, as if we had not ridden half a mile, and killed, 'And are there no other girls, Aneirin?'

And again, there was interruption. Perro growled, a horn sounded urgently from far away. I looked up. Running towards us, flushed by the hunt from his sleep in the wood, was a boar. Head down, slavering, grunting and wheezing horribly, it was a horrid sight. Dangerous always, the more dangerous now not being clouded by pain or unusual anger, it was a threat I had to face.

'The child!' I shouted. He was well away from us. I seized my spear, and ran towards him. I whistled to Perro, and the old dog, well trained, went straight for the boar like a stone rolling down a mountain. I reached the little boy, and snatched him up, struggling because he saw no reason why he should be taken from his contemplation of a grasshopper. Almost as soon as I had him, Gwenllian galloped to me. I passed her brother to her.

'Ride!' I called. She went like the wind. I looked again at the boar. The dog's blood red on his tusks, he was coming at me, roaring. I couched the spear and went down towards him, at the run, because there is no waiting for this beast. I picked my spot – and suddenly, between me and my prey, between the boar and his prey, there came a horse, and Bradwen, splendid in her haste and rage, shouting the hunting cries like trumpets sounding, came charging to save me from no danger, no danger at all. She rode between me and my adversary, and I saw her arm strike, the spear flash down. The boar changed his line, turning away, and, as Bradwen pulled up her horse, I watched it go, fast, the spear trailing from its haunch. That stroke had done little damage, except perhaps to us, because the boar, hunted before, wise to what we could, would, do, was now above all enraged.

'Cut it off! After it! Cut it off!' I shouted to Bradwen, but she hesitated, waited to lean over me and ask, 'Are you hurt at all?'

'No, no. But the boar, after it – do not let it get into the thicket!'

But it was too late, the beast was already out of sight in a clump of thorn-bushes. And then, because things happen so fast in the hunt as they do in battle, and fortunes change as suddenly and as senselessly, there were a host of horsemen around us, Gelorwid and Owain, and Mynydog's Chief Huntsman, Caradog.

'We'll have to go in there on foot,' Caradog warned me.

'I'll go in,' said Owain at once.

'If you wish,' I told him. It was my beast, but it was beyond my pride to say so in front of Bradwen. 'I shall back up.'

'I don't need anyone else,' said Owain. 'I have hunted enough boars in my time, and there is no need for more than one man.'

'Let me come with you,' Bradwen put in. But I was saved argument by Caradog, who only observed, 'Two in, on foot, and the rest mounted around the thicket. That is the rule here. Bradwen, take anything that comes out beyond that withered tree.'

Owain said no more. He went in front of me into the

thicket. The thorn-branches tore at our clothes, at our faces. The grass in the spaces between the trees was rank and thick. The trees were in full leaf now in late July. We could see little, we could only listen and smell for him, snuffle like a dog for the scent of pig sweat and ordure. It is better to do this without dogs: they only confuse the hunter, and harm the boar little. With a bear, however, I would take dogs.

We moved silently, Owain well in front, along the path, picking here and there a spot of blood, smears only. This one was not badly hurt, not bleeding badly at all. Dangerous, then.

It was very silent. The thing was somewhere, waiting for us, waiting to charge. Owain was out of my sight around the corner of the path when it happened. I heard it come, a horrible snarling shriek, and the shout from Owain, the trampling of the feet and the breaking of branches. I had the moment of space to lean back into the thorns, out of its track, and as the boar passed me, I leaned over and struck down, into the spine, the way we do here in the North. And it rolled, dead and still, with no further ado. There was no danger, no difficulty, as Owain had said. But Owain? He came down the path, from where the boar had come, still shaken from the wind of the beast as it had charged him, and missed. It was his luck to be taken by surprise, so that he had no time to strike, and little to dodge: it was my luck that his shout had warned me, given me time to strike.

We carried the boar back to Eiddin, with the deer, for that night's feast. I sat with Gwenllian, and the little boy hid under the table between us and sucked at a marrow bone, with plenty of meat on it, that I slipped down to him. We three ate venison. But in the place of honour, Owain ate the hero's portion, the thigh, of the boar: and shared it with Bradwen.

That was how we rode out to Cattraeth, as to a hunt. We thought the Savage no more dangerous than a boar, and to our leader we gave all the honour and the praise for all that we did.

CHAPTER SIX

Gwyr a aeth gatraeth yg cat yg gawr

Nerth meirch a gwyrnseirch ac ysgwydawr

Peleidyr ar gychwyn a llym waewawr

A llurugeu claer a chledyuawr

Men went to Cattraeth in marshalled array and with
shout of war,

With powerful steeds and dark brown harness and
with shields,

With uplifted javelins and piercing lances,

With glittering mail and swords.

The Household of the Virgin rode out of Eiddin on the Feast of the Holy Virgin. The oat harvest was gathered, the barley was in, the sheep-shearing was over. Early on that morning we had heard the bell from the wood, where Mynydog's hermit offered his sacrifice.

Before we rode out, Clydno numbered us. We who rode that day from Eiddin were three hundred men and one. Each of us rode a horse, and led one, or sometimes two. Each of us was armed. Never in the whole history of war, never in all the tale of the Island of Britain, had such a wealth been spent to send so great a host into the field. Not even an army of the wealthy Kings of Strathclyde had cost so much.

Each of us wore a red cloak. Red is a wide word, a general colour. Some were red as the russet autumn leaves. Others were as red as the flower of the campion shy against the grass in spring. Owain's cloak was as red as the holly berry, a crimson we could see easily in any press of men, and the plume on his helmet was of the same colour.

My cloak was old and faded by the rain and the wind, till it looked like a bank of foxgloves, blowing in the hedges of the wet and clement west from which I had come. This was a cloak the Warden of Carlisle had given me, for singing a marriage song for his daughter, before the Savages had swept into his city, in a great raid, and killed him and his son-in-law, and carried off his daughter into slavery. For years I had kept this cloak in a chest in Mynydog's palace, against my own wedding-day. Now I wore this western colour to ride to war in the East.

We were not the whole army that marched out of the gate of the Dun, that morning, and that had to come in again: one by one, after we were numbered, so that we could ride out again for the last time. Ten days before, Cynddelig of Cardigan had ridden out with sixty men of the Household, and two thousand peasants on foot. Each of these men carried a long spear and a wooden shield, whether covered with leather or not, and most of them had hand axes or long cook's knives at their belts. They all had coats of boiled leather, enough to stop a thrust, or at least break its force: and the leather cap, rarely reinforced with hoops of metal. None of them could afford a coat of mail, and if they had ever had armour then Mynydog had long taken it away to give to one of his Household. The infantry had gone ahead by the long road along the coast, where the farms were frequent. They went slowly, and would stop only where there was easy water, because they drove in front of them a flock of sheep, for them and us to live on on the road, till we came into Bernicia and could eat what we took from the Savages. Mordei the invaders had ravaged: in Bryneich they had settled. There would be food enough there.

By the borders of the Mordei we were to meet with the foot and with the sheep. We had chosen the place. It would take Cynddelig ten days at least to reach the place on the drovers' road down the coast, where we had caught the Savages on the beach. He would go south beyond that. We of the Household would take only three days to cross the high moorland, too badly watered to risk the herd over; we would head always south-east, to reach Eudav's Hall under the Wall. Then we would sweep along the Wall, and north again into the Mordei till we had cleared the way for the infantry and their animals.

The Savages had not yet settled north of the Wall: enough of our men went into the debatable land to tell us that. Only their raiding bands came North, after the wheat harvest, when they felt full of food and beer, and vain enough to think of coming to steal from anyone richer than they were. We were rich enough to stop that when we felt like it, and the time was now. Or they would come in the spring, before the sowing, when they were desperate not only for riches but for very food, and would dare anything to gain even a mouthful of our seed oats or the starved and bony cattle kept alive through the winter. These were the times when, most years, they were most dangerous. Usually they would not raid this time of the

91

year, when the wheat was ripe for the harvest, and every sensible man would be sitting safe at home, sharpening his sickle and mending his barn, treading down the clay on his threshing floor and rehinging his flail. This was the time that Precent had caught them the year before, sweeping down on them from the North without warning, burning the barns over the rats' heads, and finding a hundred other captives besides myself to bring back to the safe and pleasant North.

But just because it was this time the year before that Precent had gone to war it was just as possible that they would choose this time to raid north into Mordei to meet us. Therefore we would clear the whole land in front of the infantry.

There had been little ceremony when the infantry marched away, partly because there is not so much you can do in dignity when you are driving a thousand sheep, besides oxen and pigs: partly because the infantry, though the most numerous, are the least important part of an army, coming only to support the horsemen of the Household, to consolidate what the cavalry have won. The day that the Household rode out was the real day of the departure of the army.

Rank on rank we rode out past Mynydog on his throne. As we passed him he cried, 'Hail to the King, the Commander!' in the Roman way. Because we *were* a Roman Army, even though we rode through the Wall into the Empire to make war. Many of us, like Cynrig and Owain and myself, had been born in the Empire, wherever we had been fostered after that. Others had been born outside the Empire, and fostered in it, in great cities like Corinium or Kenfig. So we were as Roman an Army as had ever come out of the North.

Because we were Romans, also, we passed before the llan in the woods where Mynydog's hermit had been told to pray for us, and we showed that we were Romans, because we served the Roman Gods. As we passed we shouted, 'All hail to the Virgin!' and we waved our helmets crosswise. Many, too, called on the saints they

92

worshipped, on Josephus or Jesus or Albanus or Spiritus. Gelorwid, who was wise in these things, called on a saint called Veron Icon.

Between the gate of Mynydog's Hall, and the llan, all around the Judgement Mound where the King himself sat, we passed the people of Eiddin. Not everyone in the Kingdom was there, of course, although it seemed like it. Besides those who lived close round the Dun there were people who came in from farms even three days' journey away to see the Household ride out. Oh, yes, that was the day for cheering. A herd of cattle and a flock of sheep and a crowd of farmhands, even with spears in their hands, you could see those any day: but the whole Household, more mounted men than anyone had ever seen, riding out in all their splendour, that was a sight of a lifetime.

Besides, there was none of us but had a father or a mother or a sweetheart somewhere in the crowd. Clydno waved his staff to Cynon, and led the cheering. People cut the boughs of trees, and threw them before our horses' hooves, so that the iron shoes rustled in leaves instead of clattering, and struck no sparks from the granite setts.

My little friend, Mynydog's nephew, was not sitting at his Uncle's feet to see us ride. Before we marched, he had come into the courtyard of the Dun to see us saddling up and mounting, and he had wandered round among us, the only child we would have allowed to do such a thing. He tripped over the harness and spilled packed bags, and walked fearless under the very bellies of the great horses, and we all thought it clever of him to do things like that. We all made much of him, of course, picking him up and kissing him and tossing him from one to another, squealing with delight. Then Precent challenged him with:

'What are you then? Is it a bear you are?'

'Yes, I a bear, I a big brown bear. I eat you!' and he growled in a most bearlike way.

'No, boy,' Precent told him. 'Bears don't eat trees. Bears eat honey, and I'm a tree. You climb up this tree, and see if you can find any honey.'

So the little lad climbed up onto Precent's shoulder, convinced that he was going up by his own efforts, and that Precent had not lifted him at all, and, of course, on the shoulder there was a piece of honeycomb. He ate that. Then he wanted to climb every tree in the wood, and of course on every shoulder he found something good, honeycomb or cheese or dried fruit or meat.

Suddenly, he began to look very thoughtful. I knew the signs, so I picked him up, which was daring in the circumstances, and carried him out of the Dun, and we hid behind Mynydog's throne, unoccupied as yet, while he got rid of what he had eaten. I gave him a long drink, then, from my bottle, which pleased him immensely, because it was a *man's* bottle. It was, I think, the only bottle of water in the whole army, because all the others were weighed down with bottles not of water: the mead they carried had taken all the honey of a kingdom of beehives.

When the little lad had rinsed out his mouth of the nasty taste, and then had a long drink of the cool clear water, he was eager to go back and climb all the trees again. Children are quick to recover, and this one would never own that he was beaten. But while I was trying to persuade him that even a bear can eat too much honeycomb (and loth he was to believe it), and that is how they get caught, then caught my little bear was. Gwenllian came round the mound, having consulted Syvno the astrologer to find us, I am sure, and seized him from me. She scolded us both roundly: me for forcing sweets on the child, him for letting me persuade him to eat it, and nothing was further from what we both had done.

Still, he clung to me, and gave me a long hug and a kiss. I asked him, 'What shall I bring you back from the wars? Shall it be a bracelet or a collar of gold?'

'Bring me a Savage man,' he told me.

'To ride on?' I teased him, 'Or to eat?'

'I bear – I eat him.' And he growled and chuckled by turns, and then he threw his arms around me and kissed me again. But Gwenllian whisked him away, and carried him back into the Hall, to wash the honey off his face, since he had got it up to the eyebrows, and to put a clean shirt on him, because the one he had, fresh on that morning, was already as filthy as if he had worn it a month and been a scullion in the kitchen all that time.

I went back to finish saddling up and found that Aidan had done it for me. I rode my brown gelding that day, because I knew I could depend on him. My strawberry roan mare I would ride in battle, but on the road I had her as a pack beast, not heavily laden, but carrying what I had, and there was not much of that. I took only the two horses, but there were many who took three, to carry all their jars of mead. Precent, like me, had only his charger to lead, though he would have drunk a river of mead, and not been satisfied.

'If you take too much,' he told me, approvingly, 'it only gets stolen, or left behind in the chase, and that comes to the same thing. If I want a fresh horse, I will get one easily enough after the first skirmish, and the mead on it too.'

Owain did not travel as light. He was a Prince, a Prince of Cornwall, and Precent was only a Lord of the Picts in the North, and I was nothing but a failed bard and an apprentice Judge, whatever my family might be. But Owain was a Prince. He rode on the biggest horse in the Household, a black, thirteen hands high. The son of a King rode behind us and carried his Raven banner. Cynrig is now himself King in Cardigan, and behind the seven walls of Cardigan he rules that city, with all its massive wealth. But when he rode out with the Gododdin, he owned that Owain was supreme, greater in skill and valour and in pride of family. Never has Cynrig the King been more glorious than the day when he reflected the glory of Owain.

Cynrain the brother of Cynrig led Owain's packhorses, six of them, for how could the Commander of a Household hold less state, or travel without his silver cup and his plate, and enough mead to reward his followers for valour? Owain had with him five greyhounds, that ran at his horse's heels, and made wide circles around him, raising every hare for miles, but being well trained they never gave tongue. And at Owain's saddle hung his crossbow, the only bow in the Household, because it was Owain's pleasure to hunt thus, but we would hunt the Savages like deer, with the thrown spear.

A Prince of Cornwall could never wear helm on such a day or in so important a parade. It was necessary that we should all see him to recognize him, and so it was Caso who carried it in front of him. Owain's hair curled red upon his shoulders. Over his mail he wore a shirt of red linen; on it Bradwen had embroidered the black ravens of Cornwall, with their long curved bills and legs in a different red. And his shield, too, bore the ravens. A King he looked as he led us out, more kingly than any man before or since who has ever commanded an army in the Island of Britain. Not even Arthur in his empery can look more kingly. And Arthur is not a King.

Before Owain led us out, when we were mounting, Gwenllian came back with a nice clean boy in her arms, for him to give me another goodbye hug and kiss. She held him up to me, and he squeezed me tight, but keeping his other arm around Gwenllian as children do he pulled her face close against mine. Kissing him I kissed her, and she kissed me. And weeping as women always weep when men go out to war, she wet my face and shoulders. Into my hands she pushed something warm and soft. Then she hid her eyes behind the little boy, and ran from the yard.

Gwenllian's gift was a scarf, of soft wool, striped green and white, the colours of my house, the younger branch of the Gododdin, the colours that my brother wears who is King in Mona. It could not have been made for any else but me, could not have been worn by anyone else in the Household.

So out of the Dun the Household rode, and saluted King Mynydog on his throne. Rank on rank were we of oval shields, each painted as its owner pleased. Precent carried a wolf's head, and all the little boys and girls who ran alongside us pointed at it and howled horribly, but still they threw flowers at Precent. It was always flowers they threw to him. Other shields were harder to imitate. Horses or crows were not too dificult, but who knows what sounds a dragon makes, or a lion? And there were other beasts shown which are entirely mythical, like the elephant that has two tails and two fundaments, and the tiger striped in yellow and blue. And Morien carried a painted flaming brand, so lifelike that the flames flickered before our eyes and we could almost smell the smoke.

No one, of course, had painted a bear. Even in those days, as now, the Bear was worn by no one but the House of Uther. And then there was no one of that House of an age to ride with us: if there had been, would not Owain have yielded his place to him? But even if there had been, not all that pride of family could have dimmed Owain's glory.

My shield had a ground of white. I had painted it in green, an ox-head. What else for me?

The boys ran alongside us and howled and barked, and at me they mooed, not telling an ox from a cow. The women and the grown girls stood still to watch. Many of them wept, as women often do when a Household goes out to war, whether it be to battle or to a mere patrol along a peaceful border. Others were silent, tense, thin-lipped. But it was the men, the youths grown enough to watch the sheep on the hills, but not yet old enough to ride with us, the men too old to stand the long days in the saddle, with battle at the end, and it is not very old in years you must be to be too worn out for such a campaign, and between them, the young men of our own age who were not chosen to ride, or even march with the infantry, because some must be left to thresh the oats and barley just harvested, and to bale the wool newly sheared, and to net the fish for drying and to tend the oxen, so that the women will not starve through the next winter – the men, it was the men who shouted and cheered as we went by.

This did not trouble the horses. Time and time again we had had all these men out with us, and men from farms farther from Eiddin, to shout and clash metal and run about among us waving flags. Now the horses were used to it. They would stand stock still, or run quiet and steady, in the clamour of battle.

Nor were the horses disturbed at the singing of the Household. First, when we were still close to Eiddin, when the women and children still ran close to us, we sang respectable songs, the songs they expected us to sing. These were marching songs of the days of old, that the armies of the Gododdin had sung when they marched to make war on Rome, and songs too that the Romans had sung when they marched north of the Wall to fight against Eiddin. And this, too, was proper. We were the newest Army of Rome, marching against an enemy who had never owned the might of Rome, nor served the Roman Virgin.

At last, we left behind those who were the most loth to lose us to sight. On the flank of the Giant's Seat, where we had hunted, and lain in the sun to dream, Gwenllian sat her horse with the little lad on her saddle-bow to wave goodbye to us at the last. Clydno was there, too. Not Mynydog. He sat his throne till we had all passed, and gone down the hill, and past his farm, and out of sight, and out of sound, while he strained at the last to hear what could never again be heard in Eiddin, the sound of the Household. Then, I am told, he wrapped his cloak around his face, and wept, and no one dared to speak to him for the rest of the day. But these our other dearest friends sat still, where we could see them when we looked back, for hours, while our column wound up through the woods and out onto the moors.

When we had left them behind, the songs changed. The men sang newer songs, or perhaps they were older songs, bawdier songs and bloodier songs anyway, about the shortcomings in bed and battle of Bladulf, and Hengist, and of Kings of the Irish that had come into the Island before, and that we had fought before, and beaten before. These were songs they sang at the nets, and on the sheep walks. You do not sing on the hunt, only after. I thought that singing at this time was too like singing on the edge of the forest, when you may frighten the deer away. Our prey, now, we did not want to frighten away, but rather to gather together to face us. But who was I to object? I was only the Judge.

At midday, we halted to rest our horses. Now most of us took off our mail shirts and bundled them in our red cloaks to sling across the backs of our spare horses. Mail is too heavy to wear without cause, unless you are fighting or on parade. Our helmets we could sling at our saddles. While our horses cropped the grass, we filled the helms with the ripening whinberries: the blackberries were still red.

When we remounted, one Squadron rode still armed, ahead of the rest of the Household, and spread out in a long line of little groups of three or four, a mile from flank to flank. Here, so close to Eiddin, there was no real need for this, but it was good practice. The Squadrons took it in turn and turn about, half a day at a time, to ride in the skirmishing line.

Owain with his Standard rode between the Skirmishers and the first concentrated Squadron. In case of alarm we could see, from his waving Standard, whether we were to form line to right or to left or equally on either side of our Commander.

Precent always led the Skirmishers. I rode every day with Cynon. His squadron always kept the rear. In an alarm we were not to join the line, but to ride behind it, in the centre, as a reserve. Which is the harder, to lead an army in a massed assault, or to restrain skirmishers and bring them back into the line when they wish to scatter and pursue, or to hold a Squadron ready, watching the fight, till the time is ripe to throw them in? I do not know.

This first day, however, we had no thought of battle, nor the next. We rode across the high moorlands and between the groves in the quiet valleys as if we were riding for pleasure, or for hunting. Often men let loose their hawks at grouse, or files or even whole Squadrons broke from the line to ride shouting after greyhounds that had started a hare.

Time and again we passed little huts of boughs in the lee of hills or on the edge of little woods, where the youngsters spent the lazy days of summer herding the sheep. The boys we passed out on the hills in groups of two or three. They spurred their rough ponies to ride with us a little, joining in our songs. The girls at the huts looked up from their endless gossiping over the cooking-fires and the spinning-wheels to wave at us, and shout good wishes. One would have thought that huge armies like ours, six whole Squadrons, passed every day, we disturbed them so little.

In the evening we came down to a lonely farm, where Precent had already stored up food for us, sides of smoked bacon, cheeses and butter, oatcakes that the people of the place had spent all that day baking for us. Best, there was mead for all. We slept in the woods above the farm. Some of us built little huts of boughs, as we had done when we were young and kept the sheep in summer. But most of us heaped beds of cut bracken or heather, and rolled ourselves in our scarlet cloaks. In August it was still warm enough for it to be no hardship for us to sleep with no blanket in the open air. The horses were tethered in long lines, after they had been watered by Squadrons in the streams and fed with oats.

Next day, we went on with our summer ride, under the blue sky flecked with hardly a cloud. On that morning we rode careless as before across the southern valley of the Kingdom of Eiddin, and now we climbed the hills that were the border between Eiddin and the debatable land of Mordei. In these hills, we did not see boys, or girls. The shepherds, when we met them, were grown men, well mounted and armed at least as well as the worst armed of the Household. They wore jerkins of stiff boiled leather, and capes of mail. Most carried swords. They looked keenly at us, keenly but with pleasure, because they hoped that our passing would mean that they would be free next year from this boys' work. Under the threat of the Savages, men had to guard the sheep.

That evening, in the hot and yellow August sunset, we came down to another farm. Here again we found food and drink waiting for us and for the horses. Again we lay to sleep by Squadrons in the woods, making our beds as we wished. But this was not merely a second night like the first. Tonight, it was not the boys of the farm who watched our horses, and it was not only the wolves we were afraid of. Tonight, Gwion Catseyes and his Squadron watched the horses, some sleeping in their mail while others lay awake out on the wide moor, turn and turn about.

We did not light fires that night. The first night, the girls had come out from the farm to flirt with the men watering the horses. Some of them, too, did more than flirt, and slept close to our fires. But tonight we all slept alone, as well as a man may sleep alone in an army of three hundred, camped beneath the stone walls of a tower where no women live. There were worse than wolves to watch for, and these vermin no fires would frighten. The fence round the farm was not a matter of rails and posts, but a rampart of logs, seven feet high, the upper ends sharpened in the fire. This night not even Morien lit a fire, whether to cook food or to sharpen a stake: fires can be seen at night farther than smoke by day.

We did not light fires that night. The first night we had been in Eiddin. This night, there was no certainty where we were: this was debatable land.

In the misty dawn we rose to ride again. Now, too, we brought out of the barn what Precent had packed down there, load by load through the summer, to save us the trouble of carrying it ourselves. We packed more than mead now on our spare horses. Each of us had bacon and cheese and oatmeal to feed him for a fortnight. That kind of food is easy to carry: no man of the Household died of hunger.

The heat haze lay before us as we rode through the empty heather hills. Here there were no more sheep, and no more shepherds. Sometimes hunting parties came as far south as this, but not often, and if they did, they sang about it afterwards as if it were a battle. It was too deep into the debatable land. The deer lived here.

Still Precent led the skirmish line ahead of us: still Cynon and I led the rearguard. Any man who fell so far behind the main body as to hear *our* voices knew that he was too slow and spurred forward. We rode light enough, all of us, and no horse foundered. Now we were singing the other songs, the songs we knew were of older and bloodier wars, wars before the Romans. 'The Hunting of the Black Pig', we sang, and 'Heads on the Gate', 'The Toad's Ride', and 'Blood in the Marshes'. We were a happy confident Army, the Household of Mynydog King of Eiddin, and we did not care what Savages heard us coming. Besides, we were riding to Cattraeth, though we did not know it.

CHAPTER SEVEN

Ny wnaeth pwyt neuad mor dianaf

Lew mor hael baran llew llwybyr vrwyhaf

A chynon laryvronn adon deccaf

No hall was ever made so faultless,

Nor was there a lion so generous, a majestic lion on
the path, so kind,

As Cynon of the gentle breast, the most comely lord.

On the last morning of our approach ride, we roused ourselves in the wood on the north side of the crest; we slept there in the dead ground, while Gwion watched beyond us to the South. We had slept in our mail, let it rust or not. Our horses we had hobbled by our heads, and we fed them on the oats we carried. We poured water from our flasks into our helmets for the beasts to drink. We did not show ourselves outside the wood till it was time.

When we rode out again, it was Cynon's Squadron that, for the first time, rode in the skirmish line, and that for the same reason that it had kept the rear the other days, that it had in it the hardest and the toughest men, used to war and fighting and travel. Not all of them were like that. Precent, on the far right of the line, rode with Aidan to cover him, as due to his Royal blood. I rode with Cynon, and we stayed on the far left, ahead of the others.

We came to the edge of the wood, and looked across the valley to the Wall. It ran before us, miles ahead, a grey line across the green country. Below the wall there was a wood. A strange wood. In August other woods were green. This wood was brown and grey, as if in winter. The woods below us, this side of the stream, were indeed green. Between the edge of the nearer wood and the stream had once been Eudav's Hall, and the paddocks where he ran his horses. Destruction had been complete: I could not be sure where it had been, the house where I grew up.

We walked our horses down the moorland slope, over the grass cropped now by deer, and not by sheep. I rode as one does in the scouting line, on Cynon's left, five horse-lengths behind him. The light changed as we passed beneath the oak trees, dappling patches of shadow with streaks of sun. Hard light, indeed, to see a deer, let alone tell the points: hard light to aim an arrow or a spear. Quiet too: I have lain, before now, in the wood, and seen five horsemen pass twenty paces from me, and if I had not been turned that way to see them I would never have known it. Therefore our heads were never still as we rode, turning and twisting to see all round us, all the time.

I knew every inch of this forest, in light or dark: I knew all the sounds there ought to be. There was not a hollow where I had not crouched to loose a bolt at deer or hare, or to watch the badgers playing in the full moon. I had ridden here with Bradwen and Precent till I knew every pothole, every soft place where a horse or a man might stumble. I knew, almost, every fallen branch that might crack underfoot, excepting only those of last winter. Our hooves hardly rustled the leaves, or broke the mushrooms, the millers and the redcaps, left to overgrow and turn gross. No civilized man had been here, or they would have been gathered. Cynon, too, had known these woods before, when they were still safe for a little girl to go out with the dawn to come back with a kerchief full of blewits.

It was hard to see deer, here in the August woods. It was hard to see men, too. Sometimes I lost sight of Cynon, or he of me, as we moved or halted by turns, passing or repassing each other.

There was no watching here for deer, or men. The deer had not gone by, we saw no droppings or the birds that would search them for undigested seeds. We would not see the deer here: we sniffed the air for them. Then I smelt it. I raised a hand to Cynon. He rode past me towards the smell of wood-smoke, halting by a hazel-bush, listening for anything that might have alarmed the birds. I came past him, a few yards further, while he watched me.

I leant down from the saddle to see what they had left. There was a live fire somewhere ahead, but not here: these ashes were too cold to smell of smoke. Last night's? The night before? I rode a little farther, to where they had slept, curled up on heaps of bracken. At least a dozen of them by the space they had flattened. One had left a torn shred of cloth, half a blanket, ragged and dirty, the colour hidden beneath the crusted filth. And there was a scatter of bones too, deer bones, picked clean and polished. These had been hungry men, who had killed by chance at the end of a long and profitless day, and then gorged

105

themselves on the meat, half-cooked, charred at best, and left nothing but the guts that the flies buzzed over. How many men to devour a small deer like that? A dozen? A score?

I moved forward, into the stench. Man droppings, not deer droppings. Fresh. This morning's. Last night's fire, then, lit only to cook on, then prudently dowsed. But another one, somewhere, still burning? I sat still, still as I could, looking round me, listening, sniffing. Were there eyes on my back? Were men watching me from the shadows under the trees, or from the branches over me? And if there were would they stay hidden as long as I could watch? Some men say that you can feel eyes on the back of your neck. Perhaps you can if you are expecting them. I was not positively expecting them: I merely wondered if they were there.

I waved. Cynon came forward, rode past me and halted well ahead. I did not expect eyes. But neither did I expect to find in all Britain a man so poor that he would risk his life for that filthy scrap of blanket. For the sake of that rag, he thought it worth the risk to run across behind me, from cover to cover, picking it up as he went. So fast, he thought he would not be seen. But I heard him come, and I turned to see him pull at the blanket where it had caught on a snag of a fallen branch. It held only for a moment, but it was time enough to end his life. It was an easy throw. The spear took him as he bent, in the back below the short ribs. I saw the point come out below the navel. He rolled on the ground, his knees jerking to his chin, clutching behind him at the shaft, vomiting blood, calling for his mother. There had been no mistake. This was no Briton.

If I had gone back, as I was tempted, I would have been a dead man. If I had dismounted, in mercy to finish him off, in greed to recover my spear, they would have killed me. The screams brought the other Savages out of hiding. There *were* a score of them, nearly, and they rushed at us out of holes in the ground and from behind piles of leaves, from the bushes where they hid as we passed, hoping that we would pass and let them be.

Most of them went at Cynon, sitting his horse still, his head turned away from me, guarding me from that direction from which they did not come. They went at him when I should have guarded him. Before he had a moment to turn, they had his steed by the head and him by the legs, jerking and pulling him from side to side, rocking him out of the saddle. He stabbed at them with his spear, not having time to draw his sword, and they beat at him with what they had, bill hooks and axes and cudgels.

I had time to draw my sword before the Savages reached me. I cut down the first who snatched for my bridle, and I spun the roan on her hind legs to scatter the others, giving myself space to ride to Cynon. I shouted a rallying cry:

'I ni, i ni, i ni! Awn, Awn, Awn! dere 'ma!' And from all round, I heard the forest answer:

'Awn! 'na ni! Awn! Awn!'

But they were still far away, and now the Savages had Cynon on the ground, cutting and hacking at him while he tried to cover his face with his shield and stabbed up blindly with his spear. But an axe put an end to that as I crashed into them, the mare pushing aside one man with blood streaming from his eyes and another doubled up and clutching his groin.

I cut to this side and that, caracolling my horse around Cynon where he lay bleeding, hoping that my mount would not step on him. I had to be sure that they did not play the same game with me. I found that the enemy were not mailed. My sword cut through shirt and flesh and bone, and I heard them scream. But, screaming, they still held on, beating at me in senseless rage that overcame their fear, and grasping at me from all sides as though nothing but physical contact, the violence of nails and teeth, would satisfy them. Then one of them had his fingers over the edge of my shield, jerking at me, and I nearly went down, but suddenly there were horses all

107

round me, mail shirts and red plumes and words that I could understand. The hands slipped from the rim of the shield, and suddenly there was no fighting, only Morien and a dozen others sitting their horses or sliding down to bend over Cynon.

We dragged the kill over by the heels to lay them in a long line, like hares or fallow deer at the end of the hunt. But this was the beginning of the killing, I knew. Twenty-two altogether, old and young: not a bad day, if only they *had* been deer. They had nothing worth winning – their patched shirts of soft leather, their worn-out blankets rolled and slung on their backs, tied with odds and ends of knotted string, their shoes, those that had them, with the dead toes sticking stiffly out. Only two of them had the long curved knives from which they get their name, the saxes which did Hengist's work for him on the night of the long knives, and brought Vortigern the Great to ruin for a time. Otherwise, they had iron-edged spades, three hedging-hooks and five axes, and with that they had settled Cynon.

We stripped the mail from him, and cut the shirt from the bloody shoulder. He had been struck there either with axe or billhook, between elbow and shoulder, where it is hard to pad the mail without clogging the arm. The flesh was mashed and the bone, at last broken, thrust splintering through the skin. I had never till then seen such a horrible wound. I saw worse later. Cynon, however, drinking mead, was soon able to sit up and speak, gasping, which is better than lying still and groaning.

While a committee of those who claimed to know what to do about wounds debated their incompatible opinions, I cleaned the blood from my sword with the torn blanket that had been the cause of the fight. The first Savage had stopped writhing. I set my foot on his neck to pull out my spear. This was the first man I had looked on that I had killed: now I could never be a poet again, whatever was said. I looked at him. He might have been fifteen, or a little older. The flies were already gathering in his open blue eyes. The yellow hair was blackened with soot of some kind. A man poor enough to want that blanket wore no shoes.

Morien sniffed in the air for something other than blood. He called me:

'Let us see what they were about.'

It was not far to a well-remembered clearing. Here were stacks of cut alderwood. The turves were piled ready. We followed our noses. A quarter of a mile farther, in the next clearing, the unwatched kilns smouldered. Charcoal they were making, for the Savage smiths to beat out swords against us. This forest, at least, from now on, we could forbid them.

This was the first skirmish of the campaign. Precent rallied the skirmishers to move on. Now I led the left wing with Morien: others could help Cynon. We found more stacked timber, more kilns, but no more men nor sign of any: it was just the one band that had come into our wood.

We rode down the slope from the edge of the wood to the paddocks above Eudav's Hall. Now the grass in the paddocks grew high and thick because there were no horses to keep it down, or even sheep, only the shy deer and the hare. We stumbled on the dry-stone wall, now hidden under the green, that marked the edge of the inner paddock.

Here the angle of the wall was formed by a huge boulder of granite. It was one of the Dwarves that long ago came down from the North in anger to push aside the wall. But the Magician Vergil, fearing for his handiwork, had stood on his tower and turned them all to stone where they had slept. South and West from the Dwarf Stone we had stacked the thin slabs of slate to make the paddock fence, down to the river side. And standing on the Dwarf Stone, I looked towards the river – yes, there had once been Eudav's Hall.

There was no Hall now. I rode across to it by the little stream. Nothing, now, but a mound of charred thatch and rotten beams, bright green now, the grass growing stronger and rank on it as it does when we have burnt off the heather. Below that rubbish, somewhere, was the hearth where they had cut off Eudav's head, his blood spilling on me as I sang. In one instant the world had spun, from a happy night of song and dance and argument, and mead and mutton. The Savages had burst in, screaming and stabbing about them, stinking of wheat, filthy with grease. Before I could rise, my hands still on the harp, they had struck me down, with a cudgel, as they struck down Cynon.

We brought Cynon down to the edge of the wood above the paddock, where we built our huts for the night. He was pale and sweating, biting his lips not to scream with the pain. Someone had bound the arm to stop the bleeding, and splinted it to save the smashed bone. To this day, Cynon stands as Judge beside Arthur's chair with one arm stiff and useless. But on that morning he spoke as slowly and clearly and deliberately as he does now when he gives judgement, though his teeth chattered between the words. Owain debated what to do.

'You must go back,' he said. 'Hard though it is. But you can go back in honour because you have killed two of the vermin. Your Squadron can ride back with you as a Hero, to give you a triumph.'

Cynon, sweating, looked at Owain in surprise.

'Full of men you must be in Cornwall, then, and empty of glory, to talk of honour for killing charcoal-burners, and send fifty men to escort one.'

'It is your due, to ride into Eiddin in triumph, in your shining armour, your shield at your side. And it is not safe to send you across the moors with fewer men than that: you might meet more of these scavengers.'

Cynon spat. 'Shining armour!' he grunted. He called 'Hoegi!' This was a lad, a poor man from the heather hills, who rode in the rear rank of Cynon's Squadron because he only had a cape of mail over his shoulders, and had refused to take a whole shirt from the King if it meant one less man to ride with the Household. All the same, he had killed Irishmen on the coast. 'I shall not wear this shirt

110

again before the spring.' Cynon pushed the bundle of armour at Hoegi. 'My horse will run faster without it, and it will keep your kidneys warm. I am sorry it has been torn a little: only sew up the leather of the sleeve and it will serve.' Thus Cynon the Courteous.

'I will not wash your blood from it with water,' said Hoegi, knowing that a speech was called for, 'nor yet with the blue mead, but with the blood of savages.'

Courteous as Owain was Cynon, but blunt as Precent he could be.

'Wash it as you like, boy, but do it before it starts to smell, for your comrades' sake. But call Graid, and the two of you ride with me through the wood and see that I do not fall off.'

'Ride with him to Eiddin, and see him safe to his father!' Owain ordered. But Cynon over-ruled him.

'Just send me to the crest. Then I can reach a shepherd's booth by night, if I ride this horse hard.' He turned now to Owain. 'I am one man wasted to this army already. We must waste no more.' He stood up, holding to Precent's arm. 'If these boys are going to be back with you before night, then we will have to start now.'

I pressed his hand, and so did all who could get near him, because we all believed that he would die there on the high moors. Hoegi and Graid rode with him through the wood and over the crest onto the high moors, and watched him far across the heather. We all prayed that he would indeed reach a shepherd's hut before he fell from pain and exhaustion; but we did not think he would. I have not seen him since.

I did not ride with him. I did not even wait to see him go. I rode the other way, south, across the river, with Morien and a strong patrol, to see what was there now. I splashed across the ford, where I had so often lain flat as a child to tickle trout under the flat stones, or netted salmon.

We went across the southern river meadows, that were flooded every winter and so came up fat and green every spring, food for horses though not for sheep. Then we

111

entered the Brown Wood. I called it that to myself since I had first seen it that morning, lying a long grey-dun shadow below the Wall. When I was young we had called it the Cobnut Wood, because it was that we went there for in the autumn. It was, then, a place to go to hunt squirrels, if you wanted a good cloak of rich red fur for the winter; and it was good for the pigeons that eat so well in a pie. Then, if you could lie quiet for an hour or so, dead still, you would see them all come. The tree-creeper would spread himself flat against the bark and scuttle up and down, the woodpecker would nod, nod, nod against the rotten bough. You might even see the mice run. And if there was anywhere to see the Little People, it was in that wood; though I never did.

That was before the Savages came. Now they had blasted and fouled the forest. It had happened the spring before, when they burnt Eudav's Hall and dragged me off to pull their plough. They had brought their single-edged knives, two feet long from hilt to tip, not pointed, but heavy, curved, for hedging or reed-cutting. They had cut the saplings and lighter trees, the cobnuts above all, and stacked them, and burnt them down for charcoal to beat more axes to kill more forests.

They had not the strength to cut down the larger trees. Instead, they had gone from tree to tree, from oak to ash to elm, from each stripping the bark, from as high as they could reach down to the ground, all round the trunk. If you do that in the late spring, after the leaves have sprouted, then through the summer the tree will dry slowly and the leaves will turn brown and fall. Before the autumn, you will look at a winter forest, seeing the summer sun through bare boughs. The next spring, the leaves will not bud again. The trees will be dead.

This forest, now, in high summer, was a winter forest. So the Savages destroy the very seasons of the year. On some trunks the Dead Men's Ears stood out, in places the rot was speckled and red. But there were neither leaves nor nuts nor acorns. Beneath our feet, indeed, the grass and brambles grew, and the new shoots of the alder and the hazel were green, but one spring's growth and no more. There might still be sparrows, and if you waited to see, there were perhaps still mice. But all the life of the high forest was gone. The squirrels no longer quarrelled and shrieked, we could not hear the rattle of the woodpecker that carries so far. No dove called 'Coo-coo-cooroo' for beer. Wild cat and fox cannot live on mice alone; they too had gone. All this the Savages had done.

Nothing so devastating had happened since the Wall had been built. We came out of the Brown Wood and looked up, ourselves, at the Wall, standing as still and as thunderstruck as had the animals that found it first, the hare and the deer that saw it set across their feeding-grounds, across their ancient trails, the wolf and the bear and the badger seeing that it made safe the beasts that lived to the south. Five times the height of a man it stands, and twice as thick, all made of stones so heavy that a man cannot lift them. It was raised in one night, complete from sea to sea, by the Magician Vergil, at the bidding of King Hadrian. This was one of the works that Hadrian did for the pleasure of his leman Cleopatra.

The Savages, we knew, were afraid of magic, not being safeguarded by the Virgin: therefore they do not hold the Wall, and neither do they ever walk on it. They would not be watching us. There was, besides, nothing for them to watch except a dying forest. So we could in safety, turn our backs on the Wall, and see the dun swathe of death spread east of us and west, for miles. Beyond the river we could see the Household clearing the paddock around Eudav's Hall, and building the huts in which we would sleep for several nights. Axes rang on timber and hammers on post and rail, as the horse lines were laid out. The law of Rome had returned to the land below the Wall.

Soon this land would be settled and Roman again. But before that we would ourselves carry the Law of Rome, the eternal Justice and the Divine vengeance, beyond the Wall. Not only the Law of Rome: the Roman pipes

113

sounded to us from the paddocks, chanters and drones made by skill and art no Savage can comprehend. And more than Roman music we would take: to the sound of the Pipes, Gelorwid sang the Virgin's Hymn.

CHAPTER EIGHT

Yr eur a meirch mawr as med medweint

Namen ene delei o vyt hoffeint

Kyndilic aeron wyr enouant

Notwithstanding Gold, and fine steeds, and
intoxicating mead,

Only one man of these, who loved the world, returned,

Cynddelig of Aeron, a Novantian hero.

There was no hiding that the might of Rome had ridden again out of the North to Eudav's Hall. Through the three days that followed we raised a new Hall within sight of the old. Stables, cowsheds, houses were built, and for the Hall itself, oak trunks were sunk into the ground for pillars, and stout beams laid across them for roof-trees. At the last we bound reeds for thatch to the rafters. Three hundred men worked in joy to raise a house for Bradwen. For Bradwen and for Owain.

On the fourth day, Owain called us together, the noblest that is, Precent and Cynrig af Aeron and Peredur Ironarms and myself, and young Aidan out of courtesy.

'I know that the Infantry will have reached the heights above the river at the eastward end of the Wall,' he told us. 'Tomorrow we will ride out and down the river to meet them. We will clear the way for Bradwen and then bring her back in triumph to her house.'

There was sense in this. In a day's ride we could sweep the valley from Eudav's Hall to the sea. There were no Savages for a day's ride to the West, our patrols had been able to tell us that, and they had not come against us from beyond the Wall, as they would surely have done if they had been watching. It would be safe to leave the new Hall unguarded. If the Savages were between us and the sea in force, then we would need the whole Household. So we would all ride, to meet Bradwen, who had not seen us ride out because we had already seen her ride out before us, with the Infantry and Gwenabwy the son of Gwen to guard her. When we met the Army, a hundred foot would come with Bradwen to bring her cattle to the Hall and to stay with her till Owain returned. The rest of the Foot, and the sixty horsemen who were with them, would march south with us of the Household, into Bernicia and even into Deira, and reconquer it, terrible as the wrath of God.

We rode early. We turned east, out of the valley and up onto the high and windy moors. We went parallel to the Wall over the new-blooming heather. After the first hour we crossed the road that the Romans had built to carry up their

116

tribute to the Kings of Caledon. Every year, in those days, the King of the Romans sent the King of Caledon his own weight and the weight of his Queen, and the weight of his Judge and the weight of his Bard, in fine gold. I had once seen a piece of this gold, and it was clear that it had come from the King of Rome, because he had put his own face on it, and letters which were his name. That was for fear that the Caledonians would some day ride out of their wood and come down again into the Empire, as they had done so often before, and burn Rome about the Emperor's head. It was the wood of Caledon that the Savages had now begun to kill.

Through the morning we veered away from the Wall, passing here and there the farms left empty, the houses falling into ruin. We followed the line of a little river that ran east and came down from the moors by a valley so well known to us in stories that it had no name of its own, but was simply referred to as the Dingle. But, name or no name, it was up the Dingle that the army would come to meet us.

Now we looked out from the edge of the high moorlands across the land of Mordei, from where the people had long fled. On either side of the stream we saw again the signs of the Savages. The woods were dead, every tree ringed with the cruel saxes, dead and withered away. The deer had gone out of these woods onto the high moors. The land was dead. The land had been killed.

We sat by the stream in the appointed place, two or three hours before sunset. I was with the vanguard, and as soon as I had snatched a few mouthfuls of bread and mead and hot bacon I rode forward to take some to Gwion Catseyes, who was our most forward picket. He was sitting on the ground at the edge of the wood, looking across the narrow meadow to the river and across it to another meadow to the woods, the dead woods, beyond that. He was hidden behind a dead alder clump, covered with blackberry thorns. We hobbled our horses and left them a few paces behind us, and we sat and ate and chatted.

Then of a sudden we heard horses. We had never heard

117

of a Savage who rode a horse; nevertheless, we slipped back among the dead trees and mounted again. We peered through the brittle leafless twigs of the alder and poised our spears to throw.

There were two horsemen, riding one behind the other, not quite a spear's cast apart. That we could tell by listening. It was how we had been drilled. Good, I thought, these are the advance scouts of Cynddelig's force. Somewhere behind them there will be the first knot of the horse, spread out well, and then a regiment on foot. After that there will be the sheep to feed us all the way into Bernicia. With them will be the cattle that Bradwen is bringing to stock her new Hall. She has black cows to give milk, so that when we return we will be met with new-made butter, and cheese: and she has a bull to service them. She will have spare horses for the shepherds, and hunting dogs and watch dogs, and pigs to find their own beech mast and acorns in her woods. She'll live well through the coming winter, with a hundred men, and more when we come back, to live in the Hall and work for her, and to break new farms all through the debatable land. Next summer the land will be full of Romans again, men who fled to the kind and wealthy North when the Savages burst in on them in years before. Next spring, their wives will come too: but for the present, Bradwen will be the only woman in Mordei.

The host would be moving, a great horde of men and beasts that would trample the grass and eat it wherever they went, leaving a trail a mile wide. And mingled with it, company by company, the men of Eiddin and the men of Mordei would march, and the last horsemen would ride the flanks or close up the rear. Here we would be ready to meet them. Here we would take the lead, a great army of horse and foot, to regain Bernicia.

Thirty years the Savages had been in Bernicia, living and breeding. Time and again they had swept into Mordei, turning it into a debatable land, but never in such strength as in the spring of last year. Now we could hold Mordei, and sweep into Bernicia, so that at worst this year that would be debatable land. Next year, who knew, we might hunt and fish and shear our sheep as far as York, into Deira itself, as far down as the borders of Elmet, where we could talk with Christian men again.

These, I thought, will be the forward scouts. If the wind had been easterly, I would have been able to hear already the noise of all the host. There would have been the noise of the cattle, and the sheep would have baa'd my eardrums in. I listened as hard as I could, in the silence of that hot summer afternoon, and I could have sworn, ·from one moment to another, that I could hear them coming.

The leading horseman was almost level with us. His comrade had halted, far back, too far back for what we had been taught. I had mounted, and now I rode out of the woods to him. Gwion remained hidden, his spear couched ready to throw. But there would have been no need for that. I was near enough.

This leading horseman turned to us. For the first time I saw his face when he lifted his head, and I knew him. Gwenabwy son of Gwen it was, to whom Mynydog had given command of the men who were to stay with Bradwen throughout the winter. He was scarlet cloaked, and his shield was white, with no badge or sign, since he said that a man who had lost his land to the Savages had no right to an identity till he had regained it. Gwen's land it was we were on now, between Eudav's and the sea.

He rode wearily, on a tired horse. He looked like a charcoal-burner, like Morien when I first met him, because he was covered, cloak and face, horse and all, in black soot. He barely looked at me as I came down to him, only to see that I wore red and was a friend. He did not even raise his shield from crupper to shoulder, or shift his grip on his spear, or kick his scabbard free to draw his sword.

'Well met, Gwenabwy!' I shouted to him. 'How far behind are the others?'

'In the name of the Virgin, Aneirin,' he answered me, 'have you anything for us to eat?'

I laughed at him.

'Why, Gwenabwy, have you eaten all the sheep? I hope that there are no more of you as hungry as this, because we cannot feed three thousand out of what we are carrying in our saddlebags, whatever the saints did.'

'I am not jesting, Aneirin. Have you any food? There are no more of us.'

'No more? Why? Have you been defeated? When was the battle?'

'There was no battle.' Gwenabwy waved back to the other rider, still sitting hunched in the saddle by a dead thorn tree. The horse stumbled forward a few steps, the way a steed does when it is dead tired and well blown: then it stopped again.

'Who is it, Gwenabwy? Who is with you?' He did not answer. I rode down the meadow along the bank of the little stream. The other horse had made a few more steps, and then stopped again; the rider still sat, his head bowed, his body still shrunken into his scarlet cloak. This is the way men sit after they have had three days in the saddle, herding sheep away from the edge of a racing heather fire. As long as you are riding, you feel nothing, and you always look fresh, however grimed with smoke and dust. But this is the way you slouch down when the sun sets on the last day and the sheep are safe: or burnt.

I went down to this rider, weary long before sunset, on this shaggy horse, its coat caked with the mud of a dozen river crossings, and covered with black ash over that. It stood now on the edge of the stream, too tired even to bend and crop the thick grass under its nose, or even to drink. I rode close to see who this was, mail showing below the red cloak, and an unfamiliar helmet, pointed and hung with purple ribbons, and with a hanging curtain of mail protecting the face at both sides and the neck behind. I could not see the face, because of this mail, till I rode close. Then I saw. It was Bradwen.

CHAPTER NINE

O gyurang gwyth ac asgen
Trenghis ni diengis bratwen

In the engagement of wrath and carnage,
Bradwen perished, she did not escape.

We sat by the fire and passed round the mead jar. In the beginning of dusk, we heard the story. Bradwen told it.

'All went well for the first days. We moved along the coast, a few miles only between each dawn and sunset. Each night we halted by a farm, and the people made us welcome. They always took me in to sleep under a roof. When we passed farms during the day, everyone came out to watch the Army go by. When the horsemen came, they would throw flowers in our path and cheer and sing.

'Three thousand men and a thousand animals do not pass like a cat. We ate the grass from the pastures, and broke the paddock fences. We muddied the farmers' streams, and emptied their wells and left unbearable heaps to windward of their houses. We stole their hens, and enticed their daughters. Their sons came running out to join us. One Army is like another. It could not have been worse for the people south of Eiddin if we had been a horde of Savages. And they had paid for all this. And for nothing.

'Each night, the soldiers sang around the fires they made from broken fences and the planks from barns and the very doors of the houses. The farm people did not miss their doors because they had come out to sing with us. They forgave us the havoc we caused because we were going to the South to fill up the empty land of Mordei. First we could defeat the Savages that threatened them. Then we would live there as a barrier to keep them safe for ever.

'But, at last, we crossed the river. We went out of Eiddin into Mordei. The debatable land was empty. Now we stopped where farms had been. They had been deserted. Not burnt, just left. The doors were closed, the barns cleared, the cattle driven away. They were left by people who had plenty of warning, and who thought they would soon be back. They were the men who marched with us, the regiments of the Mordei, who had gone to fill empty farms in the North. They had left their houses here in order, the buckets at the wellheads, the pitchforks in the racks by the mangers.

'But in a year, a thatched roof grows weeds, and in two or

three winters, unrepaired, the thatch falls in and the rafters rot, and the unprotected walls crumble. The buckets were green with mildew and red with the spotted rot. The tines of the forks had rusted string thin. Thistles and groundsel, dandelions and couch grass choked the gardens, starving out the lettuce and the carrots, the turnips and the leeks, that, self-grown, might yet have lived a few more years. Yet still, we found apples reddening on the unpruned branches: still, the rowanberries ripened at the forsaken doors.

'A day or two farther south, we came on houses that were left in haste. They had been burnt, and fallen in heaps of rubble. You only knew where they were if someone, riding over a mound by chance, felt the difference in the tread of his mount. The Savages had not only burnt the houses and the barns. They had filled in the wells, too, and they had uprooted the orchards. They had even cut down the friendly rowans before the door. It was now that the infantry began to turn back.'

'The men of Eiddin cannot be trusted,' said Owain, firmly. He looked around him, then, and hastily qualified, 'The peasants, that is, for the nobles are as warlike and as honourable as any, as they will soon have a chance to show. But these cravens saw what the savages had done, and it was enough to make them run away, and leave the men of Mordei to win back their own land.'

'No,' said Bradwen, a Mordei woman. 'It was the Mordei men who returned first. They had lived too long in the clement and peaceful North, where the farms are fertile and the winters mild and the land long clear. There they had pastures for the taking, and space to hunt, and they themselves lived in the houses their fathers had built. Their wives and their children were safe in the North. When they came back into Mordei, they saw what they would have to do if they wished to take their old lands once again. They saw all the work they would have to do, sweating over the sickle and the axe, trenching and clearing, building the paddock walls afresh, and raising new roof-trees. And that work, the work of years, never free from fear. All those years

123

of working armed, their swords always at their sides, the spears hanging in their straps on cart or plough, or leaning against the stable door or in the chimney corner. They would never have a night free from fear, never a night without a watchman waking over them, and themselves never to be able to sleep for fear the watchman dozed. This was not what they had marched for. They went back. There comes a time, Owain, when lost land is not worth the effort of regaining it, unless it is regained for a certainty. Certainty we could not give them.'

It was half a lifetime ago she said that. Now we have certainty. The Savages are put down all over the land of Britain. Mordei was the last land to be reconquered. Arthur with the Army of the South pinned the hateful ones there between themselves and the Armies of the North, Picts and Strathclyde men, in the wood of Caledon. Now he has resettled all Mordei, and given it to Mordred to rule. There will be peace in Britain for ever.

'They went back,' Bradwen said. She was not bitter, not rancorous, she did not raise her voice or let any emotion cloud it. She did not judge them, she merely said what they had done, and that was judgement enough. 'They did not go back singly. That would have been easier to accept, the flight of single men, frightened, weak, not daring to tell their comrades who will wake with the sun to find the familiar mounds of blankets gone from their sides, slipped away from the dying fire just before the morning. They look back from the edge of the woods just when the birds begin to sing. They half regret what they have done, and think there is still time to go back, to tell how they were taken short and went into the bushes, or to find some other tale, and they wonder what tale of the many will sound the best. But they never do go back. And they go home alone. A wise Commander does not count his troops at night.

'But this was worse. The sun would rise, and whole companies would go. They would awake, and without a word would form up as if to advance, and, instead, would

124

march the other way, into the North. Other companies, regiments, turned back at the noon halts, or even in the middle of the morning. Always they took the beasts they had driven so far. What they told the farmers they repassed I cannot think. What they told Mynydog I do not care.

'Then we came into the region of the dead forests. Now the men of Eiddin began to turn back. The men of Mordei had come to reconquer Mordei, and when they saw Mordei, and it was not what they remembered, they left reconquest to others. But the men of Eiddin expected to see a conquered land. They did not come to win it back for themselves, and they did not care if anyone lived there or not. They had come to clear the Savages from what should be now dead ground, a belt of space for armour. They had come to fight, and to destroy the Savages before they came further.

'Iron the men of Eiddin were willing to face, and the strength of humans, the shock of shields and the agony of battle, where some are brave and some flee and every man is different, and each man, in the end, fights alone and dies alone. But then they saw the dead forest. All across our front, from the hills to the sea, stretched the line of withered trees. A man may fell an apple-tree in spite, or even, demented by fury, hack at a rowan. It takes more than fury, it takes time and patience to ring a tree, and strip the bark away as high as a man can reach. And this was not one tree, but a thousand thousand trees. It was blind malice that stopped the Mordei men. It was the care and patience of all that witless horde, working for weeks on end, all across Mordei, like the spread of a blight. They had quietly, thoroughly killed the kind forest, that shelters our beasts, that gives us nuts and berries and hides the deer we eat. They killed the trees that should have given us fuel and house timbers for a hundred years. All this they destroyed in malice. And the Eiddin men turned back, all in one night.

'The sight of the wasted farms turned back the men of Mordei. The sight of the dead forest turned back the men

125

of Eiddin. But it was the burnt forest that was the end of Cynddelig and his sixty horsemen. They endured till then.

'After the trees die, and the leaves wither, when the trunks are dried through and through, the Savages set light to the forest. We came out of the dead forest into the burnt land. The charred stumps still stood, sometimes knee high. The ground was covered deep in wood ash. It had been grey after the fire; now it was blackened with rain. It was too deep, the ash, for even the coarsest grass to sprout. Now the wood is cleared, the Savages will come, next year, to heave out the stumps and plough the ground to plant their filthy wheat.' She looked around her. 'These brambles have not long to live.'

'There were no brambles in the burnt forest, no food for man nor horse. Neither grass nor berries nor mushrooms, neither deer nor squirrels. That was why Cynddelig turned back. He said to me, "Mynydog gave me these warriors and all their armour, costly beyond belief. If we go farther and the horses founder, then it will all be lost. I will take the squadron back." Three days ago, he went. We have had little food from then till now.'

'But you did not go back?' My voice showed it was the reason, not the fact, that I questioned.

'I had said that I would meet Owain at his place, and ride with him to my father's Hall, the Hall that was my father's, and is mine, and will be his.'

'And you, Gwenabwy? Why did you not turn back?'

'I don't know, boy. I just came on, like I said I would, to the old Hall.' A heavy slow man, Gwenabwy, not a fast thinker, but one it was always good to have at your back. I turned again to Bradwen.

'Where did you get this mail?'

I ran my hand over the shirt, lying over the log on which we sat. Most men wear mail made of rings that might slip on a girl's little finger. The mail I wore was counted fine: the rings would have been tight on the fingers of a month-old baby. The rings of Bradwen's mail would have slipped onto the leg of a thrush, and been a snug fit there. Such mail, they say, all the front rank of Arthur's Household wear now, but it was rare in those days. It was foreign work, made by Goths or Persians far in Africa. The leather beneath the mail was boiled hard and ridged and crested like a stickle-back. A point would not pierce the iron: a blow would be broken by the leather.

'This,' she told us, proudly, 'was a shirt that King Majorian of Rome sent as a gift to my father Eudav, one that he stripped from the body of Attil, King of the Scyths, after he killed him with his own hand. Eudav thought it was too new-fashioned for him to wear, and sent it to Mynydog to hang in his Hall as a trophy, till someone worthy of it should come to claim it. But I thought to bring it back so that someone could wear it to defend my Hall.'

Some of the Household made a hut for Bradwen out of dead boughs and withered leaves. We others slept in our cloaks on the bare ground. We took turns to watch the horses. I drew the turn before dawn. Down on the river meadow, where we had lit our fire, far from the dead trees, I saw Owain still sitting on the log, thinking what next to do.

CHAPTER TEN

Oed dor diachor diachor din drei

Oed mynut wrth olut ae kyrchei

Oed dinas e vedin ae cretei

The entrance to Din Drei was not guarded,

There was a mountain with riches for those who should approach it,

And there was a city for the army that should venture to enter.

The next day, Owain led us west again, up the valley the way we had come, and then onto the High Moors, towards Eudav's Hall, that I supposed we must now call Bradwen's Hall, or perhaps even Owain's Hall. I rode, for preference, with Precent, in the van.

'Go back, then, we must,' Precent grumbled to me. 'There is no going on this campaign without the foot. Sorry it is I am to be going home without blooding my spear, but there it is. We will have to do it next year. You did well enough, Aneirin, you did more damage to the Savages than all the rest of us put together. Next time, we shall have a champion in you.'

'We shall see,' I told him. We jogged along. We might easily have made Eudav's Hall before the evening, but a little after noon, the flank guard on the right sighted a whole herd of deer, and a squadron went off onto the hunt. They cast round up-wind of them, and drove the whole herd down on to our spears. We singled out twenty-six fat bucks, and that was enough for the Household: the rest we let run against next time some Roman felt hungry. It is only a Savage who kills except to eat at once.

This took up time, and by sunset we were nowhere near the Hall. We halted for the night on the old Roman road, looking across to the way through the Wall. We ate well of roasted venison, even though it had not been hung, and there was enough for us all. What with the thrill of the hunt and the smell of the meat cooking, there was a holiday air about the whole Household, more now than ever before. They sat in circles around the fires, and as always, when they were gravy up to the eyebrows, they passed around the mead jars and sang the old songs, one circle singing against another. We the leaders sat around Owain, to hear him, and not, at that, to hear him sing. But he only wanted to hear us. At last Peredur Ironarms asked him, straight out, 'Only one question now, Owain. Do Bradwen stay here on her farm, or do she go back to Eiddin now?'

'I will not go back.' She was firm. We ignored her.

'Someone will have to stay here with her if the men of Mordei do not come. I'll call for volunteers among the squadrons. Hard it will be to find them, I'm sure.' Precent laughed broadly. But Owain said thoughtfully, 'Hard it will be to find men who will give up the glory.'

'What glory is there in riding back tamely to Eiddin with nothing done?' asked Gwion. 'Braver surely it is to stay here on the very edge of the Savages' land, and I am thinking there is not a man who will not stay.'

'Aye,' countered Owain. 'What glory indeed?'

'What will you do, then?' we all asked him together.

'I swore an oath to King Mynydog, that I would go into Bernicia and fight against the Savages. I have not yet entered Bernicia, and I have not fought.'

'But not this year,' insisted Precent. 'Next year, perhaps.'

'Why not this year?'

'There are no infantry. It would be pointless to fight against the Savages with no foot.'

'I have fought the Irish with no foot to back me. And we won.'

'You will not chase these like Irish pirates,' I warned him. 'They will stand to fight, whether we ride or march against them. I have seen them, and I have heard them.'

'Oh, you have only seen a few of them,' Owain pushed me aside. 'Perhaps you heard them, but they were boasting to terrify you. I saw the ones you killed a few days ago, and I saw that there will be no trouble. You settled four yourself, before anyone came to help you.'

'Did I? I only remember twisting and turning where I could and striking out whether I could see anything to hit or not. And in the end, it took a score of us, in armour, to settle a score of them, naked. And Cynon is dead now, most likely.'

'We bought twenty dead, cheap enough, at that price.'

'They were charcoal-burners, not soldiers.'

'All these Savages are warriors, they are brought up to nothing else. Among us, our mothers pray that we will grow up to be poets and the pride of our families and our Kingdoms. Savage mothers only pray their sons will be good fighters. And they live on a handful of wheat a day. So underfed, it is no wonder that though they are all ready to fight, any of us is as good as a dozen of them, and that on foot. Mounted, this Household can destroy any army they can bring.'

'So it is your opinion,' Precent asked him, 'that we ought to go on against the Savages?'

'I have no opinions. I only say what I know.'

'And what do you know?'

'I know that I swore an oath to King Mynydog, that I would go into Bernicia and fight with the Savages.' He did not say 'and you swore too'. He only went on, 'Nothing was said about the infantry. Much was said about the King of Elmet. Shall we leave him to fight alone?'

There was silence for a little while. Then Gwion, from his corner, said, 'So we ride on.'

'Aye,' said Precent. 'So we ride on.'

'So we ride on,' Owain confirmed. 'Tomorrow we will go down the old road through the Wall, and burn their havods on the moors above the valleys. Then we will sweep down into the valleys, and burn their farms before they can call their men together. We shall leave the country a desert and ride through them to Elmet.'

'They do not build havods,' I told them. 'Their young men and women do not go up to the hills in summer to tend the sheep. And they do not live in single farms. They cluster their houses together, and live in crowds of a hundred people and more in one place.' I was unwise enough to add, 'I have seen them.'

'Perhaps they did so live, *where* you saw them,' Owain answered me, whom he had brought because I had knowledge beyond his own. 'But you were only in one place, in a Dun. No man could bear to live as near as that to his neighbours, except in the Dun of a King who can force them not to quarrel with him. If farms are close together, then their owners are enemies: it is a law of

131

nature, we know it well enough. We will burn their farms in the valleys and be in York before they know we are on them.'

'So we ride on,' said Cynrig.

'I will tell them.' Owain, Bradwen with him, walked across to the nearest fire. We sat silent, listening to the shout from the men there, and the bursts of laughter after it. Owain went on to the next fire.

'And if Owain would not ride on,' I asked those left with me. 'Would any of us go alone?'

'I would go, if I went alone,' said Cynrig. 'Because Cynddelig turned back.'

'I came for a fight,' Peredur Ironarms laughed about it. 'I will go on till I have one, and then I can tell Evrog the Wealthy about it, and keep the arms he gave me.'

'Turn back?' This was Gwenabwy. 'Never thought of it till now, boy.'

I looked at Precent. He answered, 'So we ride on. Now we are all dead men. But it is what we came for.'

'I sang of war enough,' I told them, 'and mourned over my betters who fell. Now I will feel death for myself, and let who will sing my elegy.'

Owain returned. All the fires were blazing up high as the songs and laughter that mocked the summer stars. Syvno looked up, and read the planets for us. Victory he prophesied from them, and booty, and no loss. Owain listened, and then said, 'True it is, good things lie ahead: the best of our lives is to come. And because of that, not all should sing. Some there are that will have to stay behind, to guard Bradwen.'

'Guard me?' she asked.

'We cannot leave you alone on your farm. Either you must go back to Eiddin, or someone must stay with you till we ride back to your own Hall. We will raise such a swarm of wild bees about us that they may try to sting us back over the border. We spent a lot of sweat in building you a new house; if burnt it must be, it would be a pity if you were inside it. Either go back to Eiddin, and that would mean only half a dozen men to ride with you, or stay in your Hall and I will leave you a squadron.'

'If you are going to ride into Bernicia, then you will need every man you can take.'

'Go back to Eiddin, then it will weaken us the less.'

'It is strengthening you need.'

'We cannot wait for strengthening. No more will come.'

'One rider more would be welcome.'

'There are no more riders. We are all the Household that will ride. We have no friends till we reach Elmet.'

'I have my father's helmet and mail. I have a sword, too.'

'A woman cannot fight.' The argument was between Owain and Bradwen, between them alone, but we listened.

'I can ride as well as any man, and as long in the day. Ask Aneirin, or Precent. Riding is the most part of soldiering – I know, I have watched you. And I have killed deer – is it harder to kill a man?'

'A deer cannot hurt you.'

'A wild boar will. I have killed them, too. My father had no son. But I gave him all a son could, in love and loyalty. Now let me give him trophies. Will you deny the right of the heir to avenge the father?'

'Whoever heard before of a woman riding to war?'

'And why else do you think I came? Why else do you imagine I brought this armour, hiding it, and a sword wrapped in my cloak? Think, as I do, of all the women that have died in war. Let me have some satisfaction for all the women the Savages have killed, some recompense for all the ruined farms we passed, a red reward for rowans all cut down.'

'Eudav is dead, now, Bradwen. It is my duty to protect you from folly, even your own.'

'Where better for me to be protected than riding at your side?'

Owain looked at us, sitting around them. We looked back, Cynrig and Precent and I, bleakly. This dispute was not ours. The outcome did not matter. We knew that who

133

came, who rode, would not return, and that was our fate, settled by the Virgin. Only Gwenabwy said, 'It is an omen, better than Syvno's stars. We rode out on the day of the Virgin. Let a virgin ride with us that fight for the Virgin.'

'Ride with us, then,' said Owain at last. 'Carry my banner instead of Cynrig, so that in battle the host will rally round you and keep you safe. Ride with us, Bradwen, the Wise Woman, sign sent from God.'

So it was for pride, and the love of Owain, that we rode at last to Cattraeth.

CHAPTER ELEVEN

Bu trydar en aerure bu tan
Bu ehut e waewawr bu huan
Bu bwyt brein bu bud e vran

There was a noise in the mount of slaughter,
there was fire,

Impetuous were the lances, there was a gleam
like the sun,

There was food for the ravens, there the ravens
did triumph.

At dawn we rode forward, towards the Wall. Where the road passed through the Wall there had once been a City, a place of great houses and castles and palaces, raised in the twinkling of an eye out of the ground by the Magician Vergil, when the King's Mistress saw here, on the Wall that she had demanded, no place of pleasure for her to spend one night. And she had slept there one night, and one night only, in a city peopled only for that one night: and when she had awakened in the morning, and passed on, all the people that had come to the City rode away likewise. And so the whole place fell into ruin.

What this town had been called by the woman who had asked for it, no one knew. We called it Din Drei. All the gold had been stripped from the roofs, stolen by the soldiers of false King Arcady. Only the walls of the houses were left. The plaster had fallen in heaps, and the grass grew in the earth of the floors. Some say that if you will scrape away the beaten earth of the floors of the Roman houses, you will find there buried beneath them flat pictures of their god in coloured stone. It is an act of virtue before the Virgin to find them and destroy, but here we had no time. Only we found in many places stone figures of those devils, weather-beaten and green with moss. Where we could without too much trouble, we broke off their hands and their noses, to the glory of the Virgin and her Son and the Dove.

Nothing moved now in Din Drei. Only rats lived there, and foxes, and wild birds. It was twenty years since any civilized men had passed through the Wall here at the Eastern end, though until the Savages burnt Carlisle there had been occasional traffic at the West. We rode through the dead city, the first Roman Army for many years, and out into Bernicia.

I rode with Precent now, always at his stirrup behind the line of scouts, who spread out on either side of the road. So, we agreed, he and I should ride every day, whichever squadron were the skirmishers. Behind us, close in front of the first squadron of the line, Owain would ride. Bradwen was always with him, the raven banner sewn to a light spear, not the stout staff. Behind were the other squadrons, in line ahead, Cynrig now leading Cynon's squadron. Gwion Catseyes always rode behind the last squadron.

Beyond the town, we followed the Roman road at first, though after a day or two we left it and kept across the open moorland. The road was overgrown now with grass, but it still felt and sounded different under the horses' hooves. If you got down here, and scraped with a knife, you would find the big stones of the old road-surface. We left this paved way to head West of South, while it went East of South into the valleys.

The skies were grey and clouded early in the day. By noon, however, when the Wall was far behind, there was only blue above, and the sun in our eyes. We all rode armed, now, of course; we were ready to fight. Our flank scouts were half a mile to either side of the road we followed, looking for prey, like the booths of shepherds. As I had told Owain, they did not find any. Savages do not keep many sheep, and only for the wool: instead of lads, they have grown men, who follow the flock on foot and keep them in sight of the farm all day. But what was strange was that we caught none of the usual bands of straggling Savages, bound one way or another across the hills to beg and scavenge on the West coast. At this time of the year, we ought to have caught scores of them going back for the wheat harvest. But there were none, as if, for some reason, they had all rushed home already.

All that first day we rode quietly, not singing, and we found nothing and saw no one. There was not a living soul up there on the high moors to give warning of our coming. North of the Wall, in good sheep country like that, we could have seen the flocks everywhere, and twenty times in a day we would have had the youngsters come out of their booths to welcome us, to talk to us and ask who we were, and who we were related to, and if we had any news of their families. But Savages do not send their children to be fostered by friends and relations far away, as all civilized men do, even Irish, but they allow sons to grow up alongside their fathers, knowing them well, and having no one tied to them by blood and fosterhood in strange places. The Savages do not love the high moors as we do. They leave them desert.

That night we slept in our cloaks on the ground, as we had done since we left Eiddin. But from that night on, we took turns in hanging our cloaks on a frame of spears for Bradwen. My cloak was always among them.

There were more days that we rode south. Still the sky was grey at dawn, and cleared later and later every day. The Household could not sing when there was no sun. The emptiness of the moors that should have been full of life weighed on us. Only here and there a rowan showed where once there had been a house.

'Have they fled before us already?' Owain asked. 'How did they know we were coming?'

'This is how they live,' I told him. 'They leave the hills empty, and they farm the valleys.'

'Perhaps they did where you were, because they were hiding in the valley for fear of us. But people do not live in valleys when they have moorlands to grow their sheep on. There is nothing for sheep to graze in the marshy valleys.'

'These are not people,' I told him. 'These are Savages. You must not expect them to behave in a human manner.'

But Owain did not answer.

Then, an hour before a dusk of an empty day, Precent and I sat our horses with the left flankers in a clump of bushes and looked down at last into a valley. The sun was behind us: nobody could look into it to see us. Precent waved, and Owain cantered over to us to look.

'Look down there,' I said. 'That is how they live. You see? The oblong wooden houses, all in a square, round an open space with a pond in it. Then there are the fields, long and narrow, stretching round the houses. Not all of them are cultivated. I wonder why? That is wheat growing there. It is ripe, and they are harvesting. See where they have cut that field, and stacked the sheaves? They are loading the oxcarts to bring the sheaves back to the threshing-floor. The Savages are going home from the fields now. Can't you smell the cooking-fires? The smoke hangs in a sheet above the yellow roofs—'

'I can see what I can see.' Owain was curt. But Precent marvelled. 'What a way to live, all crushed on top of each other, hugger-mugger. Nothing but noise and people all the time.'

Owain had waved his arm, and the squadrons had spread out on either side of us. Half a dozen men fell back from each to hold the spare horses. Precent gestured the flankers to spread farther, much farther, to sweep round the village on either side. We still sat, watching the people down there walking home from work, singing probably, though we could not hear them. It was all very still and peaceful. I thought of Eudav's Hall before the Savages came, and I looked at Bradwen, holding the standard behind Owain, and Gwenabwy of the white shield behind her. No one there had yet seen us, and thought that we could be here. Owain drew his sword.

'For One and the Virgin!' he shouted. 'Free the Isle of Britain!'

Shouting and screaming, the Household charged forward, down the slope that formed the edge of the moor into the valley. We enveloped the village and its people, lapping them on every side, as they stopped where they were and turned to stare at us a moment, before they realized what it was, and began to run here and there, each away from what he had been facing, like ants, aimlessly. They had never seen anything like this, a Roman Army all cloaked and plumed in red and sweeping against them out of the empty hills. They ran, they all ran, not away from us, or even at us, but just in whatever direction they were facing when they started to run, till some random thing turned them to run another way, because there was no direction from which we were not coming at them, all furious with the

139

vengeance of Rome. As our beaters had herded in the deer a few days before, so our flankers now herded them in for the killing. Among the deer, we had killed only the beasts we needed, and left the rest to breed. Not so here. We cut them down in the killing place.

Sometimes there were men and boys who turned and tried to fight with their sickles and ox-goads. More often they ran, and in either case they died when we came on them. We left them lying, only bending to take back our spears or drag aside bodies which lay where they might frighten the horses. I saw where three or four of them stood on an ox-wagon with axes and hedging knives, ready to defend themselves and do us what harm they could. I rode at them, finding Aidan with me, and we threw our spears from a distance and saw one fall into his fellows, upsetting them. And, not stopping, we were on them before they could push his body aside, being more concerned with his hurt than with defending themselves, and slashing at them with our long swords, we soon had them tumble into the oxen's heels. We cut through the straps of the harness, and drove the oxen before us, leaving the men writhing on the sheaves till Morien came riding up swinging a flaming torch to set fire to the dried corn.

We herded the oxen into a corner, and killed them, all of them. We brought all the wagons that were not already burning, and the ploughs, and all their weapons and tools into the centre of the village, and we had a good fire to roast our meat. We could find no oat flour, but some of our lads turned out wheat flour and tried to make cakes of that, baking them on the hot ploughshares. Few of us could stomach the stuff. We found jars of the yeast they use to turn the wheat into bread, and we threw that into the fire. We found some mead in the houses, and a great deal of beer, a drink that many of the Household had not seen before, and they were astonished at its strength. All in all, we had the means to celebrate our first victory. We fed our horses on the standing corn.

140

We had killed all the men we found in the village, and anyone else who seemed too eager to run or fight. The rest of the women we penned in a corner with some hurdles, and let them watch us eat. Tow-haired sluts they were, greasy and ill-dressed, weeping and wailing. But after we had eaten, and drunk all the beer, there were a few of the Household who found lust overcame sensibility, and all night long there were screams and laughter to disturb those of us who slept in the biggest house.

This house was divided into two rooms, and we made Bradwen a bed in the inner room, and Gwenabwy slept across the door. We leaders who were too proud to pollute ourselves in the pen sat by the fire, and passed around the mead-jar and planned the next day.

'Let us reach the old road again,' urged Precent. 'Four days riding down there, easy going, and we will reach Elmet, and there we will find whole battalions of foot to support us on the way back. And on the way, one way or the other, we can clear the filth out of York.'

Owain ignored him. Instead he asked us all, 'Do you remember the songs they used to sing of this valley?'

'Gloomy and wet it was in winter, so they say,' answered Cynrig. 'But in summer, pleasant and beautiful to hunt in.'

'Ah, the summer game that was here.' Gwion had heard this. 'Elk lived here, the size of two horses, with horns that would have served as oars for a ten-man boat. Elks like that would feed a whole village. And stags of twenty points. Red deer and roe deer you could find too—'

'And wild boar as well.' That was Gwenabwy. 'The taste of a wild sucking-pig! And where there was all that game, there would be wolf too, and bear, all the fur you could want.'

'Birds of all kinds, too, winter and summer. You would never fly your hawk for nothing, in a place like this. And in the winter, with the streams in a sullen flood, and the whole valley a marsh – pike in the deep pools, roach and

141

gudgeon . . . ' Even Precent was drawn in, against his will.

'Now, look what they have done to it. It is enough to make a man weep.' Owain could sound as bitter as you liked, when he wanted to, and it was not all pretence. 'All our lovely marshes they have drained away, to leave the ground as dry as the top of a table. And cut down are all our trees, and the groves where we used to wander. And what do they do, when they have killed the trees, and burned them, as we have seen them do this year in Mordei? They pull out the stumps and plough the ground level, to turn the fruitful forest into barren wheatfields. And that is how they can live, on a handful of wheat a day, a swarm of brown ants, witless, blind, toiling away with no art, no poetry. It is a sin against the Virgin and against God, to multiply cattle, or people, or crops, without heed. For the earth is the Lord's, and he gave it to us to keep, and not to destroy. It is only Christians who protect even the wolf.

'And how else do they live? They do not keep sheep, nor do they spare any space for the gentle cow, that gives milk, and cheese. They only keep as few as they can to raise oxen to drag the plough. And when they have worn out the ox, they kill him for the tallow and the hide only, because they eat no meat, ask Aneirin if it is not true. And that is how they manage to live here, and to grow, so that in two generations they multiply from one boatload to a nation. They will swamp us if we do not stop them. We have to undo all they have done. After that, we must bring the Army of their nation to battle, so that we can destroy them utterly in one place. And, in a few years, we and our sons will hunt in this valley again.'

For four days, then, we raged in the valleys, the one that runs East to the sea, and the one that goes South to York. We treated every village as we treated the first one. When we left that first village, we burnt every house. We had thrown the ploughshares and every weapon and tool that we found into the fire where we cooked our meat, and that not only destroyed the costly work of the

142

wheelwright – ask Mynydog's men how difficult is the wheelwright's task – but it also spoiled the temper of the iron. What metal we could pick out of the ashes, the next morning, we dropped into the well, and threw in as many bodies as we could find, to pollute it. Others we flung into the pond where they watered the cattle. We burnt the corn in the barns, and smashed the querns with hammers – their hammers.

Most of this was Morien's work. After he had set the houses on fire, he made a bundle of clothes he had found in a house, and smeared them in tallow, and tied them behind his horse with a long, long rope. Then we lit the cloths, and he galloped, the flaming torch behind him, through the corn fields, and set the evil wheat alight where it grew.

We kept the spades that were in the houses, though, and we blocked up all the ditches along the edges of the fields, and broke in all the banks. We made the women work at this before we killed them in case they should breed, and for the sake of all the women the Savages had killed in the Mordei and Bernicia, in our time and in our fathers', and who had had no sons.

When Morien had shown how best to do all this, and he had given lonely thought to this in the woods by his kilns, we spread out by squadrons and did the same all across the land, till I grew tired of the sight of smoke and the taste of half-cooked beef and of wheat cakes, and the sight of the square houses, in their long fields. In four days, a hundred villages burnt, and in none of them did we leave more than a few wailing children. The wolf and the bear, the kite and the buzzard came flocking into the houses for easy meat. Why should they not feast, and why should we not feed them? They were *our* wolves, *our* kites.

We left a trail of death and destruction everywhere the Household of Mynydog rode, and there was no one more hard in vengeance, more cruel, more thorough in searching out anything that could be of value to destroy it, than Bradwen. She led us to make a ruin of fruitful fields and happy villages for the sake of the Virgin. In ten years, or five, when the trees and the grass had grown again, and the waters of the winter floods had passed across them, the ugly straight fields would be changed to pleasant marsh, a land that Romans could hunt in and make their home. But first, what we did would be more hideous than anything the wheat-growers had accomplished. Before beauty could return, we had to make devastation.

What people we found we killed, with their livestock, and showed them no mercy. Mostly we found that when they saw the smoke of the next village rise in the still hot air they would flee, hiding in the little woods they had left, seeking refuge in what they had wanted to destroy. They did not resist. There was a thing that puzzled me, though it did not seem of any importance to Owain.

'There are no men,' I told him, 'or very few, and those either very old or very young, like those we left behind when the Army marched out of Eiddin.'

'The men heard us coming and went away without waiting for urging, running faster than the women,' he answered lightly. 'Or else there are few men among the Savages, as we have few whole rams among the flock of sheep, because one male of them can serve a whole flock of females.'

'This not to laugh at,' I insisted. 'No men, and, in the houses I have seen, never a spear, and not one shield or mail coat. And seldom even an axe or a hedging-knife.'

'They are not used to proper arms. They fight naked, like the animals.'

I was stung at last. 'Perhaps that is how the Irish fight, and how you won your famous victories. I tell you, these Savages are as well armed as we are, and fight as well, and that you will find out soon enough. I have been asking the women where the men have gone.'

'You got no answer. These witless brutes have no memory of anything that happened longer ago than yesterday.'

144

'They said all the men have gone off to a war. Some-where, Owain, the Savages have gathered a great many. It is true, the women don't know where, North or South, but somewhere there is a horde of Savages on the march. Let us hope that they have gone south against Elmet, because if they have gone into Mordei by the coast road, and missed us, then we will never feast in Eiddin again.'

But Owain only laughed at me, and because he *was* Owain, our leader, I laughed with him, and believed him when he said there was no such army, only a tale the women had made up to hide the cowardice of their men. But they had made up the same tale in every village.

It was the end of the fourth day on which we laid waste in the valleys, and we had returned to the place from which we had started. Our squadrons had gone north and east, north to the Border, and east to the sea, almost. Only half a squadron had gone south, probing gently down the road which we would follow, to York and Elmet. The leader of this section was Dyvnwal, whom we called Vrych, the Speckled, because of his freckles, and he had painted his shield white covered with spots of red to match his nickname: and that is all I remember about him, because he was a quiet man. It was on the morning of the fifth day, on which Precent had hoped we would be in Elmet, that we saw this section coming up the Roman Road towards us. Owain rode to meet them, like a King in Venery, with his Jude and his Huntsman and his Standard-bearer, in myself and Precent and Bradwen. When we came near to them, we saw that there were only a dozen red cloaks, instead of forty, and no spare horses, and the chargers they were riding well blown.

They came rushing to us as we rode down to meet them on the empty road, among the empty blackened fields of burnt wheat, all shouting and talking at once.

'A battle,' they shouted. 'We have been in a battle! Against the Savages!'

Owain shouted at them to be quiet. 'Where is Dyvnwal?' he kept on asking. 'Where are the others?'

There was a greater hubbub. Geraint, a man from the South, seemed the most coherent, and I tried to follow his voice against the others.

'We came on a village some time after noon. We rode around it and into it. There was no one there. Not a soul. Not a woman, or a child. Still we did not think it unusual. You never know what customs these Savages have. We dismounted—'

'All of you?' I asked.

'All of us. We went through their houses. They had taken their jewels with them. No silver. We pulled the ploughs together close to the biggest house. We heaped corn on it. And the yeast. We piled the benches over the ploughs. We brought the blankets and clothes out of the houses. We put on the tallow. Then Dyvnwal bent to kindle the fire. There was a shouting in our ears. They were on us.'

'Many of them?'

'They made noise for ten thousand. They were many more than we were. We each had ten to fight. They were in mail. They had those short swords. We had left our shields with our horses. We tried to get back to the horses. We had to cut our way through. I killed two; at least, I struck them and they fell. I think we here are all that reached the horses. If they had stampeded our mounts they would have had us all. We got into line. We charged back into the village. There was nothing we could do for the others. Dead, all of them. A heap of Savages around them. The Savages could not stand up to us mounted. They ran when we returned. We saw that those who had come into the village were the advance guard of an Army. They were in hundreds, thousands. We set the houses alight. We came for you.'

'You returned and left your comrades there?' Owain was sharp, scornful.

'If we had dismounted to recover the bodies, it would have been a glorious deed. Who would have sung us for it? We would have died ourselves. We came back to warn you.'

'I told you the men had gone away to war,' I told Owain.

146

'It was South they went, and perhaps they have already fought against Elmet. Now they are returning. The road South is blocked. We will not reach Elmet now, or even York.'

'The road South may be blocked, but we will still take it.' Owain turned to Precent. 'The squadrons are coming in on us now, as we ordered. Meanwhile, push some scouts down the road for a mile or two.' He ignored Geraint and his comrades; in fact, he never spoke to them again, as if they had shamed themselves, though no one who saw the hacked shields and the gapped blades, and the blood up to their elbows, could doubt that they had fought.

That night, we slept spread across the road in an arc, a mile from horn to horn, with our fires burning and tended by sentries who watched for the Savages. But they did not attack that night. So, in the morning, we rode down the Roman Road in our usual order.

The skirmishers saw the enemy about two hours after dawn. They called back, and Precent and I rode across to where we could see the enemy. They were a little group of men, fifty at most, standing full in the road, waiting. Owain came forward with two squadrons, through the skirmish line, and charged down on them. There was no difficulty there. When the horsemen were within a hundred paces of them, they broke and ran in all directions, and were cut down again as they fled. We re-formed, and moved again down the road.

We came on more groups like this. 'Marching North to meet us, all hugger-mugger, every man his own general,' said Owain. I did not think so, but I held my peace. They had more the look of a rear-guard, to keep us off the main army while it found somewhere better to fight. But now I knew better than to contradict Owain, because he was our leader, and always right.

Sometimes, they would hear us coming first, and then they would get into some kind of order across the road, and try to hold a line when we rode at them. But we always got round the flanks. If we caught them strung out, they would run before we could get at them, scattering all across the country. As we moved South, they stiffened. They stood longer. Once a group ran, as a body, into a wood. Half a dozen horsemen followed them into the trees. Only two returned. They told of men who leapt out of the under-growth to hamstring the horses, or dropped from the trees onto the riders. Even Owain did not order anyone to recover the bodies.

But all this slowed us down. Late in the afternoon, when we had covered barely ten miles, we came in sight of the village where Geraint had fought. Where the road went past the smoking ruins, not through them, there was a stake new set in the ground. On it was the head of Dyvnwal Vrych. It was not freckles now that marked his face but the cuts of knives. His private parts were thrust between his locked teeth. The ravens had already had his eyes.

There we slept that night. We lay in our armour, waiting an attack. Only half of us slept at any time. Those who lay down nestled close to their horses, and not only for warmth; we knew, those who mounted first would live. Before we slept Owain talked to us.

'Now we know the spirit of the Savages,' he told us. 'They will not stand to face us. All we have to do is show a bold face to them and they will run away. Only remember, do not fight their kind of battle. They want to catch us dismounted in small groups, or lure us into the woods. If you are ready to fight that way, like Savages, then there is no way out, because they are too many for us. We have to use our superior skill and equipment. They cannot ride, and they will never stop us, because we bring civilization back to the valleys. In two days' time, we will retake York. In four days, we will feast in Elmet.'

But Precent spoke to me quietly, in the dark, by the horses.

'A victory is when the whole of an Army runs away, not when even the smallest part of it stands and dies where it fights. We have defeated no one, because they were never afraid of us. Even when they ran, they were only taunting us.' He stood up. 'Hey, Syvno! Have you read the stars tonight? Will there be a battle tomorrow?'

'No, no battle,' Syvno cried back, confidently. 'Tomorrow will be just like today. We will ride through them, and there will be a feast after it, and you and I will toast each other.'

'Then look to all your harness straps,' Precent warned me quietly, lest Syvno hear. 'Telling the stars is as easy as telling the weather.'

CHAPTER TWELVE

Peleidyr en eis en dechreu cat
hynt am oleu bu godeu beleidryal

In the first onset his lances penetrate the target,
And a track of light is made by the aim of the darting
of his spears.

At dawn, we came down from the fires where we had slept, chewing as we rode on cold bacon and wheat cakes, and drinking from our jars of mead so that we would fight with that last taste of home in our mouths. We crossed the South-flowing river, where the Romans had built a bridge. Now it had fallen, leaving only the columns on the banks, and there were no Magicians in the Island who could raise it again. Behind us, the burning thatch laid low across the land a ceiling of black smoke under a roof of grey cloud. We were not opposed.

We moved up from the river, Precent and I on the road itself, the skirmishers spread out on either side of us. We saw the town before we saw the enemy who lay in front of it. The old town was there, near the bridge. The houses were roofless. The Savages had built their village a half mile away. They never live in the towns, even when they find them empty and waiting. They prefer to stay outside the walls, or if, very bold, they come within the walls, they place their houses in the pleasant gardens where the real people of the place once grew their leeks and radishes. Savages never live in houses of stone. They cannot mend the roofs when tiles fall, or hang doors again on metal hinges. Besides, they believe that all the houses are made by Magicians, and that if they come within doors they will fall a prey to the magic. And better it would be if they did.

The town had once been surrounded by a wall. It was ruined now, and often collapsed into a continuous mound, rather than a rampart. There was a gentle slope of rubble in the ditch that went round the walls. The weeds came close to the walls on three sides, not on the one that faced the river.

'Gone,' said Precent, waving towards the town. 'All gone, the people who lived there once. No one even remembers the name of the place.'

'Oh, yes, they do,' I told him. 'The name is clear, where the old road crosses the river. How does it go? I think I remember:

'Constantine here held his court.

151

Cold the hearth, hosts unkind.
Women weep for Cattraeth, silenced.'

'Who first sang that? Did you?'

'No, I do not know who was the first. It is an old song. By the language, it is from before the Savages came. Perhaps the town had been desolate before. Why do you ask?'

'Because it is the first verse I have heard you speak for more than a year.'

I did not answer. I felt that I had been unguarded. What had softened me? The heat of the battle yesterday perhaps, the sight of the dead. And which dead had moved me most? Dyvnwal Vrych, eaten by the crows? The corpses, stiff, thrown into the ponds and wells? Or that first boy, barefoot, in Eudav's woods?

But between where we sat and the two places, the town on the one hand and the village on the other, the enemy stood. To our left, the ground sloped down to the river. The pools shining black under the leaden sky, the rushes standing up like clumps of savage spears, showed that this was bogland. It was no ground to ride horses over. To our right, there was another wood, a rare sight in that land, but whether they were afraid again of magic, or whether they left it to feed their swine, or whether perhaps the ground was too poor for wheat, I do not know. At any rate, it was dense wood, with bushes undergrowing the trees. We had had enough of that the day before. Horsemen would not enter the wood's edge and the river swamp was five hundred paces, not less, perhaps seven hundred, certainly not as much as a thousand. Through that space led the road. Through that space we had to go. And in that gap stood Bladulf.

Oh, yes, I was sure it was Bladulf, even at that distance. I had seen him the once, and that once was enough. A giant he was. There are giants among the Savages. We count a man tall at seventeen hands: they mostly top eighteen, and only Owain of all the Household came to that. And Bladulf stood half a head taller than any of his army. His yellow hair hung braided to his waist, not cut like a Christian, and he wound black rags into the braids so that he could be told from behind. He wore a helmet of bronze, not iron, shining red through the gloom of that day. Over the crest of it ran a high ridge, worked to show a wolf's face above his own. The wolf's paws reached down to cover his nose and to spread out where they might guard his cheeks. This was no Savage work, but stolen somewhere in Gaul. He wore mail to the thigh, and trousers of stiff leather like ours.

'He will not move quickly in those,' I told Precent.

'He does not mean to run,' Precent agreed. 'That one will stand where he stands, whether his men stay with him or not. Watch that sword. He will try to come up at you under your shield. Do not let him attack you on the shield side.'

We could see, even from here, that Bladulf had a real sword, long and double-edged and pointed, such as few of his men carried. This was a sword a man could strike with, putting his weight behind the point to thrust. This was no edge that a village smith could beat out, to spoil by cutting hay or splitting wood or cracking lobster claws. I wondered where he had stolen it. It was no Roman work, too long, too big.

Owain came to us. We three rode forward, close enough to see faces. The Savages did not move, just stood firm. They began to make a noise, beating on their shields, and taking up a rhythmical chanting shout, bellowing in chorus one word again and again, perhaps a hundred times, before they found another word.

'What is the word they cry?' Owain asked.

'*Blood*,' I told him.

'Then the Bloodfield let this place be,' he told me. But it was Cattraeth, all the same.

Cynrig joined us, and Peredur Ironarms.

'Eight to one, would you say, or ten?' asked Precent. He counted nice enough, seeing they were well pressed together all across our front, and three or four lines deep in most places, close on each other's heels. But Owain replied, 'Nearer twenty to one, counting us all together, horse-holders and all. Hear that, Aneirin, hear that, twenty to one, and sing it. Oh there shall be glory for us this day, honour and glory for us all.'

We looked close at the Savages, standing there in line, waiting for us. All giants they were, that is true, all of them far taller than most of us. Many of them in the front rank had a piece or two of mail to hide their shoulders or their breasts. Most of them had the saxes they used on their farms, too long to be called knives, too short for swords, and too useful to be kept only for battle. Besides there was a forest of spears, and axes as well. And every man had a shield, not oval and leather-covered like ours but round and heavy, of limewood planks joined together, with iron bosses deep and pointed, and iron rims a hand wide. They looked a dirty lot, all dressed in their undyed garments of grey or brown coloured with only grease and dirt, a line of dun ants, frugal as the ants, not knowing what art or poetry or civilization is, needing only each man his handful of wheat to live. Satisfied with that little, too.

Behind Bladulf, a mocking parody of Bradwen, a sootdaubed giant carried his banner. It was black, long and narrow, the edges stiffened with willow canes, so that it stood out for us to see all the day, and never drooped on the staff. It was embroidered with a dragon, in white. His helmet did not, however, show the dragon's wings, but the horns they liked to wear. In the rear rank, there were men with neither helmet nor even a cap of wool or leather, and these were Aidan's horned men indeed, because they had twisted their braids in tallow to stand out like stiff horns before their heads. A strange people, among whom a horned man had honour. And we could smell them, too, even at that distance, the strange almost-sweet smell of wheat flour, leavened with yeast.

'How do we take them, Owain?' Cynrig asked. It was something, that we were able to sit there, within a spear's

154

cast of the enemy line, and discuss what we would do, as calmly as if we were in the paddocks under the Giant's Seat.

'As we always planned,' Owain answered. He did not move, though, but sat still a moment, looking at the long dun line of swaying chanting warriors. The rhythm of their voices was a seductive, diverting thing, numbing thought. But under that strange deliberate assault, not on the body but on the senses, Owain still was able to plan, to change his mind.

'No, not as we always planned it. Precent, I want you to command the reserve Squadron.'

'That was not what you promised me.'

'I do not break promises lightly. Twenty to one there may be, but it cannot yet be the whole host of the Savages. It may well be that Bladulf has hidden men in the wood, to try to take us in the rear when we attack. If they do, I want my most experienced commander to be ready for them.'

'I take it Bradwen will ride with us, then?' I asked.

'I cannot ride into battle without my standard. It is my ravens that will drink blood today, and peck out eyes tonight.'

'I will carry your standard,' Cynrig offered.

'Will you dare try to take it from her?' Owain asked him. 'I have tried to persuade her, but she insists that she will fight. I have told her to ride in the second line, not the first, in case the standard is captured. It is the only argument she will listen to. Gwenabwy and a dozen others will keep close around her. I think she will be safer in the second line than in the reserve, if there should be an attack from the wood. If you want to go and argue yourself, then you can, but I have little hope that you will change her mind.'

There was no more to say. Only Owain asked, 'Their shout has changed. What are they saying now?'

'*Victory,* they are bawling, over and over again, *Victory.*'

'For whom? Go with God, my friends.'

We turned again and joined our squadrons. Precent,

Cynrig and I rode together to the reserve line. Between us and the leading squadrons rode Bradwen; Gwenabwy rode close at her right hand, and Cynrain at her left. As we rode back, though, I heard Precent ask Owain, 'Am I to use my own discretion when to throw in the reserve?'

'No! Charge when you see we have broken through, or when you hear me call to you. Otherwise, sit still!'

Owain rode forward again. We saw him speak to Bradwen before he went to his own place at the centre of the front rank. The chant of the Savages rose louder and louder. From our ranks rose only the voice of Gelorwid, in the words of the Virgin's Hymn. We were ready to put down this proud Bladulf from his throne.

Then we of the reserve stood beside our horses and watched the opening of the battle. The Household spread out in two lines, one behind the other. The Savages suddenly fell silent, keeping their breath for their fight. Owain rode in the centre, in the gap between the two front squadrons. Oh, there is never a sight in all the world like an army of cavalry riding into action, all gleaming in red and shining iron, all the gay shields bobbing and the pennants flying, the plumes tossing as they went forward, silent now as the enemy.

Owain did not ride at the whole of the enemy's line, as he could have done if he had spread out his men as far as they would go. He made his soldiers ride knee to knee, where they could help each other, but not so close that they could not move. They trotted steadily across the empty field, an eye always for bad ground or molehills or traps dug for us by night. And the Savages waited for us, not running forward to meet our people. A spear's throw from the enemy line, the Household halted. The men of the first rank raised their arms, and a shower of spears fell on the enemy. Immediately, the second line rode forward, squeezing through the gaps in the first line, only Owain and Bradwen keeping their places. The men of the second line, now in the front, threw their spears, and then, with swords drawn, rode forward again at the walk,

156

crushing and pressing against the Savage front as if to push it aside by sheer force. But as our men threw their spears, so did the enemy, and sword rang against sword, and long pikes thrust from where swords could not reach. I saw men fall from their saddles, and riderless horses rear in the press and trot back, where they could, saddlecloths blackened with blood or their riders trailing by the feet from the stirrups.

The lines were locked for as long as it took Gelorwid, at my elbow, to repeat twice the Virgin's Prayer that he had learnt from a hermit in the South. But, at length, we heard above the din, above the screech of the Savages, the shouts of the Household, the braying of horns, the screams of men struck down, and the clatter of sword against shield and spear against mail, the voice of Owain, splendid as a trumpet of silver. We saw the second line of horsemen, pressing behind their leaders, slacken, and then the Raven banner came back towards us, and Owain riding behind it, and all the rest of our horsemen following it, in a streaming rout.

Any leader can carry men with him into an attack. Only an Owain can lead them away from the enemy, and then halt them where he pleases. The Raven banner halted where it had stood before, and the squadrons re-formed around it. Again, Owain led them forward, not now at the centre of the enemy's line but at their right flank, our left, where they held their flank against the bog. Now, of course, the ranks were reversed, and it was fresh men who first closed with the line of foot, cutting and slashing at the bearded faces below them, shearing off the tow braids with the tow heads, swords falling in severed hands. Again we could see Owain in the centre of the front line, his plumes tossing, his arms flailing as he dealt out pain and death on either side. Behind him, steady, above his head, the Ravens flew.

Yet, still, the line of foot stood firm, still it neither broke nor bent. Still we could see Bladulf, a head above his men, always meeting the centre of our attack, a demon in

157

flesh. He would not let us pass. Never would Bladulf let us ride through to York, if there were not a man to help him. Oh, it would have been no trouble to Owain to have killed Bladulf: he could have done it in his sleep. There was never a giant that Owain could not have overcome, had he fought against him one to one. But in that press, in the ranks of the wild ones, Owain could not come at him.

At length, again we saw Owain break clear, again we saw the Raven banner retreat. Again we saw our comrades turn their backs on a hail of spears. Again the squadrons re-formed. They were fewer now. Bodies lay over all the ground between us and the enemy. The spent horses could not charge again. We stood there, useless and sterile, while the very horseholders of the other squadrons took their places in the line, bringing forward fresh horses for a fresh charge.

Now Owain headed a charge on a narrower front, ten men in line, no more, and twenty deep. Owain rode in the front line. The Ravens flew in the centre of the mass. Now the spears were all thrown. With swords alone the Household rode again for the third charge, and still we of the reserve stood idle, not even mounting because that would have tired our horses. Ever more threatening was the line that stood before us, as dull and lowering as the clouds above us. This battle, I thought, is lost.

The third time, the Household rode up the field, and again Owain led them against the enemy line. At a trot he headed for the centre of the line of shields, and then at the last moment he turned his force half right, to attack the Savages' left flank. At a trot he thrust against the wall of spears, and all the Household with him — except us. The ranks of horse spread out behind their leader, men cutting and hacking overlapped him on either side. The Household was a blunt wedge, pointed at Bladulf, at no one but Bladulf. The Savage line stood; then, for the first time, it bowed. It bowed, but it did not break. They were pressed back, but their line did not break. There were no gaps.

Men thrust in from every side to fill in every vacant place, to pick up every fallen shield.

Now, if a line is stretched, then *somewhere* it must give, somewhere it must thin, somewhere it must weaken.

'Look there!' said Precent. 'See how they strengthen their left flank, not by design, but by unthinking necessity. They are thickening at the left. But as each man feels his left flanker shrink away from him, he too edges over, one pace, and then another. At the beginning of the battle, the wall of shields was as strong at either end as in the middle, and four deep. Not a hare could pass. But now on the right hand they have thinned out to a mere line of sentries.'

'If Owain attacked there,' I replied, 'they would close up again to meet him. And it is what he wants. He has come for glory. The battle to him is more important than the war. If he could send all the Savages back to Jutland with never a blow struck, he would not do it. Oh, a happy man he is today, having his fill of blood, his long count of fallen Savages. And we stand here till he thinks of calling us.'

'If Owain rides to the flank, they will indeed move to meet him. But if he holds them there in strength – have you ever heard of any foot who would stand while cavalry came at them from all sides?'

'Owain said that we were to wait till we heard his voice,' I reminded Precent.

'Indeed, if you will only listen with care you will hear his voice, loud and clear.' Precent laughed from ear to ear, laughed loud enough for Owain to hear there in all the press. 'I am quite sure I can hear him calling me to charge. I can't help it, Aneirin, if you are prematurely deaf. A dreadful affliction that can be, too, for a poet.' He swung into the saddle, and turned to the reserve squadron.

'Into line, now Romans all! One line only, one line. At the canter when we reach them, and no faster. Swords only. Ready now, all of you? Then follow me. Ride, Romans! Ride!'

159

I rode close to Precent. Aidan was on my left, Cynrig beyond Precent, Gelorwid, Morien, all my friends, rode in line. Behind us, the horseholders, men wearied in the first charge, mounted rested beasts and made a second rank. Geraint led them, still weeping for Dyvnwal Vrych.

War is cruel and a waste, war is vain and useless, war settles nothing, war is a time of misery. So we may all say, on the long march, shut up in a fortress, or in the Hall at the end of a long peace. But in the moment of battle, you do not think of that, true though it may be. There is nothing in your heart but joy, and the happiness of being committed absolutely. And of all ways of fighting, there is nothing like riding in a charge of horse, a line of forty men, knee to knee. Then no man believes in death, no man believes in defeat, no man has any thought for what lies outside the line and beyond the battlefield.

We rode silent. Every head in the enemy line was turned to their left, watching the main action. Our horses' hoofs drummed on the dry ground, threw up the dust of a long drought into our faces. Fifty paces from the Savages, Precent for the first time raised his voice. He gave no words, only a yell of triumph. We shouted with him. We saw the scattered Savages in front of us start, turn to meet us, try to group in threes or fours, and then, seeing how thin they were on the ground, and how little chance they had of stopping us, flee, some into the shelter of their fellows in the centre, and others into the bog, and even into the depths of the river, swimming for the farther bank. And the few that stood to meet us we killed with hardly a break in our stride.

Now the hours that we had drilled below Eiddin were rewarded. Still in line, at the canter, we wheeled, our pivot man halting, our flanker at the gallop. Now the whole of the reserve swept round to come at the backs of the enemy who so bravely faced Owain.

It is true. Did *you* ever hear of infantry who stood while cavalry came at them from all sides? These did not stand. Not even Bladulf stood. He, and the men nearest to him,

160

tried to form a wall, a city as it were, of their shields, and stand as a living fortress. But most of them fled into the wood. Those that stood we ignored. There were enough fleeing for us to cut down from behind. Here and there, two or three of these, overrun, would turn to meet us, striking not at riders but at horses. Now our other Squadrons could break through, where there was no longer a line to meet them, and spread wider over the field. The Bloodfield it was indeed, covered with men, dead or crippled.

Not savages alone. Ahead of us all, alone near the edge of the wood, I saw a horse fall. A crowd of Savages rallied there to thrust spears into its belly, to swing poleaxes at its fetlocks. The horse came down, screaming, rolling on the rider, and we saw the swords and axes rise and fall in the brief moment before I came up to scatter them. Oh, Gelorwid, Gem of Baptism! You were not born for this. In my grief I cried it aloud. Not for this, your sword-hand cut away, your helmet rolled far, your face beaten in with clubs, your mail shirt wrenched up above your head like the shirt of a raped woman. I had hoped to see you to your marriage bed, not to your grave. You were born for the caresses of a queen, not for the blades of the Savages. I wept for Gelorwid, and sang his elegy, as I struck down those who killed him.

Nor was he the only man to fall. Buddvan the son of Bleiddvan, that should have guarded Gelorwid's back, he too lay dead. The white hide of his horse was now as red as his cloak, with his own blood. Blood hid the sheen of his mail. He that once rode through the ranks of the enemy like an eagle through the air, now lay still on the regained earth of Bernicia.

There is no time in battle to weep for those who die. Fight on we must, and show that they have not died in vain, that their death is not empty, that from the arms of the Virgin they need not blame us as sluggards. The Savages fled before us in all directions as we avenged our friends. Only around Bladulf they stood fast, and retreated slowly, step by step, towards the shelter of the wood.

161

Bladulf himself was the rearmost, wielding not a weapon but a flail. With that he swept a space clear behind his men. No horse would be forced into that arc of death, nor would any man walk there.

We left Bladulf and his remnant to hide where they would, and swept forward to take what they had defended. His was the biggest village we had seen. Not the greatest, perhaps, in the number of the houses, but in their size and splendour. The first fugitives had reached it, and now the old men and the women and children were trying to save themselves and their cattle. Neither had they expected defeat. When we burst upon them, they left their animals and tried to save themselves: and could not.

The battle was at an end. Breathless we gathered before Bladulf's Hall. I rode to Owain's side, where he sat, Bradwen still behind him. Precent we had seen among the Savages, leaping and bounding among them like a ball in the game. Now he came to us, panting, wringing the sweat from his scarf. Cynrig, too, joined us, his saddle splattered with blood, but none of his, and Peredur Ironarms, and Aidan, counted the Savages he had killed to make himself a man, and Graid, his arm numbed by Bladulf's flail. And all the others were around us, shouting and cheering and hailing the General whose arm and mind had brought us Victory.

Oh, the sight of Owain on the won field, his face shining as we shouted, 'All Hail to the Commander, the Emperor, the bringer of all luck and fortune!' Only there was no one now to sing praise to the Virgin. Gelorwid was dead.

While some entered the Hall, and the houses around it, and heaped wood and ploughs for a fire, and drove together and slaughtered the animals, others went back to scour the Bloodfield. They drove together from here and there a crowd of Savages who were only slightly hurt, or not hurt at all, and who, amazing as it may seem, wished to live even after defeat, and were willing to submit. These they set to dig a grave. With care and tenderness we brought together the bodies of those of the Household

162

who had been killed, and the few who, though unhorsed, still lived. We could not leave anyone for the cruel knives of the Savage women, crawling about the field by night. We buried our dead on the field they had won, and after that we killed the Savages who had dug the grave. We stripped the Savage dead, and brought their armour into the Hall in case anyone thought himself half armed and wanted to take his pick. What was left we would spoil in the fire, with the weapons we found, and then throw into the river, where the Savages might dive for it if they wanted it, and not be sure of finding it. The bodies of the Savage dead were left. This was Bernicia. Were not the wolves here ours to feed?

Victory was almost complete. The road to Elmet was open before us. Only Bladulf was still alive, somewhere in the wood below Cattraeth.

CHAPTER THIRTEEN

Kynt y waet elawr
Nogyt y neithyawr

Thou hast gone to a bloody bier,
Sooner than to a nuptial feast.

We feasted our victory in Bladulf's Hall. We did not weep for those who were dead, not for Gelorwid or for Gwion Catseyes, nor yet for Dyvnwal Vrych. There was not room in the Hall to lay their empty places, eighty of them. We drank and ate their share, as they would have wished, and as we wished our comrades to do when we fell. Under the joy of victory and drunkenness of battle, we knew well enough, all of us, that there would be other battles, that Bladulf would return. But not tonight. Tonight he would not come near enough to smell his own pigs roasting.

He was rich, was Bladulf. He would not live on a handful of wheat a day. The couches in his Hall were spread with wool and with furs, soft and warm. We dribbled the dregs of our mead on the couches and wiped the grease from our knives on the sables. They drink out of horns, you know, the Savages, not from cups of pottery or glass, but Bladulf's horns stood in settings of silver.

There was plenty to fill them, too, beer, and mead as well. The bitter beer we washed our hands in, and cleaned the blood from our armour and groomed our horses and our saddles. Even the horses drank it, but we did not. But the mead, the sweet blue mead, there was enough of that in Bladulf's Hall for us all to drink and be drunk a hundred times over. And we had only one night, or perhaps two, to drink it in, because we soon would move on to Elmet, and leave Bladulf's Hall in a blaze. Tables and blankets would burn, fur and horn would shrivel, painted beams and carved pillars, wool and silver, hemp and flax, all would char away into a waste of nothingness. Why should Bladulf's Hall fare better than Eudav's? But while we had it, we would enjoy it. And we had it.

Only on the top table at the feast we of the Royal families talked of the battle over and the battle to come. Precent and I had ridden over the field after the rout, and we had seen things, noted things, that could not be seen by those who made sure of Bladulf's Hall.

'Where, then, was Elmet?' Precent asked.

165

'I suppose,' Owain answered between drinking, 'that these are the remnants who came back defeated from Elmet.'

'These men have not fought before this year,' I insisted. 'There were no new wounds, no hacked shields. Dusty they were, and tired, like men who have marched long and fast. But they have not fought.'

'Again, I ask, where was Elmet?' Precent thumped the table in his urgency. 'We have come because Elmet expects us, but where is Elmet?'

'This is the strategy we worked out with Mynydog,' Owain answered easily. 'First we have drawn their army north to meet us, and now they are well engaged with us, the Elmet men will take them in the rear.'

'But why so long?' Precent asked. 'They let us ravage in their valleys for four days. They would not have done so if they had known we were coming. They went south for some reason. They were ready for the Elmet men to come. But they have not fought. Where then are the Elmet men? Did they not come? Or have they made a treaty with the Savages?'

'Or,' put in Peredur, 'have they just melted away and gone home in the night, like the infantry from Eiddin?'

'What does it matter?' shouted Owain, lifting his face from the mead-jar. 'We have beaten the Savages without them. All the better – the more glory for us. We can crow over Elmet for ever now. I wonder how they will have the gall to face us when we ride into Lincoln.'

'We have beaten part of their army,' I warned. 'There are more Savages in Bernicia than the sands of the sea. The men we scattered today could not have half peopled the villages we have burnt already. They were only the fastest, who were the first to come up and face us, in the hope of keeping us out of Bladulf's Hall. There are more coming up, you can be sure. And, worst of all – we did not kill Bladulf. That must be our main concern. When we fight again, we must kill Bladulf: then his army will go home.'

'Let me tell everybody that.' Owain got to his feet, not quite steady, and shouted, 'Listen! Listen to me, all of you!'

Nobody took the slightest notice. Very few even heard him, and they were by now too drunk to take any notice. Owain tried again two or three times, and we beat on the table, but the only effort was that some of the others began to beat their fists on the boards in time with us, and then to sing.

'We'll wait till the morning,' Owain decided at the last. 'When we are ready to move, I'll tell them. I'll give a gold chain to the man who kills Bladulf.'

'You haven't got a gold chain,' Peredur pointed out.

'No, but Mynydog has,' Owain giggled like a girl, and spilled his drink onto his cloak and tried to brush it off, clumsily.

'Never mind, boy,' Morien shouted. 'Plenty more here.'

He leaned across three or four people to slosh more mead into Owain's cup, and over the table and over everybody and everything in between. And in the state we were all in, we laughed and thought it funny to see the liquor, over the table and the floor, shining in the light of Bladulf's candles, forty alight at a time. That night we used the tallow of a hundred oxen.

I saw Bradwen lean over to Owain.

'Now, if you *had* a gold chain, you'd give it to me, wouldn't you?'

'And how do you know I haven't? I was the first in here, wasn't I?'

'No you weren't,' shouted Hoegi from the other end of the table, because Owain, for all his air of telling a secret, leaning over to Bradwen's ear, had forgotten to lower his voice. 'I was the first in here, don't you forget it, and you came next, and ordered me out. Anything you found in here belongs to me.'

Owain and Hoegi shouted at each other from end to end of the table, and Bradwen alternately urged Owain to reply or rolled with helpless laughter at Hoegi's sallies. While this went on, Caradog the Huntsman swept the plates and horns from the table in front of him, and jumping on the board began to dance, keeping time to a wordless song of his own that he sang loud. And nobody took the slightest notice of this, or of the men who had found Savage women somewhere – women will always come where there are soldiers, whoever they are, friend or foe – possessing them wildly on the straw of the Hall floor. And other men slept on the same straw, or bowed across the table, because there is nothing but exhaustion after battle, not only from the heat of moving in armour and the labour of striking and running and riding, but also from the sheer numbness of the cessation of fear. Every man is afraid in battle: but there are few who find that fear strong enough to stop them from fighting.

There were at least three different groups singing in different corners, competing in their various songs to see who could drown the others. In one place, some Mordei men were disputing the possession of a Savage woman, or rather the order of precedence with her, with three lads from Carlisle, and each group were calling their kinsmen to join in, while the woman, unnoticed, crept off, and might have got clear away, but that she stumbled over a man from Aeron, who, too drunk to stand, was still alert enough to pull her down on himself and ravish her there.

I looked round the Hall, and I felt the clear sight of the poet return to me, against all the Law. This, I thought, is where triumph has brought us. This is the prize for victory. There sits Owain in the glory of a battle gained, and barters insults with the bastard of an Irish pirate, to the greater glory of Cornwall, whose King he will be. And Bradwen, the wise Virgin, hangs drunken on his arm, haggling for trinkets, that might have had all the land of Bernicia as well as Mordei to run her horses over, and she with men's blood on her hands. Now, for the first time since I left Eiddin, I heard voices of Romans raised in anger, man against man, regardless of squadron, Mordei men against men from Dyfed, Cardi men against all the North.

Only Precent, I thought, only Precent does not change. He sat opposite me, looking moodily before him. I leaned over to ask him, 'Who is on watch outside? By the noise we are making, every Savage in the island knows what is going on here?'

'On watch?' Prescent muttered. 'Why, Gwion, he always takes the watch.'

'But Gwion is dead.'

'What's that you say?'

'Dead! Gwion Catseyes is dead. We saw him killed. Don't you remember?'

'Oh, aye, dead then is he? Watch all the better from up there, then, won't he.' And Precent giggled foolishly and suddenly turned aside and spewed up all his supper on the floor, soiling Bradwen's skirts, and she didn't care.

CHAPTER FOURTEEN

Uyg car yng wirwawr nyn gogyffrawt
O neb o ny bei o gwyn dragon ducawt
Ni didolit yng kynted o ved gwirawt

My friend, in distress we would not have been disturbed,
Had not the white dragon led forth the army,
We should not have been separated in the Hall
from the banquet of mead.

Then I thought, if this is triumph, defeat is better. The fruit of victory is the death of the soul. Even though now Arthur has brought the Savages into subjection through all the Island of Britain, though Mordred rules for him in Bernicia Roman again, yet after this will come strife and greed and treachery. Because that is the nature of man.

I got up, holding to the table. I stepped over to the wall, which was swaying back and fore, and hard to catch at so I fell down. I found where I had left my mail, with my sword wrapped in it, and I put it on. And then I had to take it off and put it on again, right way round. It was only that night that I had noticed what an ill-made thing it was, because there was an extra lacehole on one side, and when I laced it up and pulled it tight there was a fold in the mail which irked my neck. I stuffed Gwenllian's scarf into the collar to ease it, and then with my helmet in my hand, still buckling my sword belt, I pushed my way through the throng of drinking men to the door.

When I got into the cooler night air I felt better. I stood and thought, and then I looked back into the great Hall, and into the other houses where our men were sleeping. After a while I decided that the only man missing was Cynrig. Was Cynrig, then, the only man to watch over us, and more, over the whole herd of horses in the paddock?

It was true. I found him on the far side of the paddock, moving cautiously from shadow to shadow around the resting herd, as I did myself. I whistled to him, the tune of a harvest song I myself had made. He came and stood beside me in the dark.

'You would guard them better mounted,' I told him.

'There isn't a beast that will carry me now,' he replied. 'We charged and charged again today, and pursued after it. These steeds are all worn out. Not one of them is fit to march tomorrow.'

'We must march. Otherwise, the Savages will catch us here at their mercy.'

'If the horses were fit, what about the men? Will they be

able to ride tomorrow, let alone fight? What about yourself? Are you fit to go on?

'I shall be all right if only I can have some sleep.' It was all I wanted. I was tired, my clothes were still damp with sweat, freezing me as they dried. My head ached, a drilling pain above my left eye. A Savage had stabbed at me with a long spear, to the stomach, and though he had not pierced the mail, yet my midriff was bruised. My thighs and back ached from the hours in the saddle, thrusting and striking. I wanted to sleep. And I was less tired, less badly hurt than many of the men who had ridden in the first assaults. We all wanted sleep.

'If it were not for this banquet,' Cynrig argued, 'we could all sleep.'

'There is always a banquet after a victory. How else would we know that it was a victory?' I pointed out. 'Without the spoils as immediate reward, how would we enjoy war at all?'

'These spoils will spoil us.' Cynrig pointed up to the black sky. 'Pity about these clouds. Syvno would have wanted to forecast another victory for tomorrow. He died well.'

'It is a law of God: men who foretell the fates of others never read their own.'

We stood and watched. Far on the Bloodfield, lights showed, and women wailed seeking their men. Faintly, far away, sometimes horns sounded. Wolf and bear quarrelled aloud over the slain. There were more animal noises than one would think. Were some of them not natural? We peered about us.

'Some men,' said Cynrig, 'have slept enough. Cynrain is one. There are others, of my squadron, and of my country. Will you go and fetch them out to watch with me?'

'If I can wake them,' I said, 'I will.'

I slid around the edge of the paddock, as silent as a man in search of badgers in the moonlight. Soon I was so near to the Hall that the sound of the feast drowned all the other sounds, rising like a river in spate. As I came between the houses, the doors of the Hall were opened, and half a hundred men poured out, shouting and singing, and seizing me as soon as they saw me.

'A Marriage, a Marriage!' they shouted. 'Come, Aneirin our Judge, and make a Marriage!'

'Put me down!' I told them, because they had lifted me onto their shoulders. 'This is no time for playing. The enemy are around us.'

But they shouted the more. 'A Marriage! A Marriage!' Peredur clutched at my arm as I was carried, and shouted, 'It is true. We are going to have a wedding to crown the day.'

'Owain and Bradwen! Owain and Bradwen!' Others shouted as the crowd bubbled like a pot of porridge. Yet there was a little order. One small group of men carried me to the fire of ploughs and wagons, which they revived, and they pulled one cart over and put in it a chair, on which they set me. The rest came out of the Hall, in two streams, and one, carrying Owain, went in one direction, and the other party led by Gwenabwy with Bradwen on his arm went the opposite way. The Roman pipes played, and the marriage songs went up, as the two processions wound round and round the houses, and round and round each other, in and out in the dance we know so well.

'I cannot do this!' I shouted from the cart where I had been lifted. 'I am no priest, I cannot marry!'

'No!' shouted Peredur. 'But you are our Judge. You can marry, there being no priest or hermit.'

This was true. How had this all arisen? Was it a drunken joke, or the outcome of some attempt by Precent or Peredur to change the spirit of the night, to take men's minds off some quarrel? I could not think. I was helpless in the fever that caught us all, all except Cynrig, lonely out there with the horses. There was no sending any of this crowd out to him. They would not hear my voice, or if they did, they would ignore it.

The two processions wound their way around me and about, sunwise and widdershins around the fire, passing

173

away into opposite distances, and then returning to join and approach me, led by Morien carrying a flaming torch. Gwenabwy had Owain on one arm, Bradwen on the other. Adonwy was on the far side of Bradwen, Precent of Owain. They marched, slow and solemn towards me. Was this, then, to be my bitter fate, that I should marry Bradwen, my love, to Owain, her love, my leader? Should mine be the torch to light them to the marriage bed?

What better guests to be at any man's wedding, than the soldiers of Mynydog's Household? In their dusty, bloody mail, their gashed shields, their tattered cloaks of red, they were the finest army that ever was in the Island. These were my friends, my brothers, for whom, with whom, I would fight and die, and yet, they hurt me more than they knew.

But as the procession halted in front of me, seated as a Judge on the cart, the pipes were drowned by the horns. Far we heard Cynrig's voice: 'The horses! The horses!'

The other torches glared on a sudden at the edge of the paddock. The marriage broke apart before it began. Men ran from the procession towards the lights, towards the horns, to Cynrig fighting in the dark. All that saved us was this, that all the men who had come out in the wedding procession had put on their mail for it. They ran towards Cynrig, ran in one body, and that was their undoing, running into the paddock and across it. For in a moment, the paddock fence that they had put up that evening was broken down in a hundred places, and the whole herd of horses, terrified already by the horns and the shouts, ran away from the soldiers out into the night. At one stroke, we were left without our greatest weapon, our main advantage.

But they found Cynrig, wounded but alive, for he had set his back to a tall tree by the fence where only one man could come at him at one time. And when they found him, when our army was split in two, the Savages attacked again, and came flooding at us into the village.

Before we knew what we were about, they were all

among us and around us. It was an attack, then, by an army on two hundred separate men, each one alone. In the first shock, each of us fought alone, trying to hold himself aloof in the strife, trying to take as much and as little as he could of the battle. But soon, the swirling surface of the fight, as I saw it from the cart, began to take some structure, some shape. Men found their riding partners, and set themselves back to back. And then there were groups of four or eight, and then whole sections. At first one section, and then another, set its back against the cart on which I stood, and the Household began to return from its dissolution, to condense again into an army. This had been the Savages' hope, to take us man by man and kill us each alone. And it was our weeks of drill, under Owain, that saved us from that. It was because we were a Roman army, used to discipline, that we remained an army in that awful night, worse than any dream.

The men who had crossed the paddock formed a squadron around Cynrig, and they charged back as one unit, crashing into the backs of the Savages around the cart. Their effect, in the darkness, was greater than their numbers deserved, and in a short while we were free and clear, the enemy drawing back. We stood on our dead, and on those we had killed, a desperate band in the centre of the village, around the cart, on which now Owain climbed, and we lifted Bradwen up with us. The fire flared higher, and Owain suddenly shouted, 'The houses! Precent, there are men in the houses!'

I jumped down and kept Precent's back, as he gathered two sections. We made a rush at the nearest Savages, and they did not wait for us, but fled out of the village, leaving us a space to enter the great Hall by the main doors. There were men in the houses, men that had been asleep or dead drunk when the attack came, and they were all dead now. Savages were flooding into the Hall through a door in the other end. We tried a charge, and threw them back for long enough to see that there was no one in the place to help. We snatched what fragments of our equipment we could

175

pick up – I took Owain's cross-bow, the only one in the Household – and then we fell back into the open air, while the Savages came in again to fill the room.

But they gained nothing by it, because when the Hall was full of them, they heard a crackling, and saw that Morien had thrown fire into the thatch, and that while we held one door, Peredur and a dozen men had got round to the other, and though they could not hold it shut completely, they could at least delay the Savages in getting out. The night was cloudy and calm, yet the sparks from the Hall spread everywhere, and all the village in a short time was ablaze.

We concentrated again around the cart.

'What now?' Precent shouted to Owain.

'We cannot stay here,' he replied. But what to do he did not say. We none of us knew, but then Cynrig, pushing through to us, said, 'Cattraeth. Let us get to Cattraeth. The Savages cannot fight against walls. If we can get there, we can defy them for a time, and then perhaps we can regain our horses.'

Owain considered for a moment. Then: 'To Cattraeth!' he shouted.

It was not such a march I would have liked to undertake in daylight, or mounted, or with a clear head, or fresh. We had none of those advantages. We moved in a curious series of jerks. We would form into a wedge, and rush at the nearest front of the Savages. They would, perhaps, run before us, or, perhaps, they would stand till we pressed them back and broke them. In either case, we then had a little space and time to march in a column perhaps two or three hundred paces in the direction where we hoped Cattraeth lay.

It was a bitter journey. The Savages were all around us. Bigger men than we, they were, and fresher. Their shields were better made for fighting on foot, and many of us threw down our light leather-covered baskets, meant for warding off the thrown spear, and picked up the heavy ironbound planks that stopped a sword thrust or cut with ease. Their swords were shorter than ours, and we could cut at men while out of their reach: their iron was better, though, and few of the saxes would bend as our swords often did. Spears were no great trouble to deal with, because you could get inside the man's thrust and settle him. Few of them were mailed, and there were hardly any helmets. If the Savages had been well armoured, as well as armed, we would not have lived, any of us.

By rush and by stand, we made our way from the blazing houses, where Bladulf's wealth and our own dead together came to ash. Any man who fell, fell. There was no time to help him, and if a man had not good friends, then a slight wound would do for him. It happened at last to me. I was in the front line of an attack, and as we trampled over the bodies of those who had tried to stand in our way, one of them thrust up at me from the ground. His spearpoint went up under my mail, into the muscles of my thigh, and I fell grunting with the pain. Then there were a dozen of them coming at me, and I would have been pegged to death with their spikes if Aidan had not returned to stand over me. Then Precent was with him, and Caradog, and they pulled me to my feet. Precent, the strongest, put my arm around his neck, and aided me to hop back to the main body, where there were helpers in plenty. And lucky it was, that we were then almost in Cattraeth.

CHAPTER FIFTEEN

Gwr a aeth gatraeth gan wawr
Wyneb udyn ysgorva ysgwydawr

Men went to Cattraeth before the dawn,
But none of them received protection from their shields.

Below the walls of Cattraeth, the Savages had cleared the woods away, and had heaved out the stumps of the trees. They were now busy, day by day, in clearing the scattered stones and bricks from the ground, ready for ploughing, and as we pressed along in the beginning dawn, our ranks were parted, like hairs by a comb, around carts, filled with stones picked up and abandoned where they stood, in mid-work, by men who had run to join a host.

Over that last few hundred paces, the Savages let us alone. We found the gateway in the crumbling walls, and we passed inside, into a city that had been empty for generations. The houses had no roofs, and the grass grew up through the stones of the roads. Men fell down on the hard ground, bleeding, exhausted, sobbing with pain and weariness and disappointment. Owain looked around him in the growing light.

'Courage, my comrades,' he shouted to us. 'Have courage, be cheerful. Our war has just begun. Do not let our hearts go down. The best of our lives is to come.'

We sat up again from where we had thrown ourselves. The sound of his voice was enough to give us hope again, and to persuade us that we could win this war we had come on. Aidan, kneeling by me and binding up the slash in my thigh with my scarf, the only thing I had for him to use, began to smile again. I looked closely at him, and saw the tracks his tears had cut through the dust-caked sweat on his face.

'Now we have an advantage again, greater than we lost with our horses,' Owain continued. 'Savages cannot overcome stone walls. We can hold out here till they grow tired and melt away. Then we can continue our march down to Elmet.'

I believed him, we all believed him. I knew well enough that it was not true. We had not between us food for one spare meal all around. We did not know where there was water in Cattraeth. We were no more than a hundred and fifty, half the strength that had marched from Eiddin, half of us wounded, all of us tired, many sleeping still where

179

they had fallen. Now the light was strong enough for us to look through the gate, and see the red cloaks scattered over the field outside. There were one or two heaps that stirred, and yet we were so spent that there was no one willing to go outside and fetch the dying men in. Any man of the Household who reached Cattraeth on his own, we would be glad to see; but we could, would, give them no help. Still, Owain was Owain. What he said was true for us. What he said, we believed, though it was counter to the plain evidence of our senses.

We had silence and a kind of peace for the time between seeing the first rays of the sun on the clouds till the time when it was light enough to tell a red cloak from a green scarf, for the break in the cloud closed in. And then, from far away, we heard them coming. Far away, faintly, the horns blew and the spears beat on the shields, and Savage voices shrieked their strange war cries. Owain stood up, bold, defiant, on the wall to see them come. Precent called men to him, sent them to stand here and there all round the city, to see where the attack came from. But the greater number of us he concentrated by the gateway. Morein and Hoegi took axes and cut down some of the young birches that already stood up between the houses, and we pulled them to block the gateway with a breastwork of timber and stones.

The noise of the Savages came closer, resounding through the woods, sounding from all sides, trying to frighten us, to show us that we were surrounded, that they could come at us in overwhelming strength from all sides and bury us in bodies. Yet, we knew that Savages will not rush at walls, cannot scale them and have not the patience to undermine them. If they attacked us at all here, if they did not prefer to sit around and starve us out, they would attack the gate, as they did at York.

And so they did. The noise of the enemy fell silent. For a long period, the field before Cattraeth was so still that the first crows settled on the dead outside the walls. The silence was deliberate. They were testing our nerves, hoping that our hearts would fail with uncertainty. And even in that silence, there were some of us who were so tired, or so calm that they went to sleep where they waited.

At last there came what we waited for. Out of the woods around us they came, not too many, perhaps a hundred of them. But the hundred was more than enough to threaten us, for all giants they were, the big ones. They pranced on the side of the field, along the hedges, shouting and singing spells and hymns to their demons, winding in and out of each other in long lines, beating their swords on their shields. For besides their shields, these men wore no mail, no helmets, no shirts or breech clouts even. They were stark naked, erect, entranced, rigid as if they were the dead walking. And so they counted themselves. They danced and gyrated senselessly, generating strength and momentum, losing their consciousness, their individuality, their imagination, their fear. These were the poets of war, possessed by the Muse of Hate, composing a satire of destruction, selecting their alliteration of attack, their metre of murder, before they flung themselves, of a sudden, up the slope at us.

These are the most dangerous, men who in their own minds are already dead. A sane man, a whole man – thrust at his eyes and he will sway away his head, cut at his neck and he will guard with his own sword. But men like these naked entranced warriors cannot be deflected, do not waste effort on defending themselves. Their only thought is to kill till they drop, themselves killed. Straight against the gate they came, in a horde, but they did not pass. Some of us sprang onto the breastwork and thrust down at them: others, like myself, stood close to the timbers and pushed them away with spears. Ten men stood higher still, on the walls, while the rest of us passed up to them big stones, torn from the houses and the paved streets, to throw down into the press. The enemy was forced to concentrate all his strength against the gate, where never more than twenty of his men could approach

181

us at one time. There we could hold the Savages, however mad for blood they were. It was a hard fight, a long struggle, before the last of the shirtless ones lay dead in the way. They had been able neither to pull down our barrier nor to cross it. But scarcely had the last of them crawled away across the field, than we heard again the rhythmical singing, the tuneless chanting of the Savage army.

They stood in a great horde, as always, on the edge of the woods below us, a long dun line of mindless, faceless blocks, clashing their spears against their shields and thundering out that six-syllable line, whatever it was, again and again. They stamped their feet on the ground till it shook, and the ox-tail tassels that they tie to their spears and on their belts and around their knees waved like marsh reeds in a gale. They shouted, louder and louder, not moving, as if they wanted to frighten us: to frighten us not enough to run away but enough to draw us out from the shelter of our walls. But we did not move. Owain stood at the centre of the barrier, and the Raven banner still waved over his head. Bradwen still stood firm.

And then, like a ripple of water over the sand, the dun mass began to come nearer to us. Slowly and insignificantly nearer at first, because as fast as they came out of the wood, so others thronged behind them, filling in the space, and soon all the green of the field was turning dun. But they were learning, these Savages. They knew, from that one attempt, that no charge of unsupported men could break into Cattraeth.

Therefore, their wizards came out of the line, and danced against us, trying to harm us with their magic, but they could not, because the Virgin watched over us. But they could bewitch our eyes, and with their posturings and gestures they drew our attention gradually to one end of their line, as Owain had drawn their attention to one end of their line on the Bloodfield. I had climbed, now, up onto the wall, six feet above the ground, and I too watched the dancers, till of a sudden a movement the other way caught my eye. I shouted, but by then everybody else had seen it. A crowd of the Savages had taken one of the abandoned carts, full of stones, that lay scattered about the field in front of the gate, the field they were clearing to plant wheat in. Instead of bringing oxen to pull it, they themselves took it by the pole to push it. More and more of them clustered around it, as we had around the ship, and they rolled it across the ground towards the gate. This was how they had taken York: not able to scale the wall, they had broken in the gate by night, while the garrison slept and thus treacherously murdered them all in their beds. Now they pushed the wagon towards the gate as fast as a man could run, and it was heavy, too, full of stones. We saw at once that if it hit the barricade square on it would scatter the birch-poles and leave a gap for the Savages to rush in by. Clinging to the wall, I lifted stones from the crumbling parapet and threw them at the cart. But Morien had a better device. Who else but he, at this bitter time, would have lit a fire? And it was armed with flame, a flaring torch of his own red cloak, that he leapt on the parapet with me. He waved it round and round his head, till the cart was near enough to throw it. The torch landed on the cart, and flared into the faces of the men on the farther side, running as fast as if they were racing for a pig, and they jerked away, some of them burnt, but most only frightened. And the cart swerved, and turned towards us, losing little speed, and hit the wall below us with a terrible crash.

The ruinous wall crumbled under our feet. I saw it coming, and I jumped away, but my wounded thigh robbed me both of the power to leap and the agility to land. I sprawled on the road of the city beneath the tottering wall. Morien leapt a moment later: but he had already left it too late, and he jumped from a moving surface, so that he covered no distance at all. The stones came down around us, thundering like the tide on a rocky coast in an autumn gale: I felt my ribs crack under the shower, and my knee twisted under me.

And then, following on its thunder, the tide did come in, racing between the horns of the gate as it had between the horns of the cliff, a tide of Savage feet, of Savage voices, of Savage smells, that swept above me as I lay on the ground, as I rolled over and over upon my crushed ribs, the desire to get out of the way, somewhere to safety, overruling the pain. I expected to be stabbed as I lay on the ground, but the men who rushed over me, stepping on my back, were too fixed on a distant prey to bother me. I pulled myself to the wall for a backing, and watched the Savages charge against the line of the Household. Owain held the centre, but, laying about him, as furious as Bladulf with his flail, he was still pressed back. But when I thought he was sure to be overwhelmed, his flanks being eased away from where they depended on the house walls for protection, I heard the cry of the Virgin's name, and Precent charged past me, leading the men from the circuit of the walls. He did not assail directly the backs of the men facing Owain: instead, he flung his force into the gateway, separating the Savages inside the walls from those outside, sending the attackers outside fleeing from the gate by the sheer ferocity of his face and voice. Then, while some hurriedly piled up stones in the gate, others turned on the Savages trapped inside. They killed them all, in time.

Silence came again. It is a vice of the Savages, that, repulsed once, they do not repeat the attack, but withdraw and then come at you again in a different way. Now, there was nothing to remind us that there had been an attack but the piles of dead in the gate, theirs and ours. Aidan came limping to me, and Precent with him, in their own time. It is the first rule of war, to settle with the enemy's wounded before you help your own. I asked them, 'How is Morien?'

Aidan helped me to sit up, and pointed. From under the heap of stones that had been the gatepost of Cattraeth, protruded Morien's feet. No more of him could be seen. I wept. I had brought him to Cattraeth. Morien, who had spread fire upon the enemies of the Romans; now his spark was quenched, the fire of his eyes, that used to dazzle the Savages in battle, was now put out.

It was painful enough to be lifted up to sit. When Aidan put his arm beneath my shoulder and helped me to stand, the pain of my ribs and my leg, when I stood on it, ran through me worse than any sword. I wept aloud, and fainted, I do not know how long I was unconscious, but it was long enough for my comrades to carry me a little way, and take off my mail and bandage me around the body to give some support. They washed my cuts with mead, which was all we had, there only being one well in Cattraeth, and that dry. I looked around me, to see how many of the Household were left here in Cattraeth. I saw only how few we were. Only, Owain still led us, still the Raven banner flew over us. Still Bradwen, unwounded, knelt beside me. Owain came to talk to me.

'There is an end of fighting for you,' he told me. 'There is no weapon you can lift with broken ribs.'

'I can see one weapon I can use,' I replied. I pointed to Owain's crossbow, with a leather bag holding dry strings and twenty quarrels tied to the stock. 'I brought that with me, through the night. At least we have that, whatever else has been lost.'

'Aye, I have lost heavily,' Owain agreed. It is true, I thought, near on two hundred good men have gone, that had mothers and sweethearts to weep for them: all lost, all lost, and the land of Mordei lost with them. But he went on, 'All my baggage, with my two silver cups, and the coronet of a Prince of Cornwall, all lost. And, worst of all, my greyhounds – I have not seen them since the middle of the night march. My poor dogs – I wonder if I will ever see them again.'

That was the measure of Owain, of his humanity, that made us love him – in the wreck of the Household, it was his greyhounds, which he loved, that he wept for. And I? I asked Aidan, 'When you carried me, and I fainted, I did not cry out, did I?'

'Indeed you did, Aneirin,' he answered, 'but any man

185

would have cried in that state.'
   'What did I cry?'
   'You cried one name.'
   'I called for Bradwen?'
   'You called for Gwenllian.'
   And she, at least, knew nothing of Cattraeth.

CHAPTER SIXTEEN

Disgynnwys en affwys dra phenn
Ny deliit kywyt kywrennin benn
Disgiawr breint vu e lad ar gangen
Kynnedyf y ewein esgynnv ar ystre

He fell headlong down the precipice,
And the bushes supported not his noble head:
It was a breach of privilege to kill him on the breach,
It was a primary law that Owain should ascend
upon the course.

The Savages' Herald stood on the green grass before the walls, a scarlet stain on the green. His cloak was as red as ours. More scarlet than the poppy was it, more crimson than the brave red blood. Redder it glowed than the flame of fire in a man's thatch, than the sun on a fine morning that tells of evil weather to come. There he stood on the green grass, livid against the green trees. When I closed my eyes to shut him out, I could still see him, a magic green against a curtain of red.

We stood on the wall in the breach where the gate had been, where we had first made a barrier of birch-poles, and which we now had stopped with stones. I sat on a stone, leaning against the parapet, because it hurt me too much to stand.

The Savage came slowly towards us. In his right hand he waved a green branch. His left hand he held empty above his head. Now we could see his clothes beneath the cloak. Once, perhaps, his tunic and trousers had been red also, but now they were patched and darned and scattered with pieces in all colours, yellow and green and blue and brown. Through the unmended rents, and they were many, and few of them new, we could see the flesh. He wore no armour.

No, this was no Judge, no Bard that Bladulf had sent to us as a Herald. The hand that held that green branch had never had an ivory staff, nor played on the man-high harp. On days of audience and at feasts, this man would be close to the throne, without doubt, but he did not sit at the King's side, nor stand behind his throne. Instead, he danced and tumbled before the King. He turned somersaults and walked on his hands. He juggled balls and balanced sticks on his nose. And when he had finished, he did not even have a seat at table, or a dish and cup to eat and drink from. No, he would sit on his haunches and beg like a dog, and the King would throw him a half-picked bone and a crust of ale-soaked bread to gnaw on, if he were pleased. But if the King were not pleased, then the courtiers would know it without telling. They would pelt this man with broken pots and oyster-shells, thrown with malice, to hurt, and laugh to see him leap and dodge and bleed and beg for mercy. This was no Herald who came to talk to us, under the signs of truce, across the field where our dead lay tumbled on the broken stones of the walls of Cattraeth. I told Owain, 'Bladulf has sent us his Jester.'

The envoy came closer, to within shouting distance. He walked daintily, his feet close together. He stopped and called out, *'Frith! Frith!'*

'What is that gibberish?' asked Precent. 'It is like the barking of a dog.'

'He says, "Peace, Peace,"' I told him. 'He wants to parley. Should we let him come any closer? I would not, myself. What will you do, Owain?'

But Precent spoke first, spitting. 'A Jester? I would not soil my tongue. Do not disgrace yourself, my Prince. Let me take a bow and kill him where he stands. It is a weapon I would not use on a man, but on a jester—'

I had a sudden thought. 'No, Precent, if we kill their messenger, will they not then kill one of ours?'

'A messenger to them? A Herald to them?' This was Owain who spoke at last. 'How would we ever wish to send a Herald to those Savages? What would we want to say to them? We have no need to worry about reprisals. All we have to do is to keep ourselves safe here and kill as many as we can, till the Elmet men come up. We can kill this Herald, if we want to, with impunity. But I do not wish to kill him.'

'If we are safe, then we may as well kill him at once,' said Precent. 'It will be one fewer for Elmet to deal with. If we *are* so safe.'

'Safe or not safe, it makes no difference.' Owain was firm of voice. 'There will be no killing of a man who carries a green branch. It is below the honour of a Prince, or at least of a Prince of Cornwall.' He did not say 'whatever the Picts do,' but he meant it, and we knew that. 'I will not kill that poor harmless creature.'

189

'But I am not a Prince of Cornwall, or of anywhere else,' I insisted. 'And this is no poor harmless creature. Look how tall he is. He would not come up to my breast, if I were able to stand. He is a dwarf. And now look again at his face. Do you see it as clear as I do? Hairless and plump it is as a woman's. There was never need for a razor on that face. It is neither man nor woman. It is one of those sexless things that a real man would die rather than touch. Filth is what they are throwing at us. Give me the bow, Precent. You are right. We ought to kill him – it would be an act of virtue before Heaven and the Virgin. A thing like this cannot be a Herald. Let me do it. I am the better shot.'

'Only a harmless, sexless dwarf at best: at worst a devil,' agreed Precent. 'It would not do the slightest harm to kill him. Owain, let Aneirin kill him if he wants to. Here is the bow. Lay off two fingers for this wind, to the right, and allow for being ten feet above him. Hit him first time, like a deer. If you miss him, he will run and we will have no time for a second shot.'

There was none of all the Savages I wanted more to kill. There was no need to tell Owain how well I knew this one. It would give me a little peace through the long night to come. I cranked back the bow-string, and it hurt me, but the pain of my ribs added strength to my hand. But Owain still held his hand before me so that I could not raise the bow to my shoulder.

'And a Jester,' Precent went on, seeing Owain stand so still. 'Bladulf is doing this as an insult. A Jester? Talk with him, Owain, and all the Kings of Britain will laugh at us. The Household of Mynydog will itself be a jest in every corner of the Empire, a matter for giggling at on feast-days, for mockery in Halls. There is not one of us would ever dare again go into the company of warriors. Jest with him, Owain, and it will be our own honour you will jest away, and our lives too.'

'And what kind of jester would I be if I killed a dwarf?' Owain asked. 'Would *you* want his blood on your hands,

Aneirin, grandson of Cunedda? Dwarfish blood, jester blood, will that be a thing to boast about at feasts? Will you take his head to hang on a wall, or his hide to curtain a door? Nobles fight with nobles, I tell you, freemen with freemen. A prince may aim at a King, but there is nobody here so low born or so badly nurtured that he could think of killing a dwarf.'

Owain stood up in the gap in the wall. He waved his arm. The dwarf began to move forward, slowly, cautiously, as if ready at any moment to turn and run. You have seen a bear approach the tethered kid, while you sit in the tree above with your crossbow? So he came towards us. Owain, standing there in full view, took off his helmet. He handed it to Bradwen. She took it. She had said nothing while we argued. Now she spoke, as if she had been saving her words to the end, to when there was nothing left but her pleas that Owain might listen to. She said, 'Don't talk with him. There is a treachery in his walk. Look at his gait, soft and wary. A real Herald believes in his green branch: he does not. If he does not trust us, we ought not to trust him. We have seen no enemy so deadly, Owain, since we passed the Wall. Kill him, Owain, or let Aneirin or Precent kill him.' She was almost crying. I had not seen her tears since she was a little girl. 'My love, I want to sit with you again in the Hall of Eiddin. I want to ride with you to Cornwall. Do not risk all that for a whim of your honour. There are few of us here now out of all who started. Anything the Savages do is meant to harm us. Do not talk with him. Let us only wait here till the Elmet men come to us.'

The dwarf had stopped, no more than two lance lengths away. He could tell his danger from the tone of our voices. He was too close, now, to escape if anyone chose to throw a spear at him, or launch a bolt, even if they missed the first time.

Owain looked down at him, proudly, fiercely. Never had I seen him look more kingly. I have never seen any man look more a King. If this is how Kings look in

191

Cornwall, then lucky they are there. I have never seen Gwyddno at his crown-wearing in Harlech, or Arthur in his Hall at Caerleon in the midst of all the Household of the Kings of Britain, but I swear they can not look half as kingly as Owain did that day. Even now, and there are men who were not born on the day of Cattraeth who have died of old age already, I can shut my eyes, and see him, as he stood in the breach of the walls, looking at all the army of the Savages. His red curls hung down on his shoulders like red snakes, twisting and hissing at the Savages of their own strength. His green eyes showed all the fury of the winter sea, the light sparkled in them like the white foam. From his unlaced mail coat his neck stood out brown and firm, the strong pillar of Britain, to carry that noble head, dear to us as the head of Bendigaid Vran to his followers. So we all looked in love at him, and Bradwen wept, who now knew war, and had seen how many men had died around the Raven banner that she should come so far unwounded. Owain laughed at the dwarf, who was used to it, surely, and turned his back on him, to say to Bradwen, and to all of us, 'Think who I am, and who is the man you have chosen. Mark's son of Cornwall am I, that shall be King of Cornwall after him. I will lay at your feet, Bradwen, as your dowry, the heads of half a hundred Kings out of Ireland, dead by my sword. And how many heads have I not piled before you in these last days, how much land have I not given back to your own people? I tell you, I am not afraid of any living man—'

'This is not a living *man*,' I had the courage to interrupt him. 'Look at that pale face, the bulging forehead, the chin that curves to nothing under the weak lips, the lank and wispy hair. This is one of the devils out of hell, or a wild beast that Bladulf has tamed to fight for him.'

'If he were a thousand devils, I would not be afraid of him. The Virgin will protect us. Let him come.'

Owain waved again at the dwarf. He came forward, still hesitant, dainty on his feet as a faun. Caso and Graid helped me to move along the broken stones so that I might sit beside Owain, my head and shoulders above the parapet. Owain leaned over the broken wall, his elbows on the stone. I was there only to be a mouthpiece, to talk between the two.

The Red Dwarf looked at me, where I could have touched him with my sword-point. He looked close at me, and sneered.

'When we made you dance for us, we did not know that you could sing. We'll have you singing for us soon. The knife it was we took to you the last time. This time it will be the white-hot iron. It sears, the hot iron, it hisses on the skin, and you see the smoke of your own burning and smell yourself roast. Oh, we will hear you sing at the winter feast.'

'Are you trying to frighten me? Think of something else to say, because you are wasting your breath on this.'

'You will be less bold when you hear my message. Ah, you are sweating already from fear, and panting. Too soon my words will come for your comfort.'

I was sweating, it was true, and my face was pale, but it was the pain of my ribs, stabbing at me as I breathed, that made me pant, that caught at my stomach till I wanted to vomit. I turned to Owain.

'He is taunting me. Next, I think he will taunt you, and all of us. We must not show anger, or take offence. He is only a dwarf.' I said this loudly, so that all could hear.

'What does he want?' asked Owain. 'Has he any authority to treat with us, or has he only come to jest?'

'It is a high price he will pay for jesting,' I answered, and my hands beneath the wall trembled on the crossbow. But Precent growled, 'If I were shaped like that, then I would welcome death, and want nothing more than to hurt whole men in dying.'

'Life, Precent, is dear to all,' Bradwen reminded him. Owain bade me, 'Ask him!'

'It may be difficult to find out what he means, rather than what he says.' I turned back to the Dwarf, who had been watching us speak, turning his head from one to another, trying to read our meaning from our eyes, and finding small comfort there. 'What have you come to ask of us? Mind you make your requests politely, now.'

'And mind you tell your master true,' he squealed back at me.

'I serve no master,' I answered him proudly. 'I am a free man and I do what I like.'

'But do you not follow this copper-headed meal-sack?'

'I follow Owain of my own free will. I obey him because I promised to do so – and I did not make that promise to him, or to a King, or to the Virgin. I made it to myself. In obeying Owain, I obey myself. I choose to follow him. After this campaign, I may choose to follow any other chieftain into battle, where ever it takes my fancy, and I will do it so long as it means killing your people.'

'That is the mark of the coward, to pick and choose whom you will follow. The brave man follows the King he is born to serve, and does not ask whether the King be brave or cowardly, wise or foolish. Would you choose to follow a coward? Or a fool?

'And who are you to talk of courage or of wisdom? Or even of men?'

He bridled, his face paled, he spat venom at me in his words.

'And whose fault is it that I am what I am? Not mine, not any man's. My manhood is this, that by land and sea I follow the King my brother, and my wisdom that by the stars I can tell where we are, and when, and my courage that I stand here alone before you all.'

'Your brother?' and I laughed. This surely, was no more than a figure of speech. All free men are brothers within one nation. And the Savages, all herded together coupling at random at their winter feasts, they could never know who was brother to whom. But yet – the tone of that squeaking voice . . . I was Aneirin, the Pre-eminent Bard. I was used, over years, to listening to voices, to judging changes of meaning in the tone. For a winter I had been a Judge in the North. In those months I had heard more truth and more lies

194

than most men in all their lifetime. I asked, not laughing, 'Bladulf is your brother?'

'His was my father, his my mother. So he has sent me, terms you to offer.'

I spoke again to Owain. 'He has authority. This turd is the King's brother. He has terms to offer.'

'No terms,' said Owain shortly. 'This is our land. Tell the Savages to go back where they came from.'

'If they were to try to cross the sea,' objected Precent, 'their numbers would fill it, and more would come walking across on their dead bodies. They breed on their damned wheat like rats in the oatstack. There is no such simple way out, Owain.' He jerked his head at the Dwarf. 'Ask him his terms.'

Owain did not forbid me again. I asked, trying to frame in the Savages' language the rounded speech I would have made in the tongues of human beings, 'And have you come to offer us a rent of money for your farms, a tale of silver for our ruined pastures, a toll of corn for our lost marshes, and ox-flesh in payment for our lost forests?'

'Better than silver the burden I bear.'

'Gold, then, to bind in our hair and pin in our cloaks?'

'Better than gold to the poor, and sweeter than ale to the thirsty, better than cheers to the minstrel, and fairer than women.'

'What, clown?'

'What, singer? What, what?' He laughed in my face, the wheat-stinking ale-stinking breath stirred in my hair. 'Life, singer, life is sweeter than all.'

'Offer us what is in your power to give. Here we are and here we stay.'

'Do you still think, then, that others will follow? Do you hope Elmet will come to your rescue? Your King sent a wild man to tell us, that Elmet and Eiddin would march into Deira. First we went South, to the borders of Elmet, wasted a day's march into the country. But the army of Elmet was not in the field, there was no coming against us in battle. That border was safe, we wasted our journey.

Then we came North, and settled with you. Do not look for help: there is none coming.'

I looked at him in hate. There was no truth in this. I did not repeat it. I said, 'Our lives are our own. Do you think you can give them to us? And after all this, after so many dead, you expect us to ride away with all undone that we came to do, that we came so far for and have not yet finished?'

'Life, singer, life. Not to ride away. Life only.'

'Life only?' I could not for the moment follow him.

'Life only. There are enough dead men.' We looked at each other closer now. He leaned closer, confidentially, to explain, as if it were some detail in a market, about a horse or a hunting-dog he was selling. 'Men we want to dig out our ditches and clean out our wells, for all are filled in. We want men to reap and to thresh, men to carry and men to pull, men to sweat, to sweat, to sweat . . . You know that, singer, you know that.'

I knew it. He saw my face change.

'Our men are dead, singer, our men are dead. We did not think ever to meet an army like yours. Nothing has satisfied you but blood, nothing but senseless destruction. Too many men are dead, and there is work to do. Axes we have in plenty, trees to cut down. Swords will beat into saxes and sickles, reeds to bundle for thatch. Spearheads will edge spades or spread into pitchforks. Now it is men we lack, fields to clear.'

I turned back to Owain. All the Household were silent to hear. The rain began to fall, began at that moment, light and thin, the rain of summer heat from a grey sky into a steamy day. So silent was the Household that we might have heard the drizzle on the stones.

'No terms,' I said. 'No terms. Slavery only. Nothing else. No terms.'

'Slavery?' Owain looked around him, looked at all the Household, at the men old in wars with the hair worn thin by the helmets, like Precent and Cynrig, at the boys like Aidan and Graid. Last of all he looked, long, at

196

Bradwen. 'Slavery? To those Savages? That is all they offer?'

'You can see why they are so confident and proud,' I reminded him. 'They are all around us, and there are still ten times as many of them as there are of us.'

'Even alive,' he smiled. 'And as many dead, Aneirin. Slavery? To these devils, these demon-worshippers? They have no mercy, no pity. Aneirin, there is more than confidence here, and less. They are anxious to have us disarmed quickly. An army is approaching from Elmet. These monsters do not want to have to fight us on two fronts at once. They want to frighten us to surrender, and into impotence.'

'Slavery, they say, or they will kill us here.'

'Or try to. If they were willing to face the fight, they would attack now, not waste their time offering impossible terms. They say they will kill us? Let them, if they can.'

'What shall I say, then?'

'Let them kill us if they can.' Owain laughed aloud, and so did we all to see him. Oh, there was never a King on his throne had half the majesty of Owain on the walls of Cattraeth, no Queen that ever had half the beauty of Bradwen, dusty and bloodstained, sweating in her mail. 'I will tell him.'

'Don't go too near him.'

'No nearer than I can spit in his face.' Owain leaned over and down past me, down towards the Dwarf.

'Non potest,' he said in Latin, for he spoke that language well as must any ruler of Cornwall; 'numquam.' And in our own language, the tongue of the Angels, that was spoken in the Garden at the beginning of the World, 'Nage! Dim erioed!' And at last, in the few words I had taught him of the speech of the Savages, 'No, no! Never!'

Have you seen an adder strike? The neck that moves, thrusting forward, the forked tongue stabbing, stinging, pouring venom that will bring low man and horse – so struck the Dwarf. The arm that moved from beneath the cloak, the left hand thrusting forward, the knife not stabbing but cutting, slashing, tearing open the throat – an adder is not so swift, so evil, so silent, so final. A short sax, not two spans long, heavy as an axe, pointless, single-edged, hidden in his ragged sleeve: it did the business.

Thus died Owain, King Mark of Cornwall's son, the hope and strength of all the Isle of Britain. His blood ran down the shining walls of Cattraeth, and stained with new death the dead Roman stones. Mark died with him, and Tristan – Cornwall died. His body fell into the Roman ditch. He never spoke again.

He was a man in years, in mind a youth, and gallant in the din of cruel war. It shall be not my part to tell thy failings, or to reproach thee with our dismal end. Rather shall I make thee live in song, until Rome fades and the world ends. Why did I see thee on my bloody bier, before I lit thee to thy wedding-couch? My Owain, my beloved friend, my chieftain – at least, thy Ravens will not peck out thy eyes.

Owain's blood poured on my sleeve, and his body tumbled into the ditch. All the Household cried out in sorrow and in horror at the treachery. For a moment, in our bewilderment, all our eyes followed our Leader, our hero, as he died. And no one watched the Dwarf. He ran away down the slope.

After the first cry, there was silence inside the walls of Cattraeth. Then it was Bradwen who led. She had not cried, she did not weep, for Owain her love that died. Bradwen the Wise, she wasted no time, no effort, on mourning. She needed only the time to set his helmet on her head, the raven plumes gleaming blue-black in the sunless light. Then she leapt over the rubble in the gateway. Gwenabwy followed her, as always.

'Kill the Dwarf!' he shouted. 'Vengeance! Kill the betrayer!'

'No!' answered Precent. 'Stand fast! Stand here within the walls. Do not go outside, where they are waiting for us. That is what they want. Stand fast!'

But there were many men who did not hear him, or, if

198

they did hear him, took no notice. They jumped from the walls or scrambled over the rubble in the gate, sword or axe ready.

'Stop, stop!' Precent shouted. He flung wide his arms in the gate. 'Hold together!'

They took no notice. But I raised the crossbow. I had a heavy quarrel, one fit for bear, with a dropping flight. Aim off, I remembered, two fingers to the right for the wind. The target was plain enough. The Dwarf stood there, stock still, a red shape on the green grass, where he had stopped first. He had no green branch now. He stood, his arms spread wide, an echo of Precent, and waited while Bradwen came down the slope at him, and Gwenabwy, and Geraint, and others, too many others. All were eager to avenge Owain. But that was my task, my duty, my joy.

The Dwarf stood still, and laughed at us, laughed at the death that came at him, helmed and plumed. I found it hard to hold the bow level and steady, my eyes blurred the red shape hard against the green grass, men crossed my sight, red plumes bobbed in the track of my bolt. There was no hurry – he would stand. The only danger now was Bradwen, that she would reach him first. She did not. I slipped the string, the bolt flew. Before the wise woman struck the Dwarf, the iron split his chest, the feathers stood out from the cloak. It was the bolt that killed him, not the blade, though before he touched the ground a dozen swords sank in him.

He died then. All our hope died with him. With him, and not with Owain. Precent and I looked from the wall, and watched half a hundred of the Household strung out in a long single line across the field. The Red Dwarf did not die in vain, did not stand still in the middle of the field for nothing, that tempted them out of the walls, tempted them out to stand, each man alone, against the horde of Savages that came at them from the woods on every side. Bradwen I saw fall first, a dozen came at her from all sides, and it was Bladulf himself who struck her deathblow, I saw him. Gwenabwy stood above her body, sweeping his

199

sword in wide swathes, as if it were he who held a flail, till
he too fell, though when it happened I did not see for the
crowd. There was no seeing single men any more in that
press. Geraint died then, and Gwydien, and others too
many to name. I shot three bolts into the throng, slowly
because of my ribs. Before I had hooked the string to my
belt for the last bolt, we saw the enemy fall back, at a
signal from a horn, to the edge of the wood. Many limped
or crawled. More did neither. All the field was covered
with dead or dying. Some were ours: most were theirs.
The silence came back, the moaning died away.

I looked at Precent. Cynrig came to us.

'How many left?' I asked.

'Not many,' Cynrig told us. 'Not a hundred, now. Most
are Picts, or men from the West, or Cardi men who came
north with me. The Cornishmen that live, or men of Eiddin,
will none of them live long. They are the ones who were too
hurt to follow Bradwen. They will follow her soon.'

'How soon?' asked Precent. He looked down the slope.
There was no movement in the wood. 'Will they come at us
again now do you think?'

'No,' Cynrig told him. 'I cannot see them facing us on the
walls again. If they thought they could ever take the place
that way, they would not have tried treachery. What shall we
do now, my Chieftain?'

Cynrig's blood was as good as Precent's, in war he was as
experienced. In those words of his, I knew there would be
no quarrel. Such disputes about blood and precedence it
was that first let the Savages into the Island, and tempted
Hengist to enter Britain.

'What shall we do then?' Cynrig asked again.

'There is no Household that ever kept in the field when
the Captain was dead, was there, Aneirin?' Precent asked
me. It was true.

'Let us go home, then,' said Cynrig. He looked around
him at the soldiers who remained, whole and wounded.
'Those who can reach Eiddin, do so. We can do no good
here.'

'We must leave here nothing that the Savages can use,' directed Precent. 'But if we are to reach Eiddin before the Savages turn their wrath north against the Dun, we must take nothing that will hinder us on the march.' He turned to me. 'Can you walk, Aneirin?'

I tried to stand. When the weight fell on my ankle, the pain scalded up my leg and into my body, and my ribs seared me like the white hot iron. I was able not to scream as I fell again to the ground. The other men who were wounded looked at me. I called on the Virgin to help me. Then I looked up at Precent, and said loudly, 'I will stay.'

The Picts and Cardi men who could still walk brought together those men who still lived though wounded, and laid them round me, against the walls of a house where I could see through the gateway. No one spoke. We knew, now, all of us, what was to be done. Bitter was defeat that clipped our tongues. We who were to stay stripped off our mail, or others took it from us. Our swords were snapped, the edges of our axes blunted, the points of our spears turned back on the stones of the wall. All these arms were carried to the dry well and thrown down. I still held Owain's crossbow. I had one bolt. I made them leave me that. The rain still fell on us: I kept the string dry as well as I could under my cloak.

Four men climbed onto the wall and brought in the body of Owain. The other bodies, it was too dangerous to fetch, that we agreed. Even Bradwen, the glorious Bradwen, we must leave to the wolf and the bear. But not Owain, not Owain. The three of us wept above his body.

'There was an end to Dyvnwal Vrych,' Cynrig reminded us. 'We saw his head on a pole, because they thought he was a leader. How much more will they dishonour the head of Owain?'

'There is but one thing to do,' Precent agreed, without a discussion, knowing what he was being asked. 'Aneirin has sung us often the song of Bran the Blessed.'

He fetched an axe, whetting it as he came. The men of the Household gathered around us, silent. Only the rasping strokes of the whetstone sounded harsh in our ears. Precent turned on them suddenly, savage, strained to a thread.

'Have you no voices? Will you let the Savages think they have cut all our throats with this one? Sing, all of you, sing! Sing, my children, and let them hear that we are here to fight them still!'

The voices rose in the old songs, the songs of bloody and successful wars. 'The Hunting of the Black Pig' we sang, and 'Heads on the Gate', 'The Toad's Ride' and 'Blood in the Marshes'. A defeated army we were, the remnant of the Household of the King of Eiddin, Mynydog the Magnanimous and we did not care how many Savages stood to resist our going. Under the music, Precent stood and balanced the axe in his hand. He hesitated.

'I cannot. I loved him too much.'

'Nor I,' said Cynrig. 'Can a King strike a King?'

'I loved him,' I told them. 'He treated me as a man. Not as a Bard, not as a prodigy, not as a marvel of nature, but as a man who loved and hated and felt, as a man who could weep and laugh and kill for himself, and not only in words for others. He loved me as a man who could do things, and in this Household do things no other man could do. For that love, I will not see him dishonoured.'

I took the axe. I could still kneel beside the body. I struck once: with the broad-edged axe, new sharpened, it was enough. The body some of the Picts took and threw down the dry well, with the weapons. Then they heaped stones in the well, jamming great slabs, the work of past ages, the bases of columns, into its mouth, so that it would be beyond the work of a thousand Savages to clear it again. No Savage would dig up his body, or use the iron again.

Cynrig tore the edge of his cloak and washed the head with mead from his flask, cleaning away the blood, closing the eyes. Graid brought a bag of soft leather he had picked up in some village. Cynrig wrapped the head in a cloth, the shirt taken from a dead Cornishman, and slid it into the bag. He drew the string tightly at the mouth and tied it. He offered the bag to Precent.

'No,' Precent told him, 'the honour shall be yours.' I looked at the two faces. Precent had always been a ruddy-faced man, Cynrig sallow and brown. Now both were the same colour, the white that comes from fatigue and desperation. They looked along the line of the men left who could still stand. There was not a man unwounded in the town. Many of them had thrown off their armour, as too heavy, and hidden it. Precent talked to them, to us who would remain, roughly, cheerfully, to hide what we all knew.

'Well, now, who's coming with me, and who's off with the Cardi?' He jerked his thumb at Cynrig. 'Most of you will go with him, and go quietly. Cast away north-west there, and make for the river. Then you can get back to Eiddin, in small groups. But I want some of you to come with me the other way, to have a last fling at them. With any luck, we can get down to Elmet in three days. Aidan, will you come and keep my back?'

The boy stepped forward, brave-faced. I was grateful to Precent for that. But I knew that he had been struck in the back with the buttend of a pike in the morning, and although it had then seemed to be no more than a bruise, yet now he was vomiting blood at intervals.

'And Caso?' Precent called.

'Might as well with you as anywhere else,' Caso grunted. How he could stand I could not think. A slash at his waist had near let out his gut: it was only held in by a bandage. So Precent chose twenty men, wounded men, who had not long to live wherever they went. There were sixty others who would go with Cynrig. More than a score of us lay on the ground to watch them make ready. Those who had buried their helmets had kept the plumes to stick in their hair with tallow, so that they would have some Roman thing about them at last. The Picts painted their faces, Precent among them. They separated into little groups of four or five. Men from the squadrons were now mixed up, seeking their own cousins, men from their native Kingdoms. At the last, the great Household of Mynydog, the first Household of all the Isle of Britain, was breaking up.

There was silence again. Nobody had the heart to sing. Only sometimes, from the edge of the wood, came the hoot of the owl or the howl of the wolf. Were they really animals? Or were the Savages signalling to one another? Or were they still there, waiting for us? Or had they all fled, appalled by that last slaughter below the walls? There was no knowing.

'Perhaps,' Precent suggested, 'they are waiting for the dark, to rush us from two sides at once.'

'Then we dodge aside,' said Cynrig, determined that he would be cheerful, 'and let them fight each other.' He pressed my hand. 'The Virgin keep you, Aneirin. One day, come to my Hall in Cardigan, and sing to us of this battle. There will always be a chair for you there, Aneirin, Pre-eminent Bard of the Island, red-speared battle ravager, war-diademed enemy-subduer.'

I never went there. Men have told me that he still keeps a chair for me, with my name carved on it, in which no other man, no, not even any other bard may sit. But I have never been to Cardigan. I knew then that we would never meet again.

'The Virgin keep your head, Cynrig,' I answered, but he only jested again, 'Which one? I have two to worry about.'

Precent knelt to embrace me.

'Do not weep for Bradwen,' I told him. 'She had her love, and did not live to regret him. Do not weep for me, for my songs live for me. Rather weep for yourself, and for the North, that shall be defeated now we have left it defence-less. Weep for Eiddin, that has spent so much treasure for the sake of the Island, and all for nothing.'

'Not all for nothing.' Precent corrected me. 'What we have done, others will do again, and waste all the North till it is a land fit for hunting again. Every stag that grazes, every moorhen that nests where we have burnt the farms and blocked the ditches is our memorial. It was not in vain. It is not yet over. Cheer up, Aneirin. I brought you out of prison among the Savages once, and I will do it again. We will drink in Eiddin again before the year is out.'

He spoke loud for the other men to hear. But he did weep. I could hardly see him now in the evening light, but I could feel his tears on my face. Or my tears. They were warmer than the rain. The Savages do not weep. They were there somewhere beyond the walls, waiting for us, in the dark. The Household drank the last of their mead. Cynrig put his bottle by my side. I pressed it back into his hand. He would need it more than I. He said nothing more, only went in silence into the dark.

Only when all was silent did I realize that there had been sound. As long as the Household were still in Cattraeth, there was still a rustle of movement. Even men who do not speak and are careful not to make a noise still make a great noise. You notice it only when it stops. We who were left knew when Cattraeth was empty. We lay in the soaking rain and listened. For a long time, there was no sound at all, not even the hooting of the owls or the howling of the wolves. Then, all of a sudden, between us and the village, we heard a voice shouting.

'Here am I Precent, King of the North, Lord of the Picts! Come and face me, if you dare!'

And at once, from that direction, there was the noise of shouting men, and of running, the clatter of armour and the clash of arms, the sogging sound of swords on leather shields. I could hear the noise as men crossed the field before the gate to go towards the village. The noise went on for some time. Then, very suddenly, it died away. There was silence. It was all over, there. There was a long time of quiet. Then far away to the west, the sound of fighting, the blowing of horns and the beating of spears on shields as men tried to call for help. And silence again.

So it went on all night. We lay in silence and listened to fight after fight, some near, some far. None lasted long. How many skirmishes I could not count, nor recognize any

205

voices. Dawn came, a gradual lightening of the cloudy sky over the ceaseless rain. About an hour after dawn, I heard a voice in the woods, screaming.

'Oh, Mam, Mam! Oh, fy Mam i!'

Then it stopped. It was Aidan calling for his mother. He was the last of the Household to fight before Cattraeth.

CHAPTER SEVENTEEN

Eurar vur caer krysgrwydyat
Aer cret ty na thaer aer vlodyat
Un ara ae leissyar argatwyt
Adar brwydryat

Carcases of gold mailed warriors lay upon the city walls,

None of the houses nor cities of the Christians any longer engaged in war;

But one feeble man with his shouts kept aloof

The roving birds.

We lay in Cattraeth in silence through the long day, under the thin and drenching rain. We waited to die. Death did not come quickly, or easily. We tore off the bandages from our wounds. My thigh would not bleed again, though I scratched at the scab with my nails. The Virgin forbids a man to kill himself: but to seek death is not the same. Death was near to us all, in any case, as we sweated in our fevers, and coughed up our lungs out of our chests, but no one groaned or cried, to give comfort to the Savages who must still lurk outside. When thirst was too terrible to bear, we sucked the rain from our clothes. Hunger is easier to withstand: there was no food left in the town, nothing to eat within our broken walls.

And it was the silence that made me break silence. All these men who had sung so merrily on the road, or riding into battle, now lay dead, or awaiting death, in silence. At last I said, bitterly:

> 'We sang up the road – it was the mead,
> That kept our thoughts as slaves.
> Shouting over the wheat-eaters we rode;
> Silent, we thirst for our graves.'

For a while, no one spoke in answer. Then Gwanar asked, 'Is that all our death song, Aneirin?'

'What other death song do we deserve?' I asked in reply. 'There will be no one to sing it, if there is.'

'A song lives,' groaned Angor, 'even if no one hears it. Sing us our death song, Aneirin. Sing us a lament for us all, for those who have died beyond these walls, and those who are dying here.'

'Sing, Aneirin,' said someone else, in his agony. 'Sing and remind us why we are here, and how we came to our end.'

'How did we come?' I asked. I thought a while, and then:

> 'Exulting, we hurried to this place,
> As if our lives were not short enough:
> To be sold off at a bloody auction,
> And brought for a feast of mead.'

When a man is dying, he is a miser of his words, and careful with his breath. He takes a long time to frame his speeches, and says nothing he does not mean. It was, therefore, a long time before Gwanar said, in reproof, 'It was not all feasting, though glad we were of it.'

'But it is better to remember laughter than sorrow,' I answered him. It took some time to compose, and then I sang:

> 'As we rode to Cattraeth, Gwanar laughed:
> He went to battle jewelled, as for a feast.
> But other laughter died beneath his blade:
> Supporter of the living law – torn by the beast.'

A voice I could scarcely hear above the song of the thrush asked, 'Was it only Gwanar, then, who did well?'

I knew the voice. I had heard it raised in song as he danced on Bladulf's table. Now he lay with both legs broken. No more would I hear his voice in the hunting-field, or in battle. For him, when I could, I sang:

> 'Caradog rushed to battle like a boar;
> Men, witless, fled before his tusks.
> Speared, he lies up in a stone thicket:
> Brave is the hunter who will follow in.
> The questing dogs are silent: for the mead
> Of Mynydog's feast has quenched his tongue for ever.'

After a time, he answered, fainter still:

'I shall live though I die. I have a song.'

Sick men think slowly. But soon another voice, close to me, said, 'If Aneirin dies, how shall our songs live?'

And thin and high-pitched as the twittering of the sparrows in the roof I heard them ask all together, cry, plead:

'Live, Aneirin, live and sing our death songs all across the Island. If you live, then we shall live, though we die.'

'I am here with you,' I told them. 'I will live no longer than you do. What good is it to sing?'

But still they whispered in their drying throats:

'Sing us our death songs, Aneirin, sing us to death as our mothers sang us to sleep.' And Gwanar said, and it was the last time he spoke, 'Poetry is the crown of the nation, and the chief product of the Kingdom. If we have died only that a poem is made, then we have died for a better thing than ever we lived for.'

And no one contradicted him, because it was a self-evident truth, as clear to the eye as is the difference between black and white, or the truth that the many is more than the one. This was the truth we proclaimed against all the world, that there is more in life than the mere growing of wheat, and breeding till the whole land is covered by the soles of men's feet, and the blue sky is blackened by the smoke of the smiths' fires, and the song of the little birds is drowned by the harsh voices of men talking in dead-footed prose. Our open, wild land is a poem in itself, even if no man sings in it: and thus we had died to keep it.

The darkness was closing in on us. As night came, then I began the task that has filled all the rest of my life, to sing the death songs of all the Household, of the Kingdom of the Gododdin. But that night, I thought only of those who lay around me, and how to give them some happiness, some pride, to take with them when they passed into the hands of the Virgin and all her saints. The nearest man to me rattled in his throat; as he did he heard:

'Those who were merely brave fled before you, Angor:
Those who were also stubborn you struck down.
Mailclad they stood in the front line,
Till you trampled over their bodies.'

And yet, dying, he had the strength to say, 'All is well done. In dying, we have made the Pre-eminent Bard of the Island sing again. Our battle was not lost.'

I sang through the night. As I sang, men answered. At first I wondered that there were so many still alive in the town, so many who called their names and demanded a last song while they still could hear it. But as the Plough revolved above the clouds, the voices were fainter than the owl. Still the rain fell softly on us, chilling to our backbones. And still no Savages came.

With the day, I looked around. The scarlet cloaks did not move, scattered in mounds around me. I lay and shivered, coughing, hot with fever and cold with dying, my bones aching, my breath stabbing me as if it were hot iron in my lungs, my leg numb. I watched the kite and the crow settle on the stones, flutter closer. I did nothing. I needed my little strength for what now I knew only I could do. I could crown and complete all we had done in battle. Suddenly, one arm waved, one weak voice was raised, to drive away the approaching birds. Mirain, with his last strength, guarded us. Now I had time to think of those who had died outside the walls of Cattraeth, who would never hear the death songs.

> 'At our first fight in the valley,
> It was we who set a meal for the birds of prey,
> And satisfied the hunger of the eagles.
> Of all Mynydog's Household who rode out,
> In gold and scarlet mailed from the Dun of Eiddin,
> There was no Roman more renowned than Cynon.'

Because I thought, then, that he had been the first to die.

At last, even Mirain was still. I sang no more. I waited. I could not die yet: the work was not over. And I was rewarded for all my effort, in keeping off death, in refusing to go, at last, to my peace in the Virgin's arms. What had I to do with peace? It was at noon that they came.

211

I knew they were there, however silent they were, for even after Mirain ceased to wave his arms the birds still kept their distance. And this was an offence to me. These were our kites, our buzzards: why should we not feed them? I too lay as if dead. This was a thicket no hunter entered while the beast lived. There was no matter of courage here, or lack of it: only a common prudence. I knew they would not come too soon. But I knew, too, that they would come, and that only one man could lead them, for shame's sake, if he lived, if Precent had not settled him in the night. And, at last, he came.

I sat upright, propped where Precent had left me, against a pillar, and watched the Savages come to the gap in the wall. Weary men, bloodstained and filthy with two nights and a day of hunting their enemies in the woods and bogs. Huge men, yellow-haired and stinking with sweat and mud, who had fought a long battle, and won it. But they waited at the gap in the wall, till *he* came. Bladulf came, taller than any of them, wearier than any. He stepped, delicately, over Owain's blood in the gap, and stood within Cattraeth, the first of all the Savages to stand there so long and live. He looked about him warily, expecting attack from one side or the other. He muttered charms and spells, and his wizard broke eggs before him, and poured out blood, more blood on that bloody ground, the blood of an ox, to chase away the magic of the Romans. And still I waited, huddled, still as death to the eye, my fingers busy beneath my cloak, my lashes a screen before my sight. I let him come.

He walked forward. His men came behind him. One by one, they turned over the bodies of the Household with the butts of their spears, seeking life and finding none. And at last, he was two spears' length from me. I slipped aside the cloak, and he saw the crossbow, cranked back, the string still taut and dry, my last bolt in the groove, a heavy bolt, fit for bear at this range, or wild boar.

Bladulf did not flinch. He did not move in haste or cry out. He only said, in a mild surprise, 'There is one still alive.'

'And one to die,' I answered him. And as I jerked my finger to loose the quarrel, someone I could not see, round to my right flank, flung a handful of pebbles in my face, and another on the other side, with a long pole, knocked up the bow.

I sat, in fury and shame, and looked at Bladulf, alive where he, or I, should have been dead. Weaponless, powerless, I had nothing left but my hate for him. No sword, no long spear, no knife to throw, nothing left to touch him with. He looked at me, and said, 'I know you. You killed my brother.'

The man at his elbow spoke too. He said, 'He killed my brother, too. And my father. And my son.'

'I yield to you, Ingwy,' said Bladulf. 'He is yours. Shall he live or die? And if die, how shall he die?'

Ingwy looked down at me. He was a fat man, streaked with dirt and sweat. He wore a string of amber beads around his neck and copper rings in his ears. He had been weeping, and the tears had made runnels on his face. Black blood was clotted on his arms, and on the naked saxe in his hand. His left ear was cut almost away from his head, and hung by a shred of skin. He hesitated a little. Then:

'What is one more dead among so many? Let him live.'

'I do not want to live,' I replied. 'Let me die.'

'Death is a reward for victory,' said Bladulf. 'Those who are defeated must live, and regret it. Go back and thank your King for me. Where are you hurt?'

I did not answer him. I still do not know whom he counted the victors at Cattraeth. He waved his hand. A number of his men came to me. Ingwy held a horn of beer to my lips, and Bladulf himself offered me a piece of wheat-bread and a piece of cold meat. The wizard knelt down and felt along my leg. He saw first the swollen,

213

misshappen knee. He jabbered like an angry squirrel, and suddenly the men around me held my arms to my sides. I thought that Baldulf had relented, and would give me the death I asked. But the wizard jerked at my leg, and I bit my lips rather than scream at the pain and the sound of grating bone and twisting sinew. But after the sudden pang, the ache was now different in quality, the throb of twisted tissues resting, returning to their proper place, not the strain of muscles under tension, hauled from their proper path by misplaced bones.

Then he looked at the gash in my thigh. He unrolled the bandage, and Gwenllian's scarf fell into the mud, and was disregarded, trodden in. He mumbled his spells, and rubbed the cut with stones and bones and a sword that a man of Bladulf's brought. Then he smeared the wound with grease out of a pot, and wrapped the whole leg in cloth.

Bladulf looked down again at me where I lay and sweated with pain, and he asked me, 'Can you walk?'

I tried to stand. My sides were fire. I could not keep on my feet. Two young men lifted me. They supported me with their arms under my shoulders, pressing on my broken ribs, but I would not cry, even though I wanted to vomit. Slowly they helped me through the gaps in the wall, out on to the green field.

This was a place of blood and death indeed. Here lay the Dwarf, and those who were killed with him: and not only those. From all sides, men were carrying in the dead, Savages and Romans, and laying them in lines, ours near the wall, theirs further away. Other men were working in the wood, cutting down trees. Bladulf asked me, 'How do you burn your dead? What rites do you use?'

'We do not burn. We bury them.'

'Then we will dig for you.'

He called Ingwy and gave him orders. He in turn collected a body of young warrriors, and they with axes and spades deepened and widened the ditch beneath the wall, making a long trench. Then, as I watched, they carried into it the bodies of the Household, or those whom they had found. Precent I saw them bring, and Caso, Graid and Aidan, and put them carefully into the earth they had fought for. Bodies they brought from the Bloodfield, three days before, Gelorwid and Gwion. Bodies were carried wrapped in oxhide, that I could not recognize, from fights in earlier days on the road. Caradog they brought out of Cattraeth, Angor and Geraint and Mirain. Morien they could not bring. Owain they would never find.

There were others, more important, that I could not see. Arthgi was not there, nor Gwyres, or any of the Cardi men who had gone with Cynrig. Perhaps there were twenty men, at most, who had not been killed. No more.

As each of the Household was brought to the long grave, the Savages, of course, stripped him of his mail. Why else had they searched for the dead? At least, of this we had often cheated them. Each of us, then, they wrapped in his own red cloak: or, if he had no cloak, then in a cloak of their own, of cloth or fur. Precent they wrapped in a cloak of sable, ermine-edged.

At the last, they took up Bradwen. As a man began to pull the mail shirt from her shoulders, Bladulf shouted, 'Stop! Let her keep it. That at least she has deserved.'

I asked him, 'You knew there was a woman?'

'We expected it. You are ruled by women. We were not surprised that you let a woman taste the luxury of battle. Among us, it has only been allowed, and that seldom, to Goddesses. She was mortal. She did not dishonour you. We will not dishonour her.'

They laid her in the grave, still mailed. All was complete. The rain still fell.

'What sacrifices do you make for the dead?' Bladulf asked me.

'We make no sacrifices. Has there not been sacrifice enough? We commend them to the Virgin, and lament their passing.'

'Then do so!'

215

I stood a moment, silent. The horde of the Savages gathered round me, looked at me, silent too. I collected myself. I sang:

> 'In haste from the feasting and the mead we marched
>   to war,
> Men used to hardship, spendthrift of our lives.
> From Mynydog's Household grief has come to me,
> For I have lost my Chieftain and my true friends.
> Out of the comfort of a King's Hall we marched,
> Where we had horses, and brides, and mead to drink,
> Yet only one man turned his back on battle—
> Cynddelig of Aeron, shame on him for ever.
> I know of no song of battle which records,
> So complete a destruction of an Army:
> Of the three hundred who rode to Cattraeth,
> None will return.
> Before we come to earth, we did our duty:
> Now may the Blessed Trinity take us home.'

I wrapped my cloak around my face. The young men filled in the ditch. I could not weep. Then Bladulf said, 'Turn and see how a warrior ends.'

They had brought their dead together. If we had lost three hundred, as I feared, then they had lost three thousand. I had never seen so many dead men. No battle in this Island, since the beginning of time, had brought so many to a bloody end. They had cut down all the green wood that stood before the walls of Cattraeth. Because the timber was fresh and full of sap, they brought weathered beams and stakes, wagons of dry fir branches and brushwood, barrels of tar from the pine trees, and casks of tallow. They stacked the wood, and laid the bodies on it, layer after layer of timber and dead men. There were as many dead men as living in that place, and there had come, now, crowds of women and children to weep. Besides this, I knew that we had killed almost as many women, and children too young to burn.

216

When the pyre was complete, there was a noise of trampling. The Savages drove into the place a herd of horses, our horses. They brought only mares, and of these all were either white or near enough to white not to be any other colour for certain. And among them, I saw my own strawberry roan. They were of no use to the Savages, who cannot ride, and who use ploughs so heavy only an ox can pull them. The wizard, then, cut the throats of all our horses with a spear, and dashed the blood over the dead men. They piled the horses on the wood, and the wizard knocked fire with his spear out of the walls of Cattraeth. And from this he kindled the pyres, the one on which the horses, the ones in which the men lay.

It was now almost night. The roaring flames stood up against the sky, and made all the night light as day. The smell of burning flesh enveloped us. The women wailed and screamed, and cut their faces with knives, and tore their clothes, dancing widdershins around the fire. There were even some who leaped, demented with grief, onto the fire and perished with their men, not quickly or without pain and screaming.

In spite of the rain, the flames roared high into the heavens, so cunningly had the Savages built this pyre, with passages and chimneys to lead the fire from the bottom to the top. The thick smoke blew its stench over all, as black as thunderclouds, a smell of singeing cloth and charring wood, and, above all, of roasting flesh. The wind from the west strengthened, and fanned the heat till ploughshares would have melted in the furnace that was made. The wind, I said, was from the West: the smoke, which in the day a man could have seen from the Wall or from the edge of Mordei, blew east in the darkness, east and out to sea.

And that, I thought, was just. Till the end of the Island, till they rise up on the Day of Judgement, the Household will hold Cattraeth, lying here in the ditch, whence no man will ever move them. They will become one with the Island which is ours, is ours and theirs, by right of birth. Here we are born, and here we die, and here we remain. But the Savages – nothing will be left of them in all the land. After they die, they are blown out over the eastern sea, back to the place from whence they came. The land is ours. They will pass.

I stood there, on the grave of the Household, and watched the end of the Savages who had come to take from us the Isle of the Mighty. The flames flared out into the darkness of the night till it gave way to the greyness of the dawn: and the blackness of the night, displaced, became the blackness of my eyes, and of my soul.

CHAPTER EIGHTEEN

Byrr eu hoedyl hir eu hoet ar eu carant
Seith gymeint o loegrwys a ladassant

Short were their lives, long the grief of those
who loved them:
Seven times their number of English had they killed.

From the noise of the wedding feast in Bladulf's Hall we awoke into the dead stillness of Cattraeth. From the noise of the funeral night before the walls of Cattraeth, I, only I of all the Household, awoke into the noise of Ingwy's Hall. To him, Bladulf had given me, and to Ingwy, therefore, fell the task of keeping me alive, as the King had said that I should live. I had rather died, with the rest of the Household. Or, if I lived, I had rather lived for ever in Bernicia as a slave, as I had done before, because life then would not have been long. But Bladulf had said that I must return to thank my King, and that, therefore, I must do.

I lay for weeks in the noise of Ingwy's Hall. It was Bladulf's Hall now, too, because we had burnt the King's own village. His family now had to crowd in and sleep where they could, in the Hall or in the stables with the oxen, or in the barns on the unthreshed wheat. There were so many.

Crowds came down, too, from the North. We had killed all we could find, but there were hundreds, thousands who we had not found, and they all came down to beg shelter and food for the winter from their King. We had burnt their houses and stables, and they had nowhere to shelter from the autumn which had started early with the rain which had fallen on us, dying, in Cattraeth, and which did not stop. They had nothing to eat. We had fallen on them at the end of the summer, when they were living on the very last of the past year's corn. We had spoilt their harvest for them, burning the reaped grain in their barns, and the ripe wheat in the fields. They came South begging for something to eat. The seed corn was gone, and their fields were flooding as the rain came down, because we had blocked their ditches. They had no tools and no oxen, nothing but their lives, and little use they were to grow wheat with in a hurry.

The nation of Savages, what were left of them, had only the crops of half their land to see them all through the winter. They fed me as they fed themselves. Each of us had a few slices of wheat-bread a day, and the wheat flour itself was bulked out with beechmast and acorns ground with the grain. But they had cut down the wide forests where any

220

man of culture and civility, where any Roman, could find food and clothing for the taking at this time of the year.

These Savages, being tied to one crop, and not knowing how to use the forests of the land, how to hunt deer or how to search for nuts and fruit, faced a whole year on half-rations. A whole year — perhaps longer, if they could not reclaim in that first winter the ruined lands in the North. Famine was near. I have seen famine. I know what it does. I could tell, among the crowds who came to shelter in Ingwy's village, who would die that winter.

All the old people would die: anyone who was over forty would not have the strength for the bitter winter on a crust a day. The young children would die — that is nothing new. In any place, out of three babies born between May and September, only one will see May again. Out of those born between September and May, scarcely one in four will live to the first May. But among these Savages, none of the last year's babies would survive. Their mothers would die, too, starving themselves to save their children, and saving none, nor themselves either. Most of the men wounded in the battle would die. That would have nothing to do with the famine. Their wounds would turn rotten, and stink, and they would grow weaker, and dwindle into death. But until they died, they would have to be fed, uselessly. There would be few Savages' babies the next year: too many fathers had been killed. The road to Cattraeth had killed far more Savages than had fallen in battle.

Now, as I watched the Savages, I could see what a great victory we few had won, and yet I did not realize it. I realize it now. We had dealt Bladulf and his people such a blow that it would be years, generations perhaps, before they would be strong enough to come again into the debatable land of Mordei. Oh, yes, this defeat of ours had been a victory, a victory such as no King of the Island of Britain had ever won over the Savages. We had lost our battle: the war was won. I know now that if we had not then so weakened the Savages in Bernicia, then Uther would have never recaptured York as he did a few years after, when the Elmet men at last came with him into the field; and Arthur would never have reconquered all the Island. The Household died so that all Britain again could be Christian, and so that the blessed language of the Angels could be spoken again from one sea to the other, in Bernicia as in Cornwall, in Kent as in Cardigan. And I saw the victory as I lay in Ingwy's Hall, I saw the seeds of it, if not the details, and blinded by sorrow and shame I did not recognize it. But since then I have recognized it, and by the grace of the Virgin I have seen the seed sprout into a tree.

But in those first days, in Ingwy's Hall, I knew only the bitterness of defeat. I only knew that I lay a prisoner, and that I lived only by the will of my enemies, that I could not decide even my own death. There were Savage girls who looked after me. They turned me in my bed when I was too weak, and they brought me the bread on which we all lived, and they dipped it in the bitter beer when I could not even chew the crust. I was, they told me, days and days too ill to speak intelligibly in any language, days sweating and wasting, and I could remember nothing. The girls gave me brews of herbs the wizard had made to stop the sweating and bring down the fever. And they did all this as carefully and as gently as they looked after their own wounded. And some of us lived, and most of us died. Me, they *made* to live. I knew, if they did not, that this was my punishment, that I although a Bard had taken up arms, and fought, and killed.

Bladulf and Ingwy I saw daily, at sunset, when the one tallow dip was lit in the Hall. Then they came in, with all the other men from the fields where it was now too dark for work. Bladulf dressed like the meanest of his subjects, though who was the meanest no one could say, and he worked as they did. He would come in from the dusk, dropping with weariness, his shirt wet with the rain and sweat mingled, his face and hands thick with mud.

When I was able to stand, and walk a few paces, I was allowed – I could easily have been prevented, and was not – to go out of the Hall. Then I found out where

222

it was, because I had been carried there unconscious. It lay north of Cattraeth, being one of the farms we had not had time to burn on the day of the first battle, though we had seen it in the distance. But not a thousand paces away, Morien had fired the corn, and further from it, towards our line of march, we had blocked ditches. The fields were now flooded from the rain, which could not run off. The farms beyond had been burnt.

Here it was that Bladulf worked, as one man among many, taking his part in clearing ditches, in building houses and barns anew, and raising fences. He worked with his hands. I saw him, himself, digging with a spade in a clogged gully, to let the water run down into the river. I saw him again, with axe and nails, setting together the framework for a house, a house for his people, not for himself. Nothing distinguished him from his people who worked around him, but that he did nothing to his own profit.

That is why I would not call Bladulf a King, whatever his birth. It is not the place of a King to work with his hands among his people, or even to tell them what to do from hour to hour. The mark of a King, beyond birth, is wisdom, and after wisdom, wealth. And wisdom cannot be shown in the heat of the day's work, nor wealth gathered there. The place of a King is seated on his Judgement Mound, robed and crowned, listening to his suitors and to his Judge, and, when he has weighed the particular case and the universal law and the precedents, deciding what is now to be done. But the place of a King is to do nothing himself. It is not even the place of a King to ride out to war. That is the task for the Captain of his Household, who may himself be a King some day, although that is irrelevant. If the Captain of the Household of the Kingdom is defeated, then it is no shame to the King, and he can always be replaced. But if the King were to be defeated, then the luck of the Nation is gone, and the Kingdom is at an end. There is no place for a King to die in battle, but on the steps of his own dun, as Evrog

Hael did. That is why the Kings of the Island of Britain did not go out themselves against the Savages, until at last they could send all their Households out to war together, under the one Captain, Arthur.

Bladulf, here, worked as a common man, leading his people and doing himself what he would have every man do. He sent his men miles with the ox-wagons to bring back timber from the hills, because they had long cut down all the trees nearer to where they lived. And he sent the women down into the river-beds to cut reeds for thatch, because we had burnt the straw they would have used. I saw how he made his people work from dawn till the dark came, cheering them on when he needed to, or blustering and threatening them when it was necessary. That showed me how far we had been from victory. Had we killed every man of the Savages but one, and that one Bladulf, then still we would not have a victory. Had we killed Bladulf, and no other man, then all the Savages would have been scattered and destroyed. Oh, if only Bladulf had stood to meet Owain in the fight. It would have been no trouble for Owain to have killed Bladulf: he could have done it with his little finger. I watched him, and saw that he did not understand the essence and dignity of Kingship. But I saw, too, how he recovered much of what we had destroyed. His life was our defeat.

How many poems have you heard when, after defeat, warriors forgive their foes, fall into sympathy with them, feel more comradeship with them than with those of their own nation who have not ridden to battle? It goes well in a poem. It does not happen in life: it did not happen to me. I watched Bladulf, and I grudged him his life, and I grudged every hour he worked to build his Kingdom new.

Each day, I could walk farther to watch the Savages' Kingdom rise again, stand longer with the Savage girls around me. Slim and delicate, with yellow hair like braided buttercups, their blue eyes mindless, empty, they sported like so many squirrels, so many fauns, and had no more thought for the future. They had nothing to do but attend me. The boys with whom they should have been flirting were dead, or died while we watched them. The corn they should have been grinding was burnt. The querns were silent and the looms were still. War had brought idleness to those who were too young, or too old, or too tender, to strain at raising timbers or digging in mud. These girls, Bladulf's family or Ingwy's, played with me, teasing and flirting, as if I were a toy provided for their pleasure; and indeed I might have been that in Bladulf's mind, the only booty saved from the battle.

Theirs was the only gaiety. There were no feasts in that Hall. There was no food or ale to spare, and every man took what he was allowed and tried to find somewhere to sit to eat it, among the great crowd of Savages, men, women and children who filled the Hall at night. In that continual stench of unwashed wheat-eaters, in the never-ending clamour of shouts and groans, the wailing of children and the quarrels of their parents, I almost lost my reason and my voice. I only kept myself in a whole mind by repeating, beneath my breath, the verses I had already made on the men of the Household, and the names of those I would sing if, when I came again to live among men.

There were no feasts. Still, when Bladulf sat to eat, there was a moment of formality, and still, though he worked like all the others, he drank his ale, when there was ale, or his ditchwater when there was none, out of a silver-mounted horn. One night, then, in mid-September, he called me to him when he sat to eat.

'Are you well now? Can you walk?'

'I can walk,' I answered him.

'Then you must go. We can feed you no longer.'

It was true. But it was no thing for a King to say, to a prisoner or to a guest. The excuse was good; but the violation of the laws of hospitality was gross. I was, however, in no position to rebuke him. The men in Cattraeth had bidden me live. How else were they to have any memorial?

225

'I will go, then,' I replied, and stood. It was dark, and far across the river the wolves were howling. Bladulf seized my wrist, and pressed me down again to sit beside him.

'You must go, and take my thanks back to your King.'

'Your thanks?'

'My thanks.'

'For what? Have we then killed the rival who would have supplanted you? Did you send him into the forefront of the battle, as David did among the Romans of old? Or have we thinned out for you a rebellious people who now have no more to do but follow you or die?'

He remained calm, although I taunted him.

'I send you back to thank your King for what he told me.'

This was what I had heard from the Dwarf, but I hardened my face and looked at Bladulf blankly.

'He sent a messenger, a wild man, an Irishman, to tell the men of Elmet to march north against us when you rode south. But that messenger he sent to me also. He told me when you would come. To meet the onslaught of Eiddin and Elmet together we brought down all our people from across the upland moors, and even from Carlisle, that late we won. But we heard that Elmet would come first, and so we marched first against them. When we struck deep into their country, we found that they were not mustered for war. Then, when we were far away, we heard of your raid, and we marched back as fast as we could. We had not thought that so few men could do so much damage. We needed all the men from the uplands to hold you. If we had not marched to Elmet, we would have settled with you sooner; if we had not known you were coming, we could never have gathered, you would have ridden clear to York. For that we thank your King.'

'But it was only treachery that won the day for you,' I reminded him.

'There is no treachery when a man fights for the life of his people, for the future of his Kingdom. Nor was there

226

treachery to which we stooped as low as Mynydog's, who told me that you came, and when. You asked me why I thanked him – ask him why he betrayed you.'

Next day, I set out from Ingwy's village to walk back into the hills. They gave me a spear in case I met wolves, and a knife, and a few loaves of wheat-bread. I still had my own cloak. I went west, first, till I could climb up the edge of the high hills. I could look east from the edge of the moorland, into the valleys we had devastated. Where coming south we had seen a hundred pillars of smoke, now there were not ten. The valleys were laid waste. The trees would grow again, the deer and the duck come back, the fields would flood and merge and vanish as if the wheat had never grown. Our sons would hunt again over that land: Mordred hunts there now. But at what a price, I thought. I wept for the Household.

I went slowly along the edge of the old road, where I could find it. When I came to a wood, I threw away the wheat-bread they had given me. I would not soil my mouth with it again. The wood-pigeons came to it, and I made a sling out of the edge of my cloak and a small stone. I killed two, and that was enough. I made a fire, and ate again as a free man, a civilized Roman, should; I ate fresh meat, game of my own hunting, my own killing, food gained not by sweat and labour of hands but by guile and skill. The fire I lit kept away the bears. It had stopped raining. The corn had rotted in the fields, where there were not enough Savages left alive to cut it and bring it in. Now, too late, the autumn had turned sunny and warm.

A sick man, recovering from a wound, or a wounded man, cannot walk far in one day. What is shelter to the one is shelter to the other. On the third day, I came downwind to a copse, and stalked a deer, inch by inch crawling for an hour till I could cast the spear. Oh, I had meat that night, roasted to eat hot, and to carry away cold. I found a hollow to sleep in, well away from the rest of my kill, and I lit a fire in the dusk to guard me. In the morning I woke shivering, the dew wet on my clothes, and I looked round. On the far side of the hollow where I had not looked in the dusk, I saw now a low heap. I went closer. The mail was rusty, the leather green with mildew. Still the bones had not been scattered by the beasts, the rotting flesh still clung to the jaws, the row of even teeth would have told me, even if I had not seen the shield. I wept. Then I sang for him, since there was nothing else I could do:

'Tudvlch, driven from his farm – for seven days,
He slaughtered the Savages.
His valour should have kept him from harm:
Now let it keep his memory alive.'

He was the first I found. He was not the last. They were Cardi men, mostly, and a few Picts, who had struggled thus far, either alone or in a band, and had died as they marched. One or two had been buried, and I found the shields set upright to mark the shallow graves. Others had crawled, it seemed, into holes and crannies to die, hiding their pain from their comrades. There were two by the walls of Din Drei, their arms around each other, their swords drawn across their knees. One, by the blue on his face, was a Pict: the other, from the yellow and black of his shield, I knew to be from Menevia, though who I could not tell. Over were the days when I knew every man of the Household by sight, to tell him at a thousand paces. They had died sitting together, men from the opposite ends of the Island, come together to fight against the invader. Now, their backs to the Roman Wall, they still looked to the South, into the lost land of Bernicia. They were the last.

I walked down from the Wall, to the Hall of Eudav the Tall, the Hall of Bradwen, the house where I had grown up, the paddocks where I had learned to ride, the woods where I had first gone to frame in solitude the songs I would sing in Kings' Halls. The old house had burnt. A few weeks ago we had rebuilt it. Now, the work of the Household was undone and all was desolate again. No one lived there. The thatch had kept the house dry, but already the poles of the frame were rotting, since we had never tarred them. We had made it for Bradwen and the men of Mordei, and these last had never come.

Would they ever come now? I hoped that they might still come, now that we of the Household had weakened the Savages. But I knew that the hope was in vain. We had not given them that freedom from fear which they had asked. I did not sleep in the Hall. I lay on the ground, under the eye of the stars. My back was to the Dwarf Stone, the friendly Dwarf of our youth, and I faced the dead wood beyond the Wall.

The next day, I climbed the slope beyond, up on to the high ground beyond the woods. A little after noon, I saw before me the white sheep spread from horizon to horizon, a blessed sight, where there are sheep, there are shepherds. Before night I saw smoke, and I came to a hut of boughs. There I slept, as I had so often in my youth, and I had men of my own race, who spoke my own tongue, to look after me. I had returned from Cattraeth.

CHAPTER NINETEEN

Beird byt barnant wyr o gallon
Diebyrth e gerth e gynghyr

The poets of the world judge those to be men of valour
Whose counsels are not revealed to slaves

I walked the road between King Mynydog's farm and the gate of the Dun. The road was silent. The smiths no longer worked at their anvils, except a man here and there who beat out the iron tyres for carts and shoes for the horses. The sword-makers were gone, the sharpeners of iron points, the men who hammered strips for shield-rims and helmet-brims.

I passed the longhouses where the Household had slept. No longer were there little groups of men sitting at the doors, throwing dice or jackstones, playing on the pipes, drinking and telling stories, boasting of how well they rode, how well they fought, would fight. The time for boasting had passed. We had ridden. We had fought. The Household was dead.

I walked between the houses. The children peeped out at me from the doorways, hiding behind the leather curtains. They were silent. No one came out to me with flowers to throw before my feet: Precent would return no more. The parents did not look at me. They turned their faces aside. Without singing the women bent at the querns; silent, the men swung the flails on the threshing floor. The Kingdom was in mourning for the Household. I felt a dead man, sitting at his own wake.

King Mynydog sat on his throne, on the Judgement Mound before the gate of his Dun. No man came now to seek his law. Clydno stood behind him now, as before. But how should any decisions be enforced without Gwanar? Mynydog sat alone and silent, and looked, for ever looked, towards the South, towards the notch below the Giant's Seat where he had seen the Household pass away. I stood before him. I leaned on the Savage spear, and I spat upon his feet before anyone who cared to see.

'Is there Peace?' the King asked.

I said nothing. I looked him in the face. I looked down the first. The Mynydog I had known had been a man in his prime. This man was old, his face lined, his hair streaked with grey. Clydno alone answered him, at last:

'There is peace.'

231

King Mynydog rose from his throne, and came down from his Judgement Mound. He did not offer to embrace me: a rebuff here, in the face of the sun, in the eye of all, would have been too brutal for him to receive, for me to deal. But how otherwise could I have acted? He led me through the gate of the Dun, across the courtyard, into the Hall, in silence.

Dark was Mynydog's Hall. He sat alone at the High Table. Before him burned one tallow dip. The hangings were gone from the walls to make cloaks for the farm people, to see them through the winter. The arms were gone from the pillars where they had hung; gone, lost at Cattraeth. There were no weapons in the Kingdom, and few on the Rock of Dumbarton. The Kingdoms were defenceless.

Of the merry crowd who had feasted in the Hall through the summer, only Clydno remained. He sat on the side-table, at Mynydog's right. I sat at the foot of the Hall, far from them. I, only I of all the Household, had returned from Cattraeth, to feast with the King who had sent us.

'The mead is in the cup,' said Clydno, low, his voice weak and broken with long weeping, 'and the knife is in the meat. If there is anyone of pre-eminent skill, or anyone who has a tale of marvels to tell, let him speak now.'

I said nothing. Mynydog's cook put food before me, a true Roman meal: a manchet of oatcake, and porridge of oatmeal, salmon dried in the sun and venison roasted on a spit, mutton stewed with onions, blackberries and hazelnuts and mushrooms, cheese and butter and heather honey from the mountain hives. I did not touch it, nor the mead in a silver cup. I watched the King eat. And when his third cup was poured, I asked him. 'Why, my Kinsman and my King? Why?'

He did not answer. He only looked at me in wonder, as if he did not know what I was talking about. I spoke again.

'Why, Mynydog, why? There *is* a tale I could tell, of a

232

great Household that was entirely destroyed. It was the Household of all the Kings of Britain, and every Kingdom sent men to serve in it. You spent all the wealth of your Kingdom on it, Mynydog, till there is nothing left, nothing left at all, and there is no more in your house than there is in the house of King Cormac in the empty North. You have ruined your Kingdom, King Mynydog, and all your subjects; and you killed all the men who trusted in you.'

'Cynon returned,' said Clydno. 'Cynrig came back, and two Cardi men and a Pict with him. All were wounded. Three died. Cynrig has gone to the South. Cynon went with him. Three, then, have returned, out of the Household.'

'And Cynddelig?'

'It is said that Cynrig killed him. In Carlisle.'

I asked Mynydog again, 'Why, my King? But why?'

He looked down into his cup. He murmured an epigram I had first sung, years before, when I made a poem on Vortigern the Great, the Magnificent, the Wise, the Proud, the Unhappy:

'Though there be a thousand men in one house,
    Only the King knows in full the cares of war:
    It is the Chief who pays the price for all.'

He looked up at me.

'Do you think there has been one day, one hour, since the Household rode out that I have not looked around the Hall and seen you, every one? I can tell you where every man sits, every man. From the moment you gathered together, I knew the end. There was no end possible for you all but death.'

'And you sent us out?'

'I could not let you all go. I told Cynddelig, that if he could find an excuse to turn back with honour then he might save one troop. Even Owain would have saved Cynon's squadron, if Cynon had been willing. But I knew, whatever I did, all who rode out would die.'

233

'But, knowing that, you sent us.'

'I sent you.'

'Out to meet the men of Elmet, who did not come.'

'I knew they would not come. They would not follow a Prince of Cornwall. There was always jealousy.'

'And that you knew?'

'I knew.'

'And above that, you betrayed us?'

'I found the means to tell Bladulf that he was threatened from each flank; and when.'

'And after that, you sent us out. You sent out the greatest Army that has ever been gathered here, a Household that any of the Kings of Britain would have been proud of. And you sent us all, deliberately, deceitfully, to a useless death.'

'But it was *my* Household. It was me alone they came to serve. Even though they followed Owain into battle, it was the Household of Mynydog that rode out. It was not the Household of all the Isle of Britain. Elmet was not there, nor Wight, Ciren or Anderida. Think, Aneirin, what would come if there *were* one Household of all the Island, if all the Kings let their soldiers follow one General, to sweep the Savages back into the sea. But where would there be such a General, to be leader of such a Household?'

'Owain,' I said. 'Owain could have done it. Owain could have led them.'

'Not Owain. Owain was to be King of Cornwall. Would the other Kings have given a mere King such power? The man who will lead the Household of the Island must be one with no claim to any throne, but of good blood, nevertheless.

'And all his life, Owain knew he would be a King. That was how he behaved. He knew that you would do whatever he said. And you did, whether what he wanted had any sense in it or not. You followed him, partly, because it never occurred to him that you would do anything else but follow him, and because he had no doubts, you had no doubts. And so you followed him,

234

even though you knew that nothing but death lay ahead. You knew that, did you not? You knew it before you rode out of Eiddin.'

'Aye, we knew it.' The Hall of Eiddin was as silent, as dark as the streets of Cattraeth. Men had died there; had we been more alive here, in all our feasts?

'Owain was arrogant and proud. The man who will gather together a Household from all the Kings of Britain can have no such spirit. He must be a man who is used to rejection, who will be surprised to find anyone who will follow him, who will never quite expect the love men feel for him. A man who all his life had been pushed, passed from one host to another, always a stranger, never in a land or a Hall of his own, he will be willing to explain humbly, simply, what he wants men to do.'

'There is no such man.' I too looked into my cup as I spoke. My anger now was gone. That *was* how we had followed Owain, blindly, suspending our senses, as we went on a hopeless, useless ride. 'Owain *could* have done it. Any man would have followed Owain, once they had heard him. But for this dream of yours, this desire to prove that Owain's way was wrong, you destroyed him. And you have destroyed your Kingdom. Where now are the arms that should have defended Eiddin? Who now wear those suits of mail? Who now wield the swords your smiths beat out with such patience? Who but the crows benefit from the food your farmers raised and brought in to you? And where now are all those golden warriors, scarlet cloaked, who sat once with me here at table? Where is Precent? Where is Aidan? Where is Cynrain? Where is Bradwen the wisest of all women? And where above all, is Owain?' I looked around the gloomy Hall. 'Where now, is Gwenllian? And where, where, is the little boy? Mynydog, where is Arthur?'

'When the Household of Eiddin rode South to fight,' and Mynydog was calm in speech as if he were pronouncing judgement in some case of chance murder between relations or a dispute over land or sheep, 'the host of Bladulf was told. And they were told that the host of Elmet, too, was on the road. They received their challenge, and they came out to meet it. Then, as never before, they faced a threat that might well have driven them into the sea, if Elmet had indeed marched, if all my nation had been faithful, as you were. The Saxons marched, first, to meet Elmet. But when they saw that Elmet was not going to war, they turned to meet you. They expected to fight great battles, and, indeed, even though Elmet did not march, at Cattraeth they fought a greater battle than they would have expected, when only three hundred men faced them. They did not know that our army would be so few. To meet you, they brought back out of the hills their roving bands. There was not a Saxon warrior between the Wall and the Humber who did not face you. All the hill-country, between the Road to the South and the Irish Sea, was empty of them.

'For the first time for four years, a woman and child could travel by land, from Eiddin to Wroxeter, from the House of Mynydog to the House of Uther Pendragon. Gorlois Ygraine's husband is dead; they are gone who sought the child's life. Now, he can be fostered in his father's country. He will be safer there; here, how long can we hold against the Irish who come in from the West and roundabout from the North?'

'For that you spent the Household? To clear the hill-country so that your grandchild could be safer, a little safer, for a few years?'

'For that, Aneirin, for that. This is he, I tell you, who will have the humility to lead the Household of all the Kings of the Island, and the wisdom to know when to fight, and the calmness to command.'

'He alone, of all the Romans in the Island?'

'He alone, to have all that, and be also of blood to attract attention, but yet, by birth, barred from any throne of his own. Syvno saw this, he read it in the stars, Gelorwid knew it, the Virgin told him in his prayers. Even Owain knew it, Owain the Proud, the unteachable, he recognized majesty.'

'And I . . . ?'

'An astronomer may talk of the future, Aneirin, or a Priest, or a soldier. But not a Poet, because a Poet talks only of what is true, what is fact.'

'But am I still a Poet, blood-shedder, steel-bearer?'

'Go out, and ask a holier man than I am.'

EPILOGUE

Mynydog, then, sacrificed us all, the Household of Eiddin, the three hundred picked warriors of the Isle of Britain, so that, though Eiddin fell, and Dumbarton, yet Britain should live, and Rome live in Britain. I did not believe him then. Since then, I have seen it come true.

My little Arthur rode out as the Captain of a Household of all the Kings of Britain. He led warriors from Cornwall and from Orkney, as Owain did, from Cardigan and from Elmet and from Little Britain beyond the sea. Arthur killed Bladulf beneath the Rock of Eiddin. But no dead Bladulf could bring again to life Mynydog the Merciful, the Wise. Even Bernicia is ours again. Mordred governs it for Arthur and all the kings of Britain. And after Arthur, Mordred will lead the Household.

Still, though, the men of Arthur's Household must ride out in pairs as I did with Cynon. Still they must fight Savage giants in their wheatfields. Still they must find the dragon ships drifting to shore, and destroy them with iron and fire. All we did, they do.

Yet, I have never seen Arthur since, nor Gwenllian. They tell me that she still lives in Arthur's Court, in Camelot, and even Guinevere gives her precedence. Wise she is now as Bradwen ever was, and, they say, more beautiful. But she has never married.

I went out that night from the Hall of Mynydog. I walked out across Eiddin and across Strathclyde, and at last I came to the island of the monks. I stood before the Bishop in his cell, silent, and he knew my wish without words and shaved my head in front from ear to ear. I paddled the skin boat across the warlike sea to Dalriada in Ireland, and I walked to the Monastery at Bangor, founded from that older Bangor in my father's kingdom. And for my father's sake the monks took me in. There the monks taught me to read and write, and there I followed the worship of the Virgin and her son, who likewise went to their Cattraeth.

Seven years after I came to Bangor, the Virgin drove me out again in a dream, to seek a tree which bore three

239

fruits. I wandered till I came to this place, where there was an oak, with acorns on the branches, and a dove's nest in the leaves, and a sow and her litter among the roots. Here I made my llan. I cleared the ground for my garden of beans within the wattle fence. I hung my bell on a branch of the oak tree, and ever since I have remained in my little hut of withies and clay. Here I will stay till I die. And in that time, I have done my penance to the Virgin for my own sins, and for the sins of all who rode with me to Cattraeth.

I am a spoilt warrior, that I returned from a field where my Captain died. Therefore, I cannot work as a man, but only as a hermit. I am a spoilt man, and I cannot be a priest. I am a spoilt poet, who cannot sing, and therefore I must write. That was my penance. I have written down the death songs of all who died at Cattraeth, as I could find vellum. Perhaps they will come at last into the hands of someone who will take them to Arthur, or to Cynrig in Cardigan; perhaps not. Now the three hundred and three songs are ended. I am ready for my own death, so long postponed.

This was the Gododdin, the song of the Household of Eiddin. I, Aneirin, wrote it.

THE END